The

Autumn

Chickens

For Charlie, 'light of my life.'

To my *wonderful* friends, including my dear mother, Gillian, my delightful, precious children Madeleine, Roland and Harry. Thank you all, for your friendship, and I hope you enjoy the book.

The Autumn Chickens

All quite comfortable?

Then I'll begin.

If you would have told me that one of us would die before
the year's end, that summer so blue, I would have felt it
not possible. We were all so friendly, so intertwined.
True, we were entering the last trimester of our lives,
some earlier than others, but essentially it was business
as usual. We were – dare I say – young at heart.

Chapter One

Gang of Four

"Knitting is easy," said Florence, who had never
successfully knitted anything except six-inch, navy squares

as a girl guide, a role in which she obtained only partial success.

"You just get wool and needles and do stitches – one after the other."

"Well, they say knitting is coding and all that design stuff could be likened to high tech computer programming. Did you hear that Alan Turning's bagged himself the cover of the fifty- pound note?" asked Rose.

"Yes, and I hope they do a better job of him than they did with Jane Austen on those plastic tenners. She looks too agreeable, doe-faced and they mucked up the intended implication of the quotation, "I declare after all there is no enjoyment like reading!" Ha, Caroline Bingley, a keen reader. I don't think so. Though it's not as bad as Trump trying to block Harriet Tubman going on the twenty-dollar U.S bill. With knitting a pattern it *is* just one step after the other," Florence continued, flicking her long hair back.

"True, but you have to follow it," said Rose, staring at her dear friend who was unable to walk in a straight line from A to B without whizzing to Q or H first.

"Yes, but it's not as though you have to put everything together yourself from scratch and organize it and then write it in a plausible way," said Florence.

Rose resisted the temptation to point out many individual knitters designed their own woolen projects and asked, "You mean your writing?"

Florence had been writing a book ever since Rose had met her decades ago while sharing a house in London with six others.

"Maybe a set number of words a day?" suggested Rose.

"Yes, I'm really trying – but it's *sooo* hard."

"Have you tried getting into a routine with it?" offered Rose.

"Oh! That's what Catherine said – as if *she's* got one!" Florence replied excitedly. "I tried that. Did a thousand a day for months but they weren't up to scratch. I want my book to be *literary* – to touch the thinking woman. It's got to mean something," Florence explained, waving her long arms about.

"Amelia Earhart said, 'The most effective way to do it – is to do it,'" said Rose reaching for her bag; declining the offer of another cup of tea. She had marking to do. She was also reading *Mill on the Floss*, a departure from her usual crime thrillers, and finding it brilliant. She had every sympathy for Florence in her high-minded endeavour.

"Just believe in yourself. If you put in all that blood, sweat, toil and tears, it will be worth it," Rose said, walking with her friend to the front door, glancing at her watch.

"I know why you're such a good teacher," Florence smiled, adding, "You're sensible, and so encouraging."

"Ye shall reap what ye sow," Rose smiled and quietly tried to make it to the front door, but Florence was there first, still talking.

"Yes, and apparently the joy is more in the sowing than in the harvest. I do like your hair in a bob, Rose. A brown bob. When did you change it from the pageboy?" said Florence.

"About a year ago."

"Oh, it's my memory. Shot," said Florence. "You do suit a fringe. Grow it out a fraction and you'll be a perfect Cleopatra. 'Oh, happy horse that bears the weight of Anthony.'"

"It's Sara that has Anthony. Look, Doug needs feeding. He'll be sitting by the front door waiting for me," said Rose stepping a little nearer to the door.

"How do you find Year 6? Are you enjoying their relative maturity? Are SATS too awful?" Florence asked.

"Well I like the competition, and it's certainly injected some pressure into my life after years of coasting with Years 3 to 5's," said Rose.

"Catherine says you practically run that school. School plays, parent's evening, school trips, the fete, assemblies. She says you never stop. The Netball Club too. You should go for Head. You did that MA didn't you, when Steven left you? You'd be very good. You are very good with things and people. Not many people are very good at both," said Florence stepping aside and tucking her slender self behind her daughter's UPVC door. "It's the Ofsteding that killed it for me," she called after Rose. "I'd rather submit to the horrors of the Spanish Inquisition than go through that again. Have you seen that chamber in Cordoba?"

Rose knew why she liked Florence. It wasn't just for her passion, but more for her appreciation. Florence, who couldn't seem to spend more than a whole week anywhere, really loved people, loved *her*. Loved and respected her: that rare combination.

As Rose left, crunching up the Cotswold-pebbled drive, Florence felt she needed to talk some more, she, who when travelling could go days without a conversation. It had to be with someone else who knew her well, who wasn't at work on that late Friday afternoon and who lived nearby. Why didn't anyone telephone anymore? It was one thing having no one to talk with in a small Amazonian town but back in England it felt lonely. She'd call Catherine. Catherine didn't work. She had a lot to do but she didn't 'work'. Well, not what people called 'work'. She'd be folding up the sunbeds, grooming the Spaniels, dead-heading the roses and that sort of thing. Rootling in her drawstring bag, Florence pulled out a lime green Android.

"It's Florence," she said.

"Oh hi, it's great to hear from you! Where are you?" asked Catherine wondering if she was still in South America or back in England.

"I'm at the Dort's."

"Dort" is how she referred to her amicable daughter, Francesca who was now a teacher and had recently bought a house in her village of Chadbury; where Catherine and Peter owned a large house up the lane and where Florence chose to nest when she returning from years of travelling, full of tales and pregnant, managed to buy a pretty smallholding in the same village.

Catherine recalled how relieved everyone had been that the baby girl had been called Francesca rather that the suggestions Florence had been rattling off, during her pregnancy.

"Moss, Bark or Grub?" she had asked Catherine, at the same time as inviting her to be Godparent. Florence had then called out, "*Grub*, Grub, *Grubby*" trying out the name, studying Catherine's face for a reaction.

A week later, Catherine had had to drop everything, and beetle down to London, to be the birthing pal and though, perhaps Florence's best friend, still hadn't known who the father was or why he wasn't there.

"I'm picking up Ben from the station at some point and taking Hoover to the vets but apart from that I'm free. It's her eyes. I'd love to see you. Do you need picking up?" Catherine enquired fondly.

Florence declined the offer and walked the mile lane. It was a lovely time of the year and the cow parsley danced on the verges among tall purpley-pink flowers and wheaten-blond grasses. She noticed the odd campion and a clump of human-height thistles, regal, on the edge of a larger field, reputed, by the village historian – the long-legged Sebastian – to have been a Roman battle camp.

What was the fascination with the Romans, Florence pondered, stopping to admire some tiny flowers amid the lush green grass and eyeing up the neat, green balls in the developing blackberries entwined in the hawthorn hedgerow – brutal lot!

Catherine's house was beautiful, a well-kept Georgian farmhouse. It had a porch, sparkling white columns either side of a wide door that gleamed with its well-polished door furnishings and sported a plaque proclaiming it to be "Bluebell Farm". They didn't own the farm but had ten acres.

Finding the door slightly ajar, she pushed it and saw the familiar the oak floor strewn with aged Eastern rugs, leading into a state-of-the-art kitchen – unsuitably white and shining, in Florence's opinion. Hellish to keep clean she inwardly winced, with dogs too, she winced again whilst hugging her friend eyeing one of the weepy-eyed old spaniels, flat out on a high-rise, deep blue velveteen cushioned dog bed.

"God, is that a waterbed?" Florence gestured. Above it was their portrait in an acrylic, titled 'Hoover and

Foxglove' in italics. Foxglove hopped down from the bed and idled over to welcome Florence. Hoover just lifted her head and then reengaged herself in her dream.

"Well, if I had a bed like that, I wouldn't get out of it either," agreed Florence affectionately.

Catherine laughed, tutting a little. "No, no, it's just from Pershore market. Florence you look amazing but are you eating enough?"

"Dunno, I haven't cooked a meal this year. Just eat carrots and nuts," said Florence.

"Gosh you sound like a small pony. I wish I didn't have to cook every day. Peter likes his meat and two veg, and there's Ben at home, though he is easier. He can even cook spaghetti and chilli con carne now," said Catherine. "You would have thought with my degree in catering I would have managed to get my two a little further up the culinary ladder. The youth of the day seem mad for it. Food and fitness mad. All that instagraming their meal."

"Francesca is a Pescatarian. She does a mean fishfinger and lettuce sandwich," said Florence.

"I see her around the village. Is she still loving teaching?" said Catherine. "I bet with Science she'll be forever in high demand."

Florence nodded. She was tempted to ask Catherine if she and Peter still shagged, and if so when, how and where? She watched Catherine fill the kettle and Catherine, poking her ash blond hair behind her ear, informed her it had an eighty-degree boil option for coffee.

"Peter" thought Florence, continuing to wonder if he ever got her dear friend to the boil. She remembered asking Sara, one night as they had propped up a bar, if she thought Catherine and Peter still were at it and if so when and where?

"Or why!" Sara had spluttered out her wine and proceeded to illustrate an occasion upon which she has walked in on the two, years ago, "in flagrant delicto."

She, who despite herself having had many lovers, found the picture of Catherine and Peter in bed distasteful. She accepted the proffered coffee gratefully.

"Yes the 'dort's' still teaching. How are Ben and Jessica?"

Catherine replied in her customary traffic light terminology: one amber and one green, she divulged happily. It was a useful shorthand. She couldn't remember Francesca ever being on anything but 'Green'. Good job. Car. Own house. Very sweet to her mother putting her up at the drop of a hat every time she came back from her travels or wanted a break from Tom. It didn't seem quite fair. After all it was Florence that had been the single parent and had not been glued to the nest. She and Peter had been very steady and yet their two seemed a long way off independence.

As Catherine went on to fill in Florence on the various stages of her children's advancement in the ruthless job market Florence stared at the enviably attractive lighting fixtures, spotlights in the ceiling, fairy lights that lit up the high gloss cupboards and, shining down on the marble-topped island, were three low-hanging warehouse lamps.

All Peter thought Florence and said "Wow, Catherine your kitchen is super amazing. Bauhaus meets minimalist."

Catherine, she felt, would probably have kept that pale lemon painted wood with the awful lino floor and dingy square tiles and bunches of hops hanging everywhere. Catherine had changed nothing until Peter had transformed the kitchen. Some people avoided change at any cost. Not one for the new, her friend Catherine, probably why she was still with Peter. They had met so young.

Catherine was cheered by Florence's exuberance concerning their new kitchen. She, if she admitted it, found it a little harsh and the new granite flooring particularly unforgiving. It had been very inconvenient and tiresome and extremely expensive. She tried not to know what had been spent. Left all that to Peter, who had chosen everything. Catherine's touch had been the grey plastic washing up bowl with matching tea towels.

She remembered when Florence had had her own kitchen back when Francesca and Florence had lived close by. It had been such a pleasant space with a triple aspect, all with pretty views. Bohemian charm had exuded from every shabby-chic corner. She'd a noticeboard swamped in invitations, events and newspaper clippings of Obama.

She had written in black italic over the walls, lines from poems. Catherine could still see them in her mind's eye. "Stone walls do not a prison make" was above the cooker. "I met a lady in the meads" had been above the back door.

Florence looked around at Catherine's large, glistening kitchen and felt envious. She herself not only had no kitchen, but didn't actually own a kettle, pot or pan.

On leaving Catherine's, Florence had not been able to extract from Catherine a promise to depart the splendour of her country farmhouse with its dynamic, sparkling, cavernous kitchen and travel with her, by boat, from Leticia, Colombia, to Manaus, Brazil, sleeping on deck in a self-supplied hammock, to journey along the Amazon with five hundred locals, but she had made her promise to host a small dinner party to include the four of them: Catherine, Sara, Rose and Florence.

Chapter Two

The Dinner Party

Of course, the whole burden of the thing had fallen on Catherine who had been left to pin them all down to a date; never an easy thing where Sara was concerned. It was she who would source and cook the food, host the party, never mind clear up after it, but for the spirit of the thing Florence took total credit and, in a way, it was down to her that they gathered, one Thursday evening, around Catherine's glass table in the lovely Orangery complete with orange tree.

"Ah, the dream team," Peter had called them, swinging his car keys, commenting on how lovely they all looked as he headed off to the club house on golfing business.

Sara and Rose had arrived together in Rose's Focus 'Birch' thus named on the account of it being silver. Sara had parked her burnt-orange Spider on the drive of 6 Fieldhouse Lane, claiming its suspension could not cope with the sleeping policemen on the lane.

"Hasn't anyone ever heard of taxis in Chadbury?" she complained, thinking she may have to borrow a pair of wellies from Catherine's gruesome collection in the boot room as her strappy grey suede sandals would be ruined on the lane.

They stood on the top granite step between the large, white columns and admired the flower tubs whose abundant midsummer blooms spilt over the pair of stone Pointers lying down beside them; blues, oranges, pinks and yellows in the green pots their petals still wet from a recent watering. Rose rang the bell. Sara, a few inches taller, reached passed her, to ring the bell again and then almost immediately banged the brass knocker too.

Rose clutching fizz and chocolates noticed a stick with a pretty, plastic butterfly amid the flower display, and twanged it.

"What is the obsession with butterflies nowadays?" asked Sara.

"Yes – birds are *so* yesterday."

"I think saying "*so* yesterday" is *so* yesterday."

"I think you'll find that we are both quite yesterday."

"We all look quite good for our age. I used to think of us as, 'the four seasons,' a brunette, a blonde and a red head and me. Of course, I've rather spoilt it now that I have lightened up," said Sara.

"I did love your hair black, but you really suit that colour. It softens your face. We're the brunettes now. Sounds like a Phil Spector band," said Rose.

Catherine, followed by Hoover and Glove, answered the door and hugged, first Sara, and then bent lower to Rose, very heartily as well as trying to subdue the dogs who also loved Rose and wanted to show it.

"No sign of Florence on the lane?" she asked, graciously accepting the gifts and ushering her old friends into her nest or rather into the straight-out-of-*Vogue* kitchen with its ochre range and saffron glass panels.

"She's *always* late," Rose said.

"Yes, and never brings anything. Where is she back from this time? For someone who is so hippy-cool she sure does a lot of carbon," said Sara. "I don't know if I could do that. Just sell my house, give up my job and travel. I mean it must be five years and she had such a sweet place. What's going to happen when the money runs out?"

"Well, she's got Tom," said Rose, who had no one.

"How does he put up with her and her travelling?" queried Sara.

"Well they obviously have something going. They've been together for years. Maybe he likes her going away so that he can immerse himself in his painting," Rose added.

The three women opened a bottle and continued to discuss their friend who had shocked them when she'd suddenly sold up and set off around the world on one adventure after another.

"Remember when she saw that stuffed parrot in the Pitt Rivers Museum?" started Catherine.

"Yes," replied Rose. "Next thing she was off to New Zealand. It was a Kakapo. I don't think she ever saw one there. Well, not in the wild."

"Well I suppose a captive live one is better than a stuffed one," allowed Sara. "The thing about Florence she'd have you think she was blown here and there on the winds of sentiment, but she clearly has a steely core that enables her to do exactly what she pleases. It's quite incomprehensible to me."

"Interesting," said Catherine who didn't have Sara down as a natural people pleaser but as rather an unbending individual.

The conversation drifted past Florence, to Rose and which class she was teaching. The women had become very familiar with Staunton Primary School and now the staff, to them, were like characters in a book.

"How long is it since you left Chadbury?" Sara asked.

"Fifteen years," Rose said.

"Is that head still at Staunton? She must be getting on. Surely, she is retiring soon?" continued Sara, helping herself to a large black olive, by way of a cocktail stick.

"She's still as sharp as a pin," Rose assured them, "and the children are quite in awe of her. The discipline at the school is amazing. Never a hint of real trouble. Everything runs like clockwork. I read about exclusions and bullying and think we must just not get it at Staunton."

Sara picked up another olive and stared at Rose, disbelievingly, but didn't question further.

"We're 'Outstanding'," said Rose proudly.

Catherine, who knew much more about Rose's life as a teacher, chipped in how hard the staff all worked and that they were lucky to have Rose. Sara thought OFSTED had gone too far and that the tail was wagging the dog. She'd picked this up mainly from Florence's days working at Pupil Referral Units and her bitter resentment of the inspections and the rigidity and deformity they engendered.

Neither Sara nor Catherine could believe that Rose was still single after that shock break-up several years ago. In some ways, she was the best-looking of all of them, thought Catherine. Those dark, long lashes, glossy brown hair and lovely wide-set blue eyes. Clean living and exercise had kept her fresh-faced and fit and she was so nice: capable and balanced too. Surely there was a man out there for Rose?

"Well at least she's got Doug," Sara whispered to Catherine as they nipped back to the kitchen for nuts and parsnip crisps. "Does she dye her hair?" Sara went on. Catherine pulled a face at Sara and said she didn't think so. They joined Rose again on the terrace and firmly but gently interrogated her further about her singleness.

She brushed their suggestions aside stating that she was too busy to find a man, or have a man, and that she was all right as she was, though she didn't rule it out in the future. Sara couldn't decipher if she meant it or had just said it to shut them up. She did seem to have a range of good people in her life and was always busy. Sara, who had never thought very highly of teaching as a career choice, concluded that by and large the teachers seemed very pleasant to one another and over the years had forged bonds and become dear. She couldn't think of one person who she'd kept up with from her days at law and her property business was a one-man band, though she was on good terms with some estate agents and handymen, but nothing you could call friendship.

As it was such a beautifully warm July evening, they went past the impressively set table in the conservatory and out to the terrace where the view over the rolling farmland was stunning. Chadbury was a pretty place. It sat in a triangle of quintessentially English villages between the Malverns, Bredon Hill and the Cotswolds.

"I wonder where she is?" said Catherine, sounding on the verge of being put-out.

"Does she even have a mobile?" asked Sara and added quickly, "Oh yes. She's always sending photos of herself in the wilderness or some lush-fruited market with everyone dressed for the heat whilst we're in mid-February struggling on. Annoying if you ask me," Sara jibed.

"Well, we'll eat at eight," Catherine stated.

"Yes, I mean lateness is just pure selfishness," Sara agreed. "Hardly ever is a good reason, just arrogance!"

A few minutes after eight Florence swept in, a long figure dressed in pale jeans, a white blouse and a peaked cap, her locks spreading round her body beneath it.

"I knew you'd be on the terrace!" she laughed, cigarette in one hand, tinny in the other. "Oh, I'm not smoking really – don't tell Frankie," and put it out on the grass, picked it back up and flicked it into the laurel and placed her can on the elegant stone balustrade that encompassed the terrace. She hugged everyone, in turn, murmuring compliments to all and how happy she was to see them and radiated such enthusiasm that they immediately forgave her.

'There was something so refreshing about Florence,' thought Sara, although as an ardent reformed smoker with twenty years of abstinence, she was a tiny bit agitated, by the faint whiff of tobacco on her dear friend: she was so easy.

"I've missed you guys!" Florence repeated herself, raising her tinny to their prosecco-filled flutes and insisted, "We don't see enough of each other! We must do a holiday! Oh, goody a starter. This is a real treat for me. I'm 'ravishing'.

Florence went on to dominate the conversation, gushing forth on what crazy fun festivals were and that the four of them should do one. She extolled their virtues and how when they were set in glorious park land and when bathed in English sunshine that there was nowhere else on earth she'd rather be.

Catherine said she wasn't up to date on the music scene, and Florence replied many of the bands were decades old. Sara stated she'd never camped and never would and Florence said 'glamping' could be a very luxurious experience these days. Rose mentioned something about King Henry and his Cloth of Gold and how in Tudor times the French and the English Courts had had a mammoth Camping Party. Then she asked what the loos were like, and Florence had answered, "Varied but you can pay for plush!"

A tasty green soup was served first in elegant, white bone china bowls with large, round spoons. It appeared along with flatbread, heavily seeded. The unsalted British butter was delicious, Florence thought, as neither Francesca nor Tom ever bought it.

Next came Fish pie topped with mash and accompanied by homegrown courgettes and string beans – donated by a neighbour. Homemade apple crumble followed. Catherine explained the apples were Bramleys from her mother's freezer. Her mother and she were both finishing off last year's, to make room for this year's batches. Cloves and cinnamon bark were to be found throughout the sweet tasting apple alongside sultanas. Those with parents discussed them. Catherine and Sara dominated this conversation as they'd known each other's as children. Rose was the only one of them to have two left and went up North most holidays to visit. Florence's mother had died quite young while she was at Teacher Training college. Florence burnt the candle at both ends that year and had never really stopped.

The apple crumble came with cream or custard, as Sara was still very keen on custard and chatted to Catherine about their school puddings, naming them and putting them in order of preference. When Florence poured some custard on top of her cream Sara tutted and told her she'd be licking her bowl next. Florence gave her a sideways glance and sighed, "I will." And then wrinkled up her nose exposing a decent set of teeth.

"Do you still have that gorgeous New Forest?" said Florence. "Your paying pony guest and that stunning warmblood of yours that nobody rides?"

"Yes, Rollo is keeping Mima company. They're lovely together," said Catherine.

"Shame he's been gelded. They would have made beautiful babies," Florence said swigging her beer.

"Do you remember Mr. Chubbs, Sara?" said Catherine.

"God yes, we used to live for that place!" said Sara.

"Every Monday morning. It was, 'Who do you want to ride on Saturday?'" said Catherine.

"I can still picture that row of ponies in the stalls, saddled up and ready to go," said Sara.

"Henry," she started and then Catherine joined in and they continued in unison, "Whiskey, Tempo, Bingo and Corgi" and laughed.

Their memory of the horses, in loose-boxes along the yard, didn't exactly align and they couldn't agree if Killibegs or Apache came after Flash. Talk followed, of blissful Saturdays spent when old enough to, 'stay the day', when Mr. Chubb, kindly, let them remain at the yard after their ride to muck out, fill the water buckets and untack or tack up various ponies.

"It would be called child exploitation now," mused Catherine.

"Or worse," suggested Sara. "I mean can't you remember having to run round the ring with a leading rein giving the beginner's opportunity to learn how to rise to the trot. I mean we were all pubescent, and doing a bit of rising and falling ourselves?"

"I remember you seemed to get out of any hard work but used to like to stand by the jumps and put the poles back when they'd been knocked off," said Catherine. "I think you liked watching a good crash."

"Yes maybe," agreed Sara "You were all over the grooming and feeding and forever stroking and patting the ponies."

"A toast," interrupted Florence, "to our proposed week away. And too, to a line drawn under Brexit. Florence glanced at Catherine and Sara who glanced at each other and then down in mute complicity.

"A step backwards, in my opinion," said Florence and swigged her bottle.

The women reminisced, chatting hopes and fears when Florence, quite tipsy, burst out, "For my birthday I want a ferret, preferably blond with black tips, female – *and* – fully-handled from a pup. That part is extremely important as they have a very strong bite."

"You're really selling this. Sounds like you need exhausting by a daily grind," muttered Sara.

"You're never here!" interjected Rose.

"Ah, and that's Part Two. I'd like you all to take turns looking after it whilst I'm away or in non-ferret friendly digs."

Catherine looked at Sara and Sara looked at Catherine and they both looked at Rose who had a widening smile of incredulity. Florence who noted that they were not on board said unequivocally, "well that's what I want" and flicked her wavy reddish-blond locks over a shoulder and stared at Catherine as if she should expect support.

Catherine remembered those horrid months. years back, when Peter declared himself in love with Florence. He had been pitiable, desolate and demented and wrote an Ode to Florence entitled 'A Pair of Green Eyes'. Her Peter, who though mildly affectionate, had never displayed much appetite for romance, had taken to poetry and sighing. He'd even investigated the line in Florence's kitchen "I met a lady in the meads" and discovered it was from Keats', 'La Belle Dame sans Merci' and muttered the verse around the garden,

I met a lady in the meads,

Full beautiful—a faery's child,

Her hair was long, her foot was light,

And her eyes were wild.

Catherine had hardly recognized him and still couldn't listen to "Jolene" without shooting pain resurfacing. Her life had hung in the balance – her nuclear family being her life. Florence had behaved well; told him plainly that he wasn't her type and she wouldn't even like him as a brother and had taken herself off to Sri Lanka for three months teaching English as a second language near a tea plantation, leaving Francesca with her step-gran and grandpa who came to stay at Fern Cottage so Francesca could carry on at school locally.

"I've had my chances at a settled life but with the exception of Fern Cottage it never worked out for me for long," said Florence looking at her friends one by one. "You've all got so much. I think it's the very least you could do in the spirit of our long and enduring friendship!"

Catherine looked at Florence with an element of pity and asked, "Can't you get Francesca to get another dog? It must be hard for you after all those animals you once kept."

"You did have a lovely set up," agreed Sara. "If you like that sort of thing."

Rose added, "Its' not the same at Fern Cottage now, no ducks, pigs, chickens. They do have a couple of horses there, though I'm not sure if anyone rides them. It's all very ship-shape. I so miss, Hilda, with her feet over the gate watching the world go by. What sort of goat was she?"

"Golden Guernsey," replied Catherine on Florence's behalf, who was looking downcast.

"It was much lovelier when you had it," Rose stated, and Catherine agreed.

"It is hard to look back and not miss the space, the village, the animals, Francesca, the log fire in the winter, the orchard and that grounded feeling you get when feeding leftovers to your pigs and chickens over the garden fence. All that cycle of nature stuff. Franks, went all vegetarian," said Florence. "Called me a serial killer, for dispatching the Tamworth cross Sandy and Blacks, the ones after, the Old Spots. You know, Maud and Mabel."

"You didn't slaughter them yourself?" asked Sara.

"No. I went out," admitted Florence sheepishly and not disclosing she could still hear the squeals of her dear Gloucesters, in her mind's ear, and nowadays found it very creepy when people talked of how to rear animals to enhance their flavour. She automatically thought of the witch, in Hansel and Gretel, and the children in cages.

"They were so darn clever. I swear I only had to show Maud, once, how to stand on that upturned tin bath, to get a reward. Bracken, never got the idea."

"Well, Spaniels. Tim, nice but dim – brains the size of a shriveled nut," admitted Rose, who felt Doug, her Border Collie, a Mensa member of the dog world. "Whoops, sorry Catherine!" Rose, who was rarely quite so undiplomatic, apologized, and then burst out laughing.

"Be rude about my children but leave Hoover out of it. Though, Bracken wasn't the brightest in that litter. Did you ever get her ears tested?" asked Catherine.

Florence's face clouded. It was barely a week after Bracken's death, that she had whacked a FOR SALE sign up, and left the village. Fern Cottage had been priced to sell and had been snapped up. Catherine turned away and asked Sara what she wanted to do for her birthday. Sara explained that she wanted a spa weekend, somewhere elegant, Vienna maybe.

Florence brightened and said she'd heard that they held balls there. "You can hire out huge wigs and wide dresses in the style of Marie Antoinette," she said.

"Oh, that would be lovely," agreed Catherine.

"Sounds expensive," said Rose. "Tallinn's more my budget. Its architecture may not be Austro-Hungarian baroque but it's very nice. Medieval, all sturdy walls and turreted towers with heaps of folklore. I'm not sure of the costume side of things. They looked more peasant style."

"Do you remember what fun we all had in Rome?" said Catherine.

"Yes," said Sara, "I can't believe that was over fifteen years ago."

Florence was waiting for an answer to her question about the ferret and still thought herself in with a chance. She had worked out Catherine as the main source of the ferret care as she had pets already, plus she had the added support of Gavin, who came to help out, a couple of days a week. Besides, she still had Ben, her youngest, at home. She doubted if Catherine would handle the ferret as, although an animal lover, was not the boldest of types. Rose would but then Rose was busier and would have to remain backup. Florence knew Sara would not lift a finger unless it was to unzip her purse and hand out gold sovereigns.

She thought it wise not to pursue the subject again that evening and enquired as to whether any of her friends did keep fit or yoga. One of them was usually following a new regime for perfect health. Sara had retired from Zumba, blaming a knee injury. She was considering a personal trainer with whom to work with on Hampstead Heath. Rose said she'd read they once again grazed sheep on the Heath and briefly recalled the picnics they'd had there. She appeared, still to be the most active of them, with a twice daily dog walk, a Wednesday evening netball session and plenty of P.E. at school.

Florence claimed that most of her exercise, when she wasn't exploring, was on the dancefloor or in the bedroom and claimed she had no need of a gym as she'd given up her car and now had to walk everywhere and carry everything. She then, corrected herself to tell them she did 'lady press-ups', every morning, to improve her upper body strength in case she had to get back into the boat quickly while wild swimming. Sara was still undecided if Florence really did swim in Caimon-infested waters as she claimed.

"I wouldn't use the word *infested*," Florence had said, "as Crocodylia have been around for many millions of years before us. If anything, *we* are the infestation."

None of her friends shared her fascination for murky water or crocodiles. Florence put her interest down to childhood Panto-trips to Peter Pan. The supper party ended quite early as it was a school night.

"Oh, I hope your husband doesn't mow us down on his way back from the golf club," Sara said hugging Catherine goodbye and insisting they were fine to walk and didn't want her to call him.

"I suppose Uber is a foreign word in Snoresbury," she whispered to Florence.

Chapter 3

Reflections

The moon was bright. They had torches, too. Catherine draped bright yellow jackets over them reassuring them that it was better to be safe than sorry.

"You're such an old worrywart," Florence had complained but took hers anyway. Thus, they embarked on the late-night mile walk back to the village.

"This is going to take forever. Are you sure you are over the limit?" Sara complained. "I can't believe you and Catherine used to jog it every day."

"The three of us did for a while," said Florence. "Catherine was fine on the way down, but she used huff and puff on the way back."

"Yes," Rose recollected, "she didn't like to talk and jog, did she?"

"Your book, Florence, what's it called?" said Sara.

"The Yellow Rose," said Florence quickly, "I think."

"It sounds a bit of a bodice ripper," scoffed Sara, gently.

"Do you remember Catherine and her Mills and Boon phase?" she added.

Florence thumped her.

"You ought to know better than to assault a lawyer," she remarked.

"I would have called it, "The Red Rose" if I wanted to signify romance. A yellow rose is for friendship," she asserted.

"I'm not sure if the reader would know that," commented Rose. "I mean I did, but then my name is Rose. Eleanor Roosevelt had a rose named after her, all very nice but wasn't so pleased to hear it described as being, 'no good in a bed but alright up against a wall' I used to like the odd Mills and Boon, too. They probably are full on now, if they still exist.

Sara laughed.

That was the trouble with exposing your ideas thought Florence, they just get shredded. She nearly stopped to take a beer from her bag but didn't.

"What's it about?" said Sara, in earnest, the walk coupled with the velvet sky, softening her.

"Oh, you know, the toll of achievement," said Florence staring ahead.

"Oh," said Sara processing the statement and wondering if Florence had just come up with it.

"Who are the characters?" asked Rose.

"It's a timely discussion on family and friends. Blood is thicker than water, but it isn't always as refreshing," said Florence.

Florence who was walking in the middle of them now turned to her and explained it was drawn very loosely from Greek mythology with splinters of historical sources.

"Oh, like Shakespeare and Plutarch?" said Rose enthusiastically.

"Well I suppose," agreed Florence not liking the analogy. "I'm trying it from a different perspective, which I do believe Shakespeare did with Anthony and Cleopatra."

"What history told by the losers?" asked Rose.

"I think that is a matter of definition. Depends how you rank prostitutes. The book is about a road taken by a torch-bearer. This road veers way away from the main drag and is perilous. It's difficult, lonely. Things happen on it. Not very nice things. It's a typical quest novel but laced with hope. I guess to sum up the theme, I could just say it was about human sacrifice. And as for the characters? You'll have to read it and see." Florence sighed and no longer wanted to expose herself. "Did I hear you had applied for Assistant Head, Rose?"

"I told Catherine not to tell anyone," said Rose.

"Catherine didn't tell me," Florence said.

"About time too, Rose," said Sara. "You are too good to be just a classroom teacher, especially primary."

"I think that's what you call a backhanded compliment," said Florence.

"I'm insulted," said Rose. "Of course, being a landlord is such a worthy occupation."

"Oh, Ladies let's not squabble," said Florence enjoying the drama. "How many millions have you made on your backside Sara?" she added.

Rose started laughing, soon joined by Florence.

"My rents are less than market value you know?" said Sara, deciding that she definitely didn't want to go to Vienna, Istanbul, Berlin or any of the capitals that had been bandied around over dinner with these two.

First stop, was Rose who was glad to be back at her house, and quite relieved when Sara declined to come in. They had hung around Sara's Spider long enough for her to administer the breathalyzer-test, produced from the glove department. She was in the clear so drove off for her monthly visit, to her mother's in, nearby, Leamington Spa.

Once inside, Rose let Doug out, who peed dutifully in the back garden. She admired his beautiful coat and thought him very superior to the spaniels up the lane. He trotted back in and sat down beside her, in her front room, where she contemplated her professional life.

Had she done the right thing applying for Assistant Head she wondered deciding to put the kettle on. Both Florence and Sara, had told her she was worthy of promotion. She had a good life she felt, as she poured the milk. She was comfortable in her job with her home and dog, her friends and family. She still had both parents in a good marriage and a brother with children, all with whom she was on excellent terms. She liked her life so why had she sought change. It was a long time since she'd been out of her comfort zone.

She sat down on her armchair with her tea and Doug by her side and recalled her teacher training. Could it really be over thirty years ago? The school, in the East End of London, had been enormous, Victorian in red brick with a roof top playground and not a blade of grass in sight. It was just before the arrival of the National Curriculum, and though late eighties, had a sixties vibe.

There had been a large white rabbit that just lolloped, free-range, around the building. There was team teaching with vertical classes. The children, mainly refugees, were a huge mix of nationalities though largely from Africa and Asia and the staff were mixed too with a liberal ethos.

The broadness of her first situation had given her some worldly wisdom; she felt, a slither of understanding of how different were the lives of people, even within quite short distances of each other. She thought of Florence's novel and wondered if she had or should include slavery. The subject was huge and the more research she did, the more it surfaced.

She buried her hand into Doug's white ruff and felt the gorgeous softness, as she enjoyed the pinkness of his exposed tongue, and took a sip of hot tea.

She had joined a large classroom that swarmed with seven and eight-year-olds, active on various tasks until they were called over for "mat time" where they fell under the spell of two of the most charismatic teachers Rose had ever seen, Myra and Eileen.

Myra and Eileen, who she remembered went to the pub at lunchtime and indulged in alcohol, shocking by the standards of today. Myra who was unusually tall, slim and elegant with a long, serene face and brown, straight sleek hair usually worn in a ponytail down her back exuded calm. She looked lovely in whatever she wore or whatever she did. Habitually in pale jeans and plain shirt adorned by a long scarf that and when she swirled it, would fall back into exactly the right place. She only ever once raised her voice – and Rose could still hear it.

"No. No. No."

It had rung out, across the huge classroom and stopped the children in their track.

Eileen, louder, was a different kettle of fish but she, too, had those children enchanted with her shining blue eyes, Celtic freckles and wild wavy auburn, mid-length hair – a woman full of zeal. She was a matador and shook a red cloak at the children throwing them the gauntlet.

So what, if they were refugees. So what, if they were poor.

"What is oil?" she would ask, holding a picture cue. "Where does it come from?"

This was a time before classroom computers, and how the children had scampered around to investigate and how amazed they were to learn of oil's constituents!

Along with the discovery, were songs and dancing and so much joy.

A probation year followed in Tottenham. She had been amazed that Mrs Sadler and Mrs Davis had been the head teacher and deputy, both black, and further amazed by her surprize at how brilliant they both were at their jobs. She'd been ignorant. Now she realized that she had been surprized because she'd never seen black women or men in charge of anything. These two women, she held in such high esteem, were very likely to have been exceptionally talented. The head put on some wonderful dramas and during them an extra positivity emanated the airways of the school, already a beacon, in a concrete high-rise landscape of underprivilege. The deputy had gravitas, a quiet dignity, that just gained respect.

Now years later, Rose thought of some of the children and wondered what had happened to them and how different their lives, for better or worse, would have been if they hadn't been absorbed in Tower Hamlets melting pot. Trajectories were odd. She had once thought that what you put in loosely equalled what you got out but accepted now the randomness of life. For one child a boat, another left behind.

She thought back to the appealing Vietnamese children she'd so fallen in love with back in that tall, red-brick East End school, just prior to the hatching of yuppie land. The two young girls, perfectly featured, so bright and quick and Christopher, an African refugee rehomed at Broadwater Farm, so clever, calm and beautiful. How children can teach you so much. How life could teach you so much.

The few weeks at Bow followed by the eight years at Tottenham had made her a teacher. She had a longing to go back there.

Here at Staunton where, happy as it was, one week ran into another, a term became a year, a year became eight, eight was marching to eighteen. She was losing count now. If she wasn't appointed Assistant Head here, she would move.

Florence was feeling faintly disappointed with the evening. They'd swerved the ferret. She hadn't even opened the can of lager she'd walked home with. She'd meant to swig it on the walk home but never got around to it so it had stayed in the drawstring pouch she carried on her back. The bag was covered with images of Freida Kahlo with a monkey companion. She had bought it in Buenos Aires, one January Sunday morning.

She'd nearly fished a can out when Sara had completely missed the concept of her title. Had she no understanding of how precious a book could be to its writer? Thank goodness, she had kept her powder fairly dry.

Placing the can into the fridge behind the bottled water and nutritional food stuffs; live yoghurts, leafy greens and humous. She considered the clean and orderly fridge and it reinforced her perception of her daughter as being in a 'tidy desk, tidy mind' category. Though what had Einstein said of the tidy mind?

The can was semi out of sight. She preferred to leave a small footprint when staying at peoples, her daughter, no exception. The house was quiet. There were no sounds, except the humming fridge which faintly reminded her of the generator in a jungle hide.

Francesca had gone to bed. She had elected to teach secondary and went to bed early on week nights and was overall a morning sort. Florence, who could drink and talk through the night again contemplated genetic heritage, this time in relation to circadian rhythms.

She gathered her faithful bag, Freida looking at her watchfully and took it to bed. In a neat bedroom with a single bed and green gingham curtains. She placed the bag on a chair that sat in the corner of the oblong room and remembered her week at the backpackers, in the Paris of South America, where she had been as central in Buenos Aires as Mayfair was to London and where on Australia Day she'd partied day and night with an Australian couple and danced and laughed, on the roof top, through the small hours.

In South America they didn't start until midnight. It was barely eleven and the village even on this perfect summer night was sleeping. No wonder Sara called it 'Snoresbury'. They did seem happy though. Contented. A Lady Bird book from her childhood, *The Discontented Pony* crossed her mind. She could almost still remember the pretty bay pony on the hardback cover. Self-knowledge stung. She needed to get back on the road again – that, or get a job.

It was very inconvenient without a car in the village. Tom would have to pick her up and the neediness of it made her squirm. An aunt once told her that men liked to be useful.

Tom was good for her as well as good to her. He'd kept her clear from her excesses, though it had certainly meant leaving parties early.

He who holds the car keys drives the car. Though there had been a tricky stretch, Florence knew it to be a good relationship. It had stood the test of time and she felt blessed. Look at Bathesheba Everdene, she'd once told Catherine.

The town, small and delightful in the honeyed Cotswold stone, had a very pleasant vibe with endless tea and coffee shops where she could scribble ideas and second-hand shops to swap clothes in. It had a train station too. But could that certainty wear her down? No, she would take the bull by the horns and go adventuring again. She looked forward to seeing Tom the next day, but would book her flight back to South America, in the morning. It wasn't as though she hadn't asked him. It was his choice to stay.

She would continue her journey along the Amazon; source to mouth. The world was her oyster. She might even have Carpe Diem etched onto her skin somewhere in downtown Manaus. She went to bed feeling happier.

Catherine's kitchen had thrown Sara. It was so state of the art, so dazzlingly modern. The wooden stools had gone from the breakfast bar replaced by chic white plastic. So un-Catherine!

Sara remembered, a decade ago, being perched on one of the old wooden stools after helping Catherine in with the groceries. They were having a cup of tea and Catherine had yet to sit down when Sara had had an odd physical sensation.

Something was happening between her legs. She'd excused herself, feeling awry, possibly some emission, something on her inside thigh as she hastened to the bathroom.

Once, locked in the loo, her suspicions were confirming as she watched her seven-week pregnancy escape and in those few seconds, she knew her course was changing, maybe by the biggest single event in her life, but she had tidied herself up, flushed the plug and washed her hands, returning to her best friend, in the kitchen, as though nothing had happened.

She thought of Anthony and texted him goodnight with three kisses.

Chapter Four

About Time

A week later, Sara called Catherine, announcing she was on her way over. Catherine guessed that Sara would not be dressed for the country and that she would have to put the dogs away which could be a performance. Catherine would ask them and they'd look at her. Catherine would ask them, more firmly, and receive nothing but looks again. Catherine would then command them, in a low fearsome tone, and still they'd look at her fondly. Finally, Catherine would resort to food or an old, green plastic fly swat that she'd whack against the kitchen table. Food worked better, especially when rationed. A gravy-coated Boneo, split in two, on this occasion, did the trick. She felt, as she had managed to keep herself trim despite being at home and middle-aged, she owed it to the dogs not to overfeed them. Hoover was over ten now and Catherine realized in Cocker years, that was getting on.

Her children had been brought up with dogs as she had and her mother before her. They could compose a dog family tree, which started with Bertie, the Boston Terrier, a long-legged ectomorph. Catherine appreciated her doting dogs. By day, she and they formed a triad.

'Sara,' she thought and shifted a few items back into their proper place. Sara had no room for pets in her high-gloss, urban life-style. Not in her Belsize Park apartment, nor the house in South End Green where Sara and Anthony had committed to co-habit once Sara had deemed his children independent enough not to cause friction. What a fuss she'd made if ever they left a cereal bowl out on their alternate weekend visits. No wonder she steered clear of pets. Goodness knows what she'd make of her clutter, as she swept a counter clear of condiments. At least, Peter had forced them to update the kitchen. She would have been happy to have kept it. It wasn't broken. She had liked the solid wood cabinets painted lemon and the old stools. They had had a country feel and she was still shocked by the stark modernity of this new version and shuddered to think what it might have cost.

It was the hottest day that year. At least Sara wouldn't be cold. Catherine could remember once overhearing Sara saying to Rose, "I'm freezing. Not everyone's into Long-John's."

Sara pulled up in her runaround Mercedes hatchback, gun metal grey. She parked right in front of the front door.

How Catherine hated the glorious view of her front garden and paddock, with a possible glimpse of an equine head or two hanging over the five-bar gate, blocked by a car. It was Sara though, and Catherine could forgive her dear and oldest friend anything.

Sara pushed through the opening door and they kissed each other. Catherine gave up at two but awkwardly received a third.

"Where are the dogs?" Sara enquired sniffing the air. "I do love Hoover. I still think of that terrible time when your Cairn got drowned in the brook. Sweet little thing. He was so delightful with his long pale gray coat and face as bright as a button. What was his name?"

"Voltaire," replied Catherine. "Alert, fearless and gay according to 'The Observer book of Dogs'. Catherine remembered the little head bobbing up and down and then up no more leaving nothing but swirling whirlpools before the chaotic waters disappeared, angrily, under the bridge.

"A little too fearless," remarked Sara. "And your Hungarian Vizsla was shot. Sheep worrying, wasn't it? Beautiful animal that, had 'a line of beauty'. Please don't tell me you are going to take on a ferret for Florence. The cheek!"

"You used to be such a keen animal lover?" Catherine said. "No, even with gardening gloves, I'd be scared. They have needle teeth in an iron-jaw. I'm going to suggest a pair of guinea pigs. Florence told me she once got so lonely in Peru she nearly bought one from the market as a travelling partner."

"Why didn't she? Could have saved one from the plate?" asked Sara.

"Oh, she met some Brits. One girl, who was studying monkeys, started to cry when Florence offered her a piece of Cadbury's Fruit and Nut. They bonded over a mouthful of chocolate and spent the next fortnight joined at the hip."

"Erhh. Who would want to hang around with a group of students? Disgusting," said Sara.

"Florence said she spent the whole two weeks weeping with laughter. Apparently, Isabella was a very good monkey impressionist and taught Florence Capachin," said Catherine.

"I can just imagine them in a restaurant. Anyway, what is her book all about?" said Sara.

"I'm not quite sure. A dissenter. Oh, and something about how power can so easily be abused. Who will guard the guardian?" said Catherine.

"She told, Rose and I, it was about human sacrifice," said Sara.

"Maybe she means people trafficking. They say it's all over the place," said Catherine. "Very topical. Oh, and something along the lines of save one soul, save the world."

"She told Rose and I, it was about torch-bearing. It sounds awful. A foolish attempt at high-brow. What is the entomology of high-brow?" asked Sara.

Catherine shrugged her shoulders and said "Google, it."

"Big-head," Sara suggested. "You know, she'll expect us to read it."

"I want to read it," said Catherine.

"Well you do have the time," said Sara.

"Florence has something to say," said Catherine.

"If she cares so much about stuff why doesn't she do something. She's on constant holiday. Anyway, I'm not stopping long," Sara kicked off and proceeded forth in a near monologue for the next twenty minutes, mainly explaining to her patient friend, the whole debacle of the damage, occurred to her buy-to-let, in North London, by a 'water ingress.'

It was at a garden flat in East Finchley. The saga involved a whole cast of pantomime villains including Caspar-the-deep-voiced Insurance broker; Jeremy, a senior-aged junior who very much liked the sound of his own voice; Jane, an efficient but hardly ever-present letting's manager and the main contractor Parvel – or 'Parvel the Marvel' as Sara referred to him, with deep sarcasm.

It was he who, she felt, had misdiagnosed the leak initially and not being able to admit it had caused Sara to lose faith with him and his set of workers. She had called in the big boys via her insurance and that had landed her out of the frying pan and into fire. Now embroiled in a ridiculous protracted system with multi-party involvement, all with their annoying rules and regulations, and none of them seemed to know what the other were doing she watched and waited as they dismantled the *whole* flat until she was sick to death of the affair.

Then, there were her troubles in Great Rissington, with a virtually unemployable woman, with an Amazon habit, who, after stacking the entire house with boxes, couldn't or wouldn't pay her rent or move out.

Catherine listened kindly whilst supplying them both with coffee and biscuits.

"About time you did something with this place Catherine. At least you got rid of that awful kitchen, though I miss the stools in an odd way. Peter behaving himself? Kids alright?" Sara asked before draining her coffee. Picking up her key fob she had said, "Still a councilor? They must love you. First trustee to the Schoolroom and then on the Parish Council. You are so easy to co-opt. School Governor, once too, I believe. And the coffee afternoons for the community. Where would we be without Volunteers?"

Catherine waved her friend goodbye her from the raised stone steps admiring her greatly, watching the smart, determined woman adeptly and abruptly execute a three-point turn and whizz down the drive, no doubt, back to the super highway of her life.

Catherine felt sloth-like and turned her thoughts to The Chat Shack where she and Rose, for a decade, had served tea or coffee with biscuits, run a raffle, a 'bring and buy' and a book-exchange along with the occasional quiz. The original cast now really showing their age.

Initially, these "senior citizens" had walked upright and helped bring out the chairs and now they shuffled and stooped. Then drivers, now passengers, but still the little party smiled in the face of the adversity wearing them down. It was still an oasis. Catherine remembered Anne, the grandee, so fond of public speaking. She would rap her spoon against a cup, waiting for silence, before projecting herself onto a stayed audience. She'd once announced: "We are very lucky this afternoon to have Catherine, a very important person in the village."

Ha, that had warmed the cockles of Catherine's heart. No one had ever said that before and, for a while, she had battled to keep their bus routes. She decided to visit Anne later that day and considered what to take her.

Catherine remembered, with fondness, her first evening as a councillor. It had had the feel of the *Vicar of Dibley*. They'd actually unearthed some unclaimed war bonds. These meetings were only once a month. They gave her a standing in the village, an identity. Her self-image seemed to slip lower and lower year on year until recently she was really rather confused by her position, her use. Did she have a use? Was she useless? Of course not, she was the lynchpin of her family; Rose had assured her one dog walk.

It still troubled her, sometimes hourly. Peter, her children, her friends seemed so absorbed by their own lives. Sara had her empire-building. Rose her teaching. Florence travelled the world obsessed by rivers, absorbed by wildlife, bunking up with people half her age in backpack inns. Peter sat on the pinnacle of his career and between golf and work they did little together but eat, sleep and watch TV; yet weren't they happy?

She was Ferdinand the Bull, sitting under the shade of that solitary tree, smelling the flowers. She loved her garden which encircled their house with the ramshackle greenhouse, the bluey-green garden shed where the lawnmower and garden chairs overwintered, the flowering potted plants, her tomatoes, her strawberries of five different varieties this year; her Wisteria that clad the front of the farmhouse, her glorious five-foot high perennial border, alongside the sweeping well-mown front lawn. The cottage style border was home to Lilac, Wild peas, Foxgloves seven foot high that year due to the mini-monsoon that June, Euphobia, Pyracanthus, day lilies, Crocosmia and wall to wall along the back of the stable block there were roses, multi-variated, sweet-smelling and colourful: her pride and joy. But was it enough? She felt loose, and as if her loose-end was getting looser.

Maybe she should join an art class, Pilates group, do something more for world poverty. She'd been meaning to do Lend with Care ever since Florence had raved about it. Catherine wondered if she could persuade her friend to swap ferret for guinea pig. She remembered her children's guinea pig, Guinness, who had shared a stable with a highly-strung spotted rabbit. One day, she'd entered the stable to tend them and was confronted by the rabbit, its head, entangled in a haynet with its beautiful black and white spotted body, paws to the front, a metre from the ground: hanging hard and still.

All those small animals had filtered out when the children grew up. Only Jess's horse now remained, the Belgian mare, Mima. Once they'd rampaged through the cross-country course amid a torrent of Pony Clubbers, in high competition, now Mima retired early, to the paddock at the bottom of the garden, to be admired and in the summer to be offered stalks of Cow Parsley over the gate and Jess gone to the city.

At least, Catherine thought, she was going to spend a week away with her friends. Maybe now was the time to insist Peter and she took their long-promised 50th birthday trip to a long-haul destination. It was years overdue and still continually postponed by Peter.

Catherine decided to speak to him on the matter that very weekend, after his Saturday golf session. She enjoyed travel and had done very little of it during her long marriage.

In their twenties, Sara and she had travelled, for three months, on a bus, together with eighteen others, from London to Katmandu. It was the most adventurous, laid-back time of her life. She was grateful to Sara for persuading her, back in the days when Sara and she were inseparable.

A hoard of them had boarded the thirty-year old Leeds double decker outside the Enterprise Hotel in London. It would be their home, to eat and sleep in, for the next ten weeks. A 'night drive' through Belgium took them to Munich beer festival, all be it with a stuffed gear box.

They had given her the log book, a possession dear to her heart:

We got to Munich campsite at 12 noon so everyone sat around

in the sun and had a bit of a rest. The place is really filling up.

By late evening it was a shambles. Everyone (almost) is pissed.

Catherine could still remember the weight of those heavy stein glasses and the yellow stretchers darting, here and there, picking up casualties. She imagined it might not be the same, today. She couldn't quite remember how they'd all managed to sleep on the bus but remembered, by day, they had seating but, at night, everything flattened out. There was a kitchen on the bottom deck but no loo. You peed outside or at a pit stop. By day six they had arrived in Venice. The weather had been perfect, but Catherine remembered being violently lost when in a maze of canals with no clue to where the bus was.

She remembered how they'd taken the catering for the large group, in turns, and remembered a little argument she and Sara had had when making a stew. Sara had tried to put whole onions in the mix and Catherine had wanted her to chop them up. That was the last time she could remember Sara cooking. It was always out to dinner, with her, or out to lunch.

Catherine felt an urge to be outside, on such a fine day, so stepped into the garden. Mima ambled forth to the gate, along with her new sidekick Rollo, a strawberry roan New Forest. Catherine felt him, 'a cheeky chap.' She liked his stockiness and his delightful habit of raising his upper lip. The day was passing by.

Times change, maybe she should too, as she looked at the shadow cast between her and her beloved roses and was reminded of the lines by TS Elliot

'Come under the shadow of this rock.

And I will show you something different from either.

Your shadow at morning striding behind you.

Or you shadow at evening rising to meet you.

I will show you fear in a handful of dust.'

Ten o'clock, and Peter not back from his golf club? Ben was in his bedroom on the computer. The dogs curled up, asleep. She climbed the stairs.

The morning after the night before, Catherine was gripped by the sense of a new beginning. There was a limit to so much thinking and she felt it was time to finish with procrastination and make tomorrow become today.

Clearly the village posts, the mothering of grown children, being a part-time wife to a golf-obsessed workaholic were no longer enough. Even her beloved Spaniels were not enough. If she didn't want her life she should shake the dice. Dance a new tune. It was going to happen. It had to start, to be followed through. Once in free flow she might not be able to go back but she couldn't be stayed. Desperate for change, hungry for new, she would have to stand up for herself. Catherine continued to stroke her dogs.

She'd tell Peter when he got back. They would have to go abroad, a great holiday to Angkor Wat or The Great Wall. She had spent thirty years worrying about Peter, fitting in. He could make the effort to sit out a long-haul flight for once in his life. She would stop that dull ache of time passing her by, of having no control, no say. Just time pushing. She would have her say. What did she do these days? What should she expect? She did things barely half-heartedly. Nothing is the wage of nothing. No satisfaction. No kudos. No respect. They would book an exotic holiday. She would go away with her friends and then she would, refashion her life, to make it count.

The dogs were cheerful to see the leads with the promise of new smells and a trip out. Rose, high from her netball session, was pleased to see Catherine hovering round the front door.

"You should have gone in and made yourself a drink! You have key!"

"I know and I know you're busy Rose, but I really wanted to book this trip, and thought I'd better just check things with you."

"I'm not too busy for you Catherine. Cup of tea? Put the dogs in the garden," said Rose with a lovely smile.

First, with lightening efficiency Rose booked the flights. At a more leisurely pace, after perusing Rose's newly acquired, Lonely Planet Guide with accommodation-possibilities already underlined, between them and Trip Advisor, they nailed the accommodation. Four nights in the Lithuanian Lake District and three in the capital of Vilnius.

"Let's phone the others. Sara did say it was her treat," said Rose. "Sara did say she'd pay for the flights. Do you think she'll reimburse us?"

"Oh, we'll let her pay for some meals. She'll probably pass them off as expenses," said Catherine calling first Sara and then Florence.

"The cat's in the cradle," she said excitedly. "It's Lithuania here we come."

Chapter 5

'Plenty Makes Us Poor'

Weather-wise, August was proving to be mixed. Rose and Catherine were out on a dog walk. Catherine's mojo had, partly, returned. Side by side, they swung dog-leads. She poured while Rose listened, nodding. Rose's dark hair, in its neat style shone and her face was as intent as a doctor's evidencing symptoms. Her prognosis, in total agreement with Catherine's, was 'aimlessness'.

"In the words of our august poet Wordsworth, you suffer, "The weight of too much liberty," she'd said.

Catherine said nothing but didn't think the quotation summed up her situation at all. It dawned on her that she might be in a gilded cage. What liberty? She was hostage to fortune. Bound. Rose was free, not she. 'Weight,' did come into to it and she was under a great deal of it: family responsibility. It was if she were under a giant nest and twig after twig was falling; burying her.

She was aimless though, that much was true. The blind assassin had been a stealthy foe and crept up on her and left her as helpless as a shuttlecock battered by anyone who fancied and took aim. Back and forth, back and forth, between opposing forces and on top of that, at the mercy of the weather and high wind.

Rose, after explaining to Catherine the difference between aims and objectives, and not at all convincing her there was any difference, had come up with three classics:

a) Charity work

b) Creative pursuits

c) Job

This trio was hardly new to Catherine but the time had come to act. Family and friends though precious were not enough. They simply did not have time for her. Anymore delay on her part would lead to a weakening of a perfectly fine edifice built up over decades, the weakening of which would hurt her more than anyone else, of that she could be sure. So, she would have to stop being that shuttlecock and take control of her game. Bat and bat until her game was upped and she could rid herself of the nasty feeling of under fulfilment, under everything; including under everybody's feet.

"You're a brilliant cook and you did catering at uni. Why don't you do something with it?"

"Oh, I've cooked every day for years. I'm out of date," shrugged Catherine which struck Rose as defeatist.

"How did this situation rise? How did I miss being a professional? Was I not bright enough?" she'd asked Rose.

"Of course, you were bright enough. Besides, look what you *have* achieved!" said Rose, wondering what Catherine thought she ought to suddenly become mid-fifty and thinking, too, that it wasn't as if any of them were super bright.

"I'd like to be remarkable, outstanding at something, maybe painting," said Catherine. "I've a great life, I know, but I met Peter and was swept me off my feet. You should have seen him. He couldn't do enough for me! Then the children, the house, the animals. It was all so involving but now I'm," she paused pulling, Hoover firmly away from a scent she was lingering on, and then checked herself.

"I wonder if I could have been a lawyer?" Catherine said "I mean they inspire such kudos. Sara is so self-confident, so smart. People just gravitate towards her. Lawyers are respected. Everyone just knows they must be intelligent, driven, together."

"And resented," said Rose "Well, in some cases. They can work long hours and they seem to have to be Partners or something to make the big money these days and the worthier parts of law seem to get the least respect unless of course you are a successful barrister or an equal rights crusader."

"Sara never was a Partner, was she?" said Catherine.

"No, I suppose Sam was a lot to deal with. I was thinking about him the other day. Anyway, she got into property. I hope she and Florence can rub along on this holiday."

"Oh, they'll be fine. I am sooo looking forward to it!" assured Catherine.

"There's another one," confided Catherine. "Florence, she had such an interesting career with all those expelled teenagers, and now just goes where ever she pleases. I guess, having 'put in' to society and potting a pension, she *can* just float."

"Well, it wasn't quite that simple. Can't you remember she was on her knees by the end. Single parent. Demanding career. And don't forget she had to sell her house to fund her travelling," said Rose.

"Yes, but she knows what she wants and goes after it like a bloodhound. She's so certain. Sniff, sniff, sniff and she's off up some river in the jungle," said Catherine.

"She does seem to have Wanderlust, she probably has the DRD4-7R gene." said Rose.

"Well, when I think of her in those dug out boats in the Amazon I just think she is at the helm of her life. Don't they call it "agency"? She has agency. She is 'navigating' her own path," said Catherine.

"Well yes but she doesn't actually steer the boat?" said Rose.

"I think Tom, would have her down as Water, in the Chinese Five Element Medicine," said Catherine. "I'm Earth, apparently. Becoming an Artist appeals to me. Who knows I might have talent?" she laughed.

"I'm sure you might, but half the time with these things it's 99% application and 1% inspiration," Rose suggested, agreeing to go along to an Art Class for a session if Catherine found one. Catherine decided Tom might classify Rose as Wood.

She remembered how supportive Peter had been in the early days, so interested in her catering degree, and so pleased for her when she'd started professionally, a road that had stumbling blocks and had soon come to an end. The hours were long and they didn't need the money.

After booking "A Day in Oils' for herself and Rose, she dashed up the stairs in twos, and arriving in her en-suite bathroom admired her new elongated cream metro tiles which complemented the elegance of the aquamarine and cream-motif wallpaper that she held so dear.

She swished her mouth out with mint flavoured mouthwash and ran her tongue along the roughish edge of an upper molar, the one that was blighting her life, and yet she was too petrified to seek a solution for. Maybe dental treatment had been the only fly in the ointment throughout childhood.

"A Day in Oils, booked all day Saturday," she texted Rose and paused delighted, on the threshold of a new beginning. She would give it a real go, even try hard!

She would transform the Orangery into an art studio. It had excellent light, a mass of space and such a pretty outlook on to the terrace with the further backdrop of the black iron railed fence one could see through to open farmland. The dogs could hang out, flat on their sides, faithful muses as she toiled towards achievement. Tom might hang them in his gallery. One day her exhibition would be unveiled, astonishing her nearest and dearest, and society. Society rated Art. She could purge herself from being filled top to toe with vilest mediocrity. Shuddering at self-indulgence, she checked her daydreams, remembering it was an art lesson. No more, no less.

Rose, punctual, picked up Catherine. The day was on. Catherine had provided the picnic of two easy peel orange spheres, two apples, two bananas, not ripe enough to cause mayhem, and doorstop sandwiches made with mature cheddar. She would have liked to include grapes, olives and tiny vine-ripened tomatoes but felt it impractical.

"It's alright for you," Catherine confided. "You're used to classrooms and you do art. How is your application going?"

"In," said Rose smartly.

"Ah," said Catherine with a turn of the head and a broad smile conveying congratulations.

"I'll put on the Sat Nav." said Rose. "We're making good time."

"Did you bring any 'Woodland scenes'?" Catherine asked.

"I did," said Rose.

"I bet if Florence was here, she'd be wearing an artist's smock."

"Yes," laughed Rose. "Olive green with a fetching beret!"

"Oh, tilted just a bit too far. She'd knock up something very bold in minutes," said Catherine fondly.

"And get paint everywhere," remarked Rose. "Oh, and Sara would turn up in Chanel, perfect make-up without a hair out of place and treat paint if it could cause disease."

"Not really fair," corrected Catherine lightly. "Sara used to get stuck in with paint when she started on those refurbishments. She did no end of rubbing down and painting Victorian windows. On a ladder, too. Cleared the guttering, fixed the odd slipped tile, all that stuff. Got down and dirty. No long fancy nails then."

"Strange we are all such friends when you think how different our lives are now?"

"I guess," said Catherine enjoying the ride. "Gosh it's pretty countryside. I'm so glad you could come. It makes it twice as good for me, at least twice! I think I must be essentially a herd animal."

"Aren't we all?" said Rose fondly remembering the general warmth and bustle of the school life. The cosy story times she had with her young pupils, squashing cross legged on the mat, with a thumb near their mouth or leaning against a best friend, hanging on her every word. "Though Sara might not be," she ventured.

"Maybe she's a Queen Bee? I mean she's made enough Royal Jelly!" Catherine laughed. "I'm a little disappointed that the class is 'Woodlands'. I love trees but I'm not that keen on plain landscapes. I like animals and people in my art," said Catherine.

"Sneak a squirrel in," suggested Rose who liked to find solutions.

"It's just a bit of fun really," said Catherine.

"Yes, and I can put it on my next CV if this application backfires on me!" laughed Rose.

"You can see why the Cotswolds are world famous."

"Yes," said Rose her eyes glued to the road; her hand clasping the wheel as if it might escape.

"The Sat nav says we are only four minutes away. We must be coming in the backway or something. This looks like a common or a deer-park."

Almost as they parked the skies let forth heavy drops of rain. Catherine felt the wetness on her face and forearms before unleashing a large navy umbrella. Rose scrambled for her raincoat and the backpack containing their picnic and her inspiring Woodland scenes that they'd been asked to bring along.

A woman parked alongside and, in the spirit of camaderie, Catherine approached and enquired if she, too, was here for the Art Class.

"Indeed," Brenda smiled emerging with her large, ruddy face with on- trend, red hair-tips.

She was portly and middle-aged. Her dazzling shirt, shouted out, that the wearer, was not willing to step aside into the margins, before old age, death and obscurity; a battle against the tide indeed.

Brenda was a singer and wore her heart on her patterned sleeve. The three women made their way up the path through well-kept lawns to the Rococo Orangery where their class was to be held.

Rose and Catherine were treated to a full disclosure of Brenda's life. The death of her parents and its impact on the family farm, somewhere in Warwickshire. Her brother wanted to sell. Her sister didn't. However, it turned out that it had, in the spirit of primogeniture, been left solely to brother who feeling that this was unfair to his sisters in this day and age, and who wasn't a farmer, had the will changed so it split three ways. Now he wanted to sell but his sister did not and Brenda, was in two minds in the middle.

"Yes, she wanted to keep it!" Rose had exclaimed on their journey back, "but only to visit occasionally. Happy to leave all the hard work and expense to the brother who clearly didn't want to be hobbled down with a dirty great farmhouse, so his sisters could occasionally visit or go on to their friends about the family farm."

"Yes, I suppose it's unreasonable," agreed Catherine wondering if that was how Rose viewed her house, a great millstone. She thought of Rose's neatly built semi. What they did hold in common was they were all in "autumn" now and winter was just around the corner. The talk of bereavement had reaffirmed her sense of an ending.

"You're lucky having both parents still," she said to Rose knowing what a good relationship Rose enjoyed, with both. They were very proud of Rose though Catherine guessed they would have preferred her nearer, and that Steven hadn't deserted their daughter after robbing her of a chance to have children with his insistence that the world was full enough. For the first time in her life, a penny dropped, and Catherine considered a life without children might indeed be just as happy if not happier.

"I feel nearer to death, now Dad's died. Losing a parent, bumps you up the Ferris Wheel," said Catherine. "And, of course, I miss him and mum's now on her own."

Rose said nothing.

"'Pushing up the daisies' Catherine said, "stops just being a euphemism." She considered daisies, sucking out her minerals to flower, but who got buried these days?

"Do you remember Sara saying she wanted to be buried if she couldn't be frozen or cloned," said Catherine. "That she wanted to be sitting up in an open coffin. Very candid," continued Catherine.

"Macabre," added Rose. "She'd be in a well-cut business suit with an expresso in hand."

"Bolt upright, with that red lipstick," agreed Catherine.

She remembered once when they were very drunk a discussion on how they wanted to be seen out had evolved. Something, Catherine had never done with Peter. Florence had been full of it, continually changing her mind; first, a white wicker coffin and then a cardboard one they could graffiti.

She'd wanted to be buried as a bride and have her daughter as a flower-girl walking in front of the coffin, singing Ophelia's flower speech. 'And there's pansies, that's for thoughts. There's fennel for you, and Columbines,' she'd half-sung explaining that her humanist ceremony was to include an open mic, where all the mourners should file past, write on the coffin or recount some ditty and swig a drink.

"That might take a long time," said Rose.

"That's what Sara said and on the presumption that more than a handful would turn up," said Catherine.

"I suppose it depends how long she lives" said Rose, "as to the number of her mourners?"

Catherine continued, "Florence said that if a plot was out of the question her burnt ashes were to sprinkled on the junction of the Rio Tabatingo and the Rio Madre de Dios and Sara had asked her who the hell was going to do that. Florence had suggested posting them to a nearby back- packer's inn. I asked her if the Danube or Tiber would do and then you suggested Merry brook or the Avon and asked if Tom had any part in this and Florence had said they were to be buried together, entwined. If she were to go first he should be 'encouraged' to join her."

Chapter Six

The Art Class

Killian was a good teacher. Better teacher than artist, thought Catherine, who was not a fan of modern Art, especially not abstract landscapes.

His most useful tip was, when looking at something to squint. It helped you pick out the main outlines, the dark showed up more. They all tried it.

Rose delighted, was already playing out the scene it would create back in the classroom.

Killian emphasised there was no obligation the final painting should look anything like its starting point. From the beginning, he assured them, anything could and should happen. He was very dismissive of copying, considered it had been done to death.

Catherine couldn't swallow this concept and rather thought it the case that no-one these days practised enough to be able to copy well, and certainly nothing matching the Dutch Masters or Millais. At Tom's gallery there was nothing that resembled anything in the photographic sense.

Now one need only show a glimpse of what something might be. This very, very, impressionistic style would be easy for even the youngest children, thought Rose. She was giving Killian her full attention and was becoming rather hopeful on the outcome of the day and itched to get started. She didn't enjoy too much theory and thought TTT or Too much Teacher Talking was taking place.

Catherine was quite happy to jot down notes. Rose had bullet pointed two:

Don't have to copy

Screw your eyes up as defines shape better

Killian continued expressing that painting should be 'a journey.' He showed the class two he'd done earlier, reminding Catherine of Blue Peter.

Dot, who had already asked several questions, although around fifteen years older than anyone else was twice as animated. She volunteered that his paintings had been quickly executed. Even Rose cringed when Dot had said, "I bet that one didn't take long."

Killian had shaken his head, emphatically, and explained that it had taken "hours," to deliberate on which colour to fill a particular section. He showed some cut out colours, Matisse, near death, had produced, to prove his point.

There was a whiff of loneliness within the class. At the drop of a hat, Dot spoke. It was if the painting was only a backdrop and the real story lay in the group. Mixed paint meant mixed people.

Brenda, Catherine, Rose and Dot shared a stout wooden table at lunch and looked over each other's sandwiches. Dot offered homemade currant rock buns round to everyone in the group.

Catherine glanced at Rose and surmised that she'd not known many lonely moments. Of course, there had been her abrupt abandonment, but Rose had always had that lovely school with all those welcoming children with cheerful faces, the corridors adorned with their 'masterpieces' or photos of smiling staff, herself, a member of the inner circle; a full-timer and long serving member, near the top of the tree.

There was the uplifting morning singing, the excitement, the structure, the discipline, the order; the promise. Oh, Rose didn't know anything at all about loneliness thought Catherine. She was cosy in the school bubble; a womb.

Catherine conceded Rose had known pain, as she studied her friend's eager manner as Rose shifted from one resting leg to the other and seemed to be willing Killian to stop talking about his painting and let them get on with their own.

Catherine remembered back to the flooring of Rose. She remembered, more clearly than yesterday, the phone ringing late one, late, Thursday evening.

"He's left me," Rose's gentle voice waivered. "He's left me and he's not coming back."

Catherine had told her to stay put, and had been there in the ten minutes it had taken to grab her bag, put the dogs to bed, briefly explain to Peter and drive the mile to her friend's house. Catherine had let herself in with her spare key and found Rose upstairs looking into the abruptly half-emptied wardrobe where Rose's clothes remained neatly hanging.

She was staring at them as Jude the Obscure might have stared at his children, on opening his. Her world as she had known it, sweet, full and wholesome, had emptied: ended with a bang and a whimper. The wheel had turned.

Catherine turned her friend around so her back faced the wardrobe and held her very close for the first time. They had sat on the marital bed for a good few moments, in silence, with Catherine holding Rose's hand firmly as if she would never let it go. She had hung her head forwards, in sympathy.

Gradually, their breathing slowed right down and time crawled by until the silence stopped soothing and started to oppress. Catherine suggested tea and Rose murmured she'd have coffee; decaff, to be found decanted in a mint green jar. Most things were decanted at Rose's: everything having a place.

Catherine assured her dear friend she was baffled by the situation, astonished. Rose, by this time had started to cry, silently with tears rolling and rolling, shaking her head and saying, "I just can't believe it."

Catherine had snuggled into Peter that night and couldn't easily think of life without him. That, had been years ago. Things were different now. Wounds had closed and wounds had opened.

Rose was in an exuberant good humour on the way home, heralding how great was Killian's technique with the toothbrush and turps. She would introduce the children to the joy of 'Spotting' after Sandy had rigged up protective sheeting, she said continuing, "They don't get paid enough for what they do and not even paid for the lunch hour."

"Many teachers haven't kept up with the other professions let alone, with business, though of course the media would have us think that everybody else is earning a fortune. That or starving," Catherine remarked calculating that Rose probably earnt a fraction of what Peter and Sara did.

"Yes and no bonuses," laughed Rose suspecting that Peter's new Audi was the result of last Christmas's bonus. "Unless of course, you count a box of chocolates and a, 'Best Teacher' badge. We'll be using acrylics, as I don't suppose the school budget will run to oils," Rose continued.

"Yes, well, oil is tricky. I could imagine some of the parents getting pretty cross if any damage was incurred to uniform or furnishings," said Catherine. "I didn't know the prices of those oil paints varied so. I have to have some of that very brilliant fuchsia,"

"Me too," agreed Rose.

"And some of that glorious dark lilac!" enthused Catherine.

"Yes," said Rose "You could use one of them sparingly as part of your 'bold statement'."

"Didn't Killian comment on your 'brilliant use of colour?'" Rose recalled.

"He did!" said Catherine. "I really enjoyed that class. I didn't know that oils could be manipulated so."

"Yes, I know," said Rose who hadn't had quite the success of her friend and had the indignity of having her work pointed out as an example of 'muddiness' where she hadn't got the knack of when to blend and when to let dry.

"Oh, Killian seemed to call every painting either too 'muddy' or too 'busy'," Catherine said dismissively. "Leave a place for the eye to rest on," she mimicked.

"What was all that about tonality and why can't you use more than two or three colours?" queried Rose.

Later Catherine discovered that if you took a photo and then edited the piece it could appear far more proficient. She had "What's Apped" some impressive images over to her children and had been texted back with "Brilliant art, mum!" by Ben who had cheered her up no end.

Driving home Rose suggested that they might paint together one evening. Maybe with a bottle.

"Yes, what a great idea. Painting with Prosecco," Catherine suggested proudly.

"Or painting while pissed," offered Rose who seldom if ever got pissed.

Catherine was further lifted by a suggestion from Sara that she should come.

"Get Florence along, too!" she'd added. "I wish I had more time. I would have loved to have been at the class. It sounds a hoot. I've had a nightmare this week. Three change-overs and five, FIVE places I should be at once. Whitstable, London, Worcestershire, Warwickshire and Gloucestershire. And Sam's Lucy is over from Australia between jobs and boyfriends. Painting with Prosecco sounds fabulous."

Catherine was delighted with the idea saying how they could all paint in the conservatory. As she put the phone down on Sara's clipped voice, she felt a warmth and enthusiasm, as Killian had claimed, the start could throw up a whole different outcome. She fantasized about adorning her conservatory's walls with works of art from her friends. Their gallery.

She felt connected, happy and looking forward. She would spruce up the ample space and put up fairy lights. The shambolic cocktail cupboard could be cleared out to store paint and equipment, a range of which already acquired. It had felt good. She hadn't yet allowed herself to purchase an easel feeling she should earn that though she couldn't prevent the flight of fancy involving easels on the lawn, along with pastel coloured, iron tables and chairs with everyone scampering around with paint brushes and silken head scarves with a "Oh, that's so good, darling."

Peter seemed in good spirits, too, and asked her if she'd had a good class. Catherine had hidden the fruits of her labour under newspaper on the top of the grand piano and he hadn't asked to see them.

"How's Rose?" he had asked.

Catherine asked him about his day and he said something like "We're getting there, we're getting there." Then he had asked what was for dinner and disappeared into his study.

Catherine had thought he seemed a little friendlier than usual but felt it could have just been due to her own uplifted state of mind. She started to wonder if they should do more as a couple. Wasn't it a danger when the kids left, the glue flew? Didn't you have to make sure that you bonded safely, in other ways, like a weekly dance class or buying a holiday cottage.

She imagined how Peter would have got on with Killian and his class and dropped the notion, as soon as she'd started it, as semi-ridiculous. She also decided she wouldn't mention too much, the subject of art. He could be quite squashing in a careless way.

Tired, she decided on an early night, she went to say goodnight but his study was empty. She climbed the stairs and entered the bedroom to find him curled up. He stirred and she told him that the dogs were away and his grey suit was out for the next day. He smiled appreciatively and snuggled up.

Lying next to him, the thoughts of her painting subsided, as she sensed a change in Peter. He seemed a little low-spirited, nicer. She wondered if she ought to cheer him up with a supper party. Long ago, they would see Rose and Steven most weekends. Peter would come home and cheerfully ask, "When are the Guardian readers due?"

Maybe Rose, Florence and Tom should come around for supper and then she remembered those days, years back, when he couldn't take his eyes off Florence and had followed her around like a puppy dog and had the gall to then complain to Catherine of the pain of unrequited love. He would have left her had Florence said the word, an act of betrayal that Catherine could never quite forgive. Peter seemed to make very light of it.

"I would never actually have gone, darling," he'd told her a year or so later but she knew that he would have. No, she didn't want Florence and Tom around Peter, after all.

She missed the early years of foursomes. Rose and she met first in London and had an instant rapport. When Rose had moved to the village, they'd dog walked together, becoming close over the years. They had shared many a happy supper night with Rose and Steven, animated with political and broad ranging discussion.

Sometimes Peter could be induced to play Scrabble or Trivial Pursuits where Rose displayed a competitive nature and knew all the two letter words and strategized to use her 'x's and 'z's on a triple letter.

Steven, a social-minded, sports-loving, science teacher was a formidable opponent at Trivial Pursuits and Peter would sometimes ditch Catherine and insist they play Boys vs Girls though this could backfire as Rose, too, was knowledgeable. She and Steven had been well matched there. They'd been a cosy couple.

Catherine felt a surge of anger at Steven. He'd come out of the mayhem he caused so well, with a young family. Was it a boy then a girl? Catherine estimated they would now be around eleven and twelve. At least Rose had been spared teaching them.

Thank goodness he had moved out of the village. The village community was tight. Everything overlapped. He'd moved on with the girl from the squash club, divorcing Rose quickly and married Megan.

Peter had met him once in the pub and came home saying how cut up Steven had been about leaving the dog and that he felt he'd been very fair to Rose by accepting a low valuation on the house.

Catherine dwelt on the notion of letting go and thought of those people who had to do it. Did it get easier when you got older or harder? Did you train your brain to rose colour memories and filter out the pain?

Outlook was so fundamental and there was probably a knack to it. She felt blessed with a glass half-full nature. Of course, she'd had that knock from Peter. Life was never the same. Always now she had one eye open, her face half shrouded from the crowd. Her slice, not easily healed so she would continue to rinse it out. She feared gangrene. After the betrayal, for years this sore wept, robbing life of colour.

Lying in his embrace, she thought to, 'lighten up'. Catherine corrected her thinking "What's all this fussing? How is this helpful?" She would take a leaf out of Rose's book and write a 'to do' list before bed. It was said that it helped remove anxiety and made for a sounder sleep.

So not to disturb Peter she wrote her list on the stairs.

Paint

Be nice to Peter

Prepare C.V.

Walk the dogs

Start Yoga class

Start Art Club

Happy with the list she returned, quietly to the bedroom, put it on the cabinet, and peeling back the silken duvet and high-grade Egyptian cotton sheet she climbed back into bed, contentedly.

Chapter 7

The Girlie Weekend

Returning to Chadbury, after two very nice nights with dear Tom, Florence found herself back at her daughter's boxy home, at a loose end.

She could, at least, make herself useful and took a look at Beatrice the Border Collie, a non-litter sister to Rose's Doug. There you had it: two of the four friends joined, cross-generationally, by dog blood.

Florence hoped 'Be-at' wouldn't be too boisterous. She took the smart red harness near the front door and slipped it onto Beatrice deciding she would not let her off it until they reached Catherine's. The sleek, young dog was far too integral a family member to risk with the chance of speeding traffic. Besides, dogs weren't treated on the NHS and vets were expensive.

This decision had been partly born of experience. Her father was in the habit of walking his neighbour's dog. This immaculately well- behaved, always-off-the-lead Golden retriever, one fateful day, instead of sitting on the curb as always, raced across the road, dying before he reached the other side. Her dad had seen it all. No one else was hurt, well at least not physically. The owner, a long-term friend, as well as neighbour, was very good and joked lightly, "No good deed goes unpunished, huh?" but Florence's father had seen the pain in his eyes. His wife had died a couple of years earlier, his children all abroad.

So, Florence kept Beatrice safely on her lead.

She noted the dogs, with the exception of the meteoric rise in popularity of the Cockerpoo and Labradoodle, believed always to be non-shedding and hypoallergenic, were all pedigrees. Where had all the crossbreeds gone? Those delightful healthy 'heinzs'. She missed the street dogs of South America. In her book, they were the best dogs. You had to go to Romania now to get hold a proper mongrel, she thought or Spain.

Florence tensed round a bend and then relaxed once past a blind spot and Catherine's large brick house reached out monumentally from the landscape amidst a canopy of trees.

There, enjoying meadow life, was a lovely herd of cattle, grazing nonchalantly. When surveying cattle, always Florence sought to pick a favourite and, then would change her mind over and over, when caught by the subtleness of another's set of brindled markings. A mixed herd was a special treasure and put her in mind of the poem, 'Pied Beauty.' 'Glory be to God for dappled things,' she murmured, wishing she had learnt more of it by heart. Her mother had a terrific arsenal of quotations, as had her late grandmother, too. Florence had read somewhere, that someone could recite *Jane Eyre,* off by heart; in its entirety.

A lovely warm breeze blew between the burgeoning hedgerows. She trundled up the lane beside the long grasses, three-foot high; wavering yellow corn in one field and cattle idling in the other. She had loved living amid the greenery of Chadbury. She would suggest a London stay for them all. Sara had the space if they doubled up. They could go dancing and have fun.

"She'll be alright with my girls, won't she?" said Catherine, relieving Florence of the lead and trotting Beatrice to the boot room. "I've just done the kitchen floor," she explained over her shoulder.

The floor sparkled as if on an advert. Florence wondered how often Catherine did it. She'd just presumed that Christine took care of all that.

"Thought Christine did all that?" she enquired.

"No, no. Only have her once a week now besides I quite like doing it."

Florence, not at all a fan of any sort of housework or even talking about it, changed the subject.

"Peter good?"

"Yeah"

"Kids, good?"

"One green, one amber."

"Well that sounds good. Francesca's fine though no sign of a boyfriend. I'd had a hundred by her age. It's all work no play with her. Teachers have to work so hard these days, can't be much fun for the kids. No wonder so many play up these days. I'm thinking of working again. I miss the PRU."

Catherine had heard that before.

"I thought you were going back to South America to finish your epic voyage?"

"Yes," said Florence, who had still not bought her ticket. She was enjoying her summer in England with Tom, family and friends and had rediscovered London.

"We should visit Sara and do some sights?" she suggested.

They could pub crawl through Camden; The World's End, The Oxford, hang out at comedy clubs, hit the Electric Ballroom, thought Florence although she realized that it might be a step too far. Catherine set down the tray she had carried; placing coasters on the glass table.

"God you need dynamite to get you out the village these days. When did you become such a homebird?" Florence continued.

Admiring the surrounding green aspect through the glass, a twinge of envy shot through Florence. She'd had all this, the apple trees, the paddock, all be it, on a smaller scale, but once, she'd had all this charm with Fern Cottage – or the Crow's Nest as she had nick-named it.

"Why did I sell my house?" she blurted out.

Catherine, who at the time thought her crazy, said, "Florence, you thought long and hard over it. You were sick and tired of all the work, the garden, the paddock, the animals and you were working so hard at the Pupil Referral Unit. Franny had left home. It was too much for one person. You were always worried about money. You said you hated being a wage slave. Selling that place set you free. I remember distinctly you, me and Rose composing a very involved for-and-against list."

"Well, I wish I hadn't," Florence confessed.

Catherine could see why but Florence appeared to her as a child with a hand trapped in the biscuit tin after scoffing countless custard creams and who was now feeling caught out and sick. Florence had been living the high life for five years. Talk about having your cake and eating it.

"Have a biscuit Florence," said Catherine, passing her a bone china teacup decorated with tall poppies. Florence turned her nose up at the biscuit wondering why her friend didn't get it that she was not, and never had been, a grazer of biscuits, however exotic the assortment. It wasn't as if she ever brandished at Catherine, a pack of cigarettes or such.

"Don't look back," Catherine advised Florence, admiring her friend's face, that chin held high setting off a strong jawline, reminding Catherine, yet again, of Pre-Raphaelite painting. She always thought of Florence somewhere middling between Rossetti's ethereal muse, Lizzie Siddal as Beata Beatrix, and Jane Morris as Venus Verticordia or even Persephone. The lucky thing was disturbingly, irritably good looking but could also, at times, appear mellow and, with those lovely strawberry blond locks, look as innocent as Botticelli's flaxen-haired Venus rising up on the giant clam.

She'd once told Florence who'd laughed out loud and said Aphrodite was the goddess of Sexual love and had been created by sea froth and the hacked off genitals of Uranus and on being born immediately gave birth to twins, Himeros and Eros.

"Uranus's Titan son, Cronus, did it," Florence had said, "with the use of a stone sickle, care of the Greek primordial deity, Earth mother, Gaea who was Aphrodite's mum. The kids at the PRU enjoyed creation stories," she'd said.

"You have had an amazing lifestyle. You still do. I would love to be that intrepid," Catherine assured her friend.

Florence, sensing it was a good time to plead her case, looked up at Catherine and over her tea that she nursed with both hands as if a tiny baby.

"I need cheering up. Can you get Sara to have us all for a girly weekend at her London place?"

"I'll certainly try," said Catherine.

"And we must go dancing, but don't mention that part to Sara," said Florence, clapping her hands, and very much cheered.

They'd been saddled with Friday rush hour on account of having to wait for Rose to finish school who made up for it with her abundant enthusiasm. She thought the sheer energy, movement and variety was staggering.

"London is a totally intoxicating soup," agreed Florence. She herself had a tiny backpack, a pale blue jersey wrapped around her slender waist and no coat.

"Really girls? One each, even!" she'd exclaimed disapprovingly when the women had arrived with their wheelies.

"Kitchen sink," Rose grinned.

"Two nights," scoffed Florence who, at twenty-seven, had circumnavigated the globe with just two matching red, Roly-Poly bags. "Remember the days when the Wheelie case was still a twinkle in some inventor's eye?" she'd laughed as they trundled to the station.

Once safely on the Northern Line, all of them with one arm hanging on to keep upright, Rose looking down at her cabin bag, shamelessly broke the silence: "You know the Mayans and the Incas, around 1500 BC had invented the wheel, but had just used them for children's toys not for building. So they did have the wheel even if it was around two thousand years after the Mesopotamians."

Within the hour the gallant band had arrived on the doorstep of an elegant, Hampstead townhouse built alongside the Heath.

"Welcome to South Hill Park. How is Jess?" Sara asked.

"Green," said Catherine.

"Ben?" enquired Sara.

"Amber," said Catherine.

"Ah," sighed Sara in relief, they were on for a good weekend, she thought as she knew Catherine could only ever be as happy as her unhappiest child. Sara credited Florence as able to bypass that parental trap, although Francesca appeared so together, it had never been an issue.

Florence was impressed by the modernity of the interior behind the Edwardian façade. She slung her backpack on the window side of the doublebed admitting she was 'well jel'.

"Zone 2 and right next to the Heath!" she'd whispered to Rose applying an ample amount of eyeliner.

They returned, freshened and changed, to Sara's bar and toasted their good fortune. Sara, not renowned for her cooking, threw a selection of cheese in front of them along with a French stick and some elegantly boxed 'Thins'.

"Starting with cheese and biscuits" she announced, "finishing with fruit," she added, dropping a bunch of red and a bunch of green grapes in front of her guests.

"Ha, do you remember that toga party we had?" laughed Sara, "Rose was doing her probation year, studying the Romans. I remember us buying sheets from the charity shops and Florence was, literally, in her toga, languishing on the staircase, feeding grapes to any attractive man by hand."

"Ah yes, that's when I met that Adonis. That was his actual name. Good-looking but very quiet. His family were mega wealthy. I could have been rich. He showed me photos, his uncle's yacht and a place which had marble everywhere and two huge Great Dane statues and *enormous* chandeliers. A little like the hotel I visited in Buenos Aires, the one that Obama and Madonna had stayed in," said Florence who, as her daughter often pointed out, was prone to crow.

"What together?" asked Sara non-seriously, adding, "What was Adonis doing with us lot in East Finchley if he was so rich? Either the uncle had a lot of nephews or those were old photos of Onassis that he'd picked up to impress gullible young women. Probably, bought them at a Seduction School."

Florence laughed good humoredly. She felt quite at home and sipped away at her fizz as if remembering good times past and thinking she should swap to lager.

"Eat something then," warned Rose. "Remember what happened last time!"

"No…" said Florence and Sara in unison.

"My point exactly!" said Rose, who had never been 'black out' drunk, unlike the rest of them. Although Catherine and Sara had left behind that sort of behaviour long ago.

It was after two when they got in; Catherine hobbling about on her kitten heels. "I don't know how people can wear high heels at the office all day, well, anywhere really. Did you ever – in the city and all that?" she looked at Sara.

"Hmmm, that should be the reason they're called *killer* heels. Thankfully I took a stand against girl torture, as did some bright spark, in early 20th Century China, when they made foot-binding illegal. I'd no more walk around in high heels than take a rusty knife and cut out my lady parts."

"I rather like them…" said Rose. "They are sexy."

"Yes, I agree with you," Florence sighed, "though, you have to lower your head down to talk to shorter people. They're not very practical and can hurt… apart from that, they do look cool."

Florence suggested that they visited the Porcupine – an old meeting spot in Charing Cross. How she had loved to browse the bookstores.

On arrival, they managed to grab a table, helped by the efficient, elbows-wide technique Sara had adopted when very young. Sara and Florence secured a table whilst Rose and Catherine bought the drinks. Catherine had raised a glass and exclaimed:

"To the autumn of our lives!"

Florence, though not as old as the others was no spring chicken, frowned and shuddered. "Great, winter next."

"Yes," said Sara, "remember girls – there's no situation today that can't get worse tomorrow."

"I wonder how old we'll be when the fat lady sings?" said Florence, wondering who would die first.

She said that she didn't like winter for more than three days a year and would be coming back as an 18th century Highway man.

"Time travels back and forth, as steady as the pendulum on a grandfather clock," she said. "I like those three-cornered hats."

"You've always had a very vivid imagination Flo," remarked Catherine.

"What animal would you come back as?" asked Rose remembering the warm-up game of 'Who am I?' or '20 questions' she sometimes used at school.

"Oh, a giraffe maybe" Sara suggested. "Or Okapi, yes an Okapi – less people around. Not many tourists in the Congo. And you?"

"Oh, a dolphin I think," Rose said.

"Better make it a male one then unless you want to be gangraped by a group of bottle noses," said Sara nonplussed.

"Sara!" exclaimed Catherine.

"No seriously, the animal world is not fluffy. It's fierce," she insisted. "I heard a chimp raped a woman once."

"Red in tooth and claw," remarked Florence who had a liking for Tennyson and had a copy of 'Mariana' in her bag, that she was still trying to learn by heart.

"And you'd be a Hook-nosed Sea Snake," she laughed.

Sara laughed tilting her head, her nose not the least bit aquiline.

"They inject a neurotoxic venom five times more potent than a cobra," Florence added.

"Lighten up ladies" a gentleman bystander chipped in and the four of them gaped at him. His name was Terence and they bought him a pint of 'Hell's Camden Ale'. He was visiting his son who was at Dental School for technicians, in Gower Street. From then on, he was to be known as, 'Terence the Tapir.' Aptly named as he, nonthreatening and nosey.

Catherine picked both, a dog and horse, and couldn't decide. She had been nicknamed 'Pony Perks' at Prep School hanging out with Donkey Dale but dogs were now more prominent in her life.

Florence said Sara was to be a porcupine, as they'd been in the Porcupine, and that she was ill-suited to be the shy and retiring Okapi and was better suited to the spikey Porcupine or maybe a raptor. Sara told Florence she was a butterfly or possibly a mink. Florence disagreed and had herself down as a Brahman cow and ignored Rose protestations that it had to be a *wild* animal as Catherine had been allowed both dog and horse. Catherine offered to be a wolf but everyone shook their heads, even Terence.

"On the canine front," Florence said, "I bag the fox, the *long-legged* fox, it's a separate species apparently that only some have ever seen, I guess it might look like the Brazilian Maned Wolf," and swanned off to the ladies, wafting her scent glands and swaying her imaginary foxy brush behind her. Terence watched her go.

"Terence are you from Malaysia or Brazil?" asked Sara.

"I'm originally from Croydon," replied Terence.

Rose, keen for Terence not to hear her, turned her back on him, and pointed violently towards her crotch with the accompanying action of the fake razoring of her pelvic bone, while pulling a *you know what I mean* face.

"Brazilian, Terence you are Brazilian," said Sara.

Florence was quickly brought up to speed by Catherine.

"There is a third one," said Florence who couldn't recall its name. "It's smaller and hairier and somewhere on the South American continent." She then potted a tipsy evolutionary history of the tapir, involving horses, hippos and some giant hyena type dinosaur called Ic-something-saur, the skeleton of which she had recently seen in a Bratislavan Museum.

"**Con**-ti-nent" giggled Sara.

"There used to be one hundred and sixty species of elephant and now just three remain, two in Africa and of course the dear, dome-headed Asian one," said Florence who had read it at the museum.

"Verbal in**con**tinence," said Sara. Rose was very interested by this and Catherine, too, although she had one eye on Sara and hoped she wouldn't go too far.

Terence, merry by this stage, and blessed with good humour, offered to go to the bar. He had been alone in a crowd for the last twelve hours. Catherine suggested that Rose should give him a hand. She was busy calculating whether or not Terrence was married. She hadn't seen a ring and he hadn't mentioned a 'lady friend'. He wasn't bad-looking, a reasonable height and Rose had been single for several years. She was very fond of Rose, her constant companion throughout all those dog walks and talks. She was always there at the bottom of the lane, so cheery. Catherine considered that she might be bereft without her.

So, when Rose and Terence returned from the bar, Catherine stood back from the table so they could place the drinks carefully down, then stepped back in between them.

Chapter 8

Sara

The whole weekend had been a great success and the women enjoying a great deal of jollity, fell quickly back into intimacy, as old friends do.

Rose, after many drinks told Sara that she'd taken anti-depressants when Steven left. Sara wondered if either Catherine or Florence knew, or indeed, anyone. Rose had spoken as though it was a confession but it shouldn't have been. Who apologized for having an aspirin? The British were still so up-tight about all that sort of thing.

Why did she feel shocked? Disappointed, even? She imagined it was because Rose was so capable, appeared so upbeat, such a 'Zelda'. If it happened to her then it could happen to anybody. Sara felt a disappointment too, that Rose hadn't told her at the time. Were they not close?

Fun as the weekend had been, an odd feeling had descended on Sara that hung around preventing her somehow from snapping into action. She couldn't get started. That Monday morning, she couldn't be bothered to deal with any of her nineteen lets.

She couldn't even be bothered to write her 'to-do' list. She should be phoning the insurance broker to see how the leak detection was progressing or if her non-payer had at least paid some part of what she owed. She had a message from Domek to say that the showerhead needed replacing and that he could get someone to replace it for £100. That had cheered her a little.

Sara mounted the white staircase, the white steps with a strip of striped hues of blue carpet pinned down with pewter stair rods, and once in her generously proportioned bedroom mooched towards her bookcase and pulled out a book. She eyed its patterned hardback cover with the handwritten title:

A Year in the Life of an Alcoholic's Wife

She opened it at random. It took her back over twenty years.

11.30 am

'I'm sitting on the garden swing-seat and I'm getting that rising feeling; boy it is nice to have it back. Happiness is in the mind. I've fought not to contact Sam – sat on my hands and not let any "feel sorry for him" excuse or "angry with him" reason to provoke me to pick up the phone.

I've left him alone since he called 8.30am on Monday morning to see if I wasn't in too much distress after Sunday. If I walk to the phone or even get that feeling I say: "detach with love, detach with love, detach with love" and if that isn't enough I say: "let go" ... "let go" ... "let go" breathe out and feel better. I push thoughts of the past away and thoughts of the future unless it's a realistic future.

I make myself do the things I know I like. I've just planted twenty winter pansy seeds and have a whole lot more in the packet. I sent for them from the Sunday Times or Mail. It is better to live in the present as much as one can. I'd procrastinated with the seeds as I didn't know where I'd be. Now I know I'll be somewhere. There is no real rush. Panic is so destructive. I'll move when I'm ready – either to somewhere that Sam sets up or somewhere that I set up. I'll just wait and see...

Sara remembered those bleak weeks and tortured long minutes. She couldn't believe she'd ever been a *Daily Mail* reader. She from her very earliest years had been attracted as a fly to light to a single goal was caught in a web having to accept powerlessness. School, The Law, Money had been easy a track to follow. Goal after goal. Pound after pound. Then Sam came along and they danced on air.

Then came the pain.

The shame.

The secret life.

The fear.

The professionals tried to help.

"Desperate situations need desperate measures," they said.

A new language appeared with little phrases that popped up.

Tough love.

Rock Bottom

One step at a time.

Enabler.

Co-dependent.

Sara struggled to help.

The planner could not plan.

Relapse after relapse dulled her senses.

She wanted her old Sam back. The fun one.

When it manifested that life in London was too dangerous for Sam who had perhaps to allay ennui or suppress intolerable anxiety had taken to street drugs for his codeine dependency.

Secrecy, at first, and then immediate and energetic measures followed, once the cat was out of the bag, to deal with his addiction. Rehab after rehab followed. Sara waited, her life not her own. There were three in that marriage too. She read, dipping and skipping as she couldn't face it straight up.

Flashbacks of the early days when she and friends thought they could help him at home in their London flat, where you could step out of the French doors onto the suntrap of a patio, through the big beautiful shared garden, then under a little wooden gate straight on to Hampstead Heath, metres from Parliament Hill. The higher you climb. They'd flown kites together.

How his medic friends had brought him Temazepam with red wine to let him drink his way through cold turkey. How they'd taken all his shoes and boots. How they'd corralled him in and then left.

The stumbling.

How she'd sung hymns with him through the night from their wedding songs, 'Jerusalem' and 'Lord of all hopefulness.'

How she'd come back one morning her hands full with two shopping bags with food to sustain them through their trials and found a large, sleek drug dealer near her front door, in their leafy road. She'd implored him to go away. Put down her bags and begged.

To no avail. Sara felt dislocated.

Soon came the comatose body.

The syringes.

Eyes white and rolled.

The incessant pleading.

The choice.

She flicked through some more pages and landed on...the frothing, the fitting. She jolted and flicked further.

October 28th

Slow and steady wins the race.

10. 30 am

I woke up crushed or with the feeling of being crushed. A lot has happened in the last few days. It seems an age ago since the weekend and yet its only Wednesday.

I saw Sam on Sunday and it hurt.

It hurt keeping cool and listening to the counseller's interpretation of our situation.

By then they had left London and rented half a farmhouse in in a remote hamlet up a one-way track. She skipped a bit and read:

The messages from AA are sinking in. Think one day at a time. It is a battle to live in the present but when you feel the future is such a giant obstacle and the past is such a minefield, it's the best way – one step at a time – go forward.

Today I will make one personal phone call, write one letter to a friend, one business call, keep up with the housework recall the plumber (kindly but firmly). I will not let myself get tired. It hurts to much the next day.

How cut off she'd felt – no job – no routine. Just waiting and still hoping.

And then the alcohol. Street drugs mercifully left behind only for the demon drink to swoop in. Two against one.

The confusion.

The worry.

The car in a ditch.

The wooden club.

The terror.

The punches.

The struggle to keep centred, *when the centre cannot hold*.

The dragging out of bed.

The rage.

The cover up.

The visit to A and E.

To the dentist.

The choice.

She took a leaf out of the book of her younger self, and texted Domek, to say *yes,* he could go ahead and organize the shower repair and thanked him.

Uncharacteristically, she decided to cook something nice that evening. How calm and pleasant was life with Anthony. Easy. It seemed to work well. They knew where they were with each other. Sara called Catherine. Thank God for Catherine. She was always there and knew her so well.

Sara warned Catherine not to offer any assistance with a ferret for Florence. They discussed the forthcoming holiday and what to bring. Sara's sap rose and she opened her office door to check her bank statements. Money was her friend, too.

After her chat with Sara, Catherine returned to the garden, and resumed clipping the fur from her ten-year old Spaniel. She remembered the shot Vizsla, and tried to think why Peter hadn't helped with the aftermath. Maybe he'd been at a conference. She was used to dealing with household matters alone. It was her domain. Their worlds were divided. She used to wonder when she heard a couple enquire whether or not one or other of them had paid the electricity bill, back in time before everyone did it, by direct debit. To her it sounded so sweet. So collaborative.

She pondered over her marriage as she combed the newly cut fur off Hoover and scooped up the fur droppings from the lawn and threw them behind the peach rose bush. Hoover had lovely soft white silky fur and then her black hair was equally soft but of a downy, fluffy nature; suitable for a nest, mused Catherine caught up in the modern hysteria of recycling. She thought it still nesting season, mid-July.

The bird song was beautiful and she thought she heard the distinct delivery of a chiffchaff amid the melody of a blackbird and the familiar cooing of the wood pigeons, more distant. She must top up the feeders. Where was her cocky robin?

Out of all the couples she could remember it had been Sara and Samuel that had cut the most dash. Both good-looking and in their prime, so spirited. One so self-assured, one a mix of wild and gentle with a generous heart. Any fool could see they were in love. Their eyes so focused on each other with their secret empathy and both so active, it made you weary. They got on like a house on fire. Ashes to ashes.

Her marriage was very different. Fruitful, but slow and steady; lethargic even. Years after Sara's catastrophic loss she wondered if Sara really was as alright as she seemed. She had always been robust, career-minded, focused, not so much materialistic, but goal driven.

Catherine remembered them as six-year-olds when she and Sara were both proud hamster owners. Her

Golden Siberian – or was it Syrian? – 'Hammy' had outstripped Catherine's in hamster accomplishments. She'd taught it to beg. From then on Sara had proved Catherine's superior. Sara was a worker, a trier and she had discipline with which she obtained results.

They'd shared a fierce passion for animals and Catherine could recall the dogs of their childhood: Poppy, Petunia, Rastas, Voltaire and early days spent at a well-run riding school. Catherine in the White House and accompanying farm. Her father had a factory and her mother, an artist, worked part-time at the Further Education College. Animal paintings were dotted around the house, mainly of pigs.

The riding school was set in an incredibly small plot of land thought Catherine, in suburbia. There were two rings. Black peat kept the circles ridable. The all-important letters, capitals in black on white, marked every few metres. She still remembered the boom of Mr. Chubb's voice:

"At the letter A prepare to trot … and TROT!"

There would be a line of them. The leader being of special importance and the others positioned with relevance to their rider's experience and their mounts size and temperament. Kickers were at the back and the nappy tucked in the middle.

Mr. Chubb was fair in the dishing out of the confidence-boosting rides and also, where possible, giving when possible most a go at leading the ride. It was hard work leading. Catherine didn't much like it.

Naturally, the horses were fresher earlier in the day. This worked to Catherine's advantage as her parents, with a farm, were early risers and got her to the yard for nine. This ride was for the most experienced riders and was miles the fastest. They had access to the hallowed jumping lane, a row of cross-country jumps, railed in, adjacent to the hedge-line.

Whatever happened to, 'Never give a lady a rested horse.' when little girls took over riding, thought Catherine?

Chapter 9

Regent's Park

Once again safely seated on the train, by a window with a good book at the ready, and the promise of a coffee or tea, shortly, trundling up the aisle, Florence was feeling thoroughly relaxed.

Soaking herself in good literature was a joy and, in 'The Gentle Spirit', she had found an amazing weave. Diffused with minutiae details revealing the human psyche, it was an exquisite tale of cat and mouse. Dostoevsky had it percolating with tension.

Florence, overwhelmed by his genius, was writing, more than ever, in a notebook always to hand. She was concentrating on the short 'revenge' play, 'The Starchers,' within her novel. She was investing more and more into her work, observing harder: staring at the world. Her book had grown to be so real she could almost see her new friends. 'For Every Action,' had become a passion. It was as if for years she had tinkered in the shallows and now somehow taken the plunge and was immersed very comfortably in a watery world and no longer liking to be on dry land for any length of time unless it was to glean more information on how things had ravelled, and where the kernel of truth could be located, from which to start again, to roll back up the power ball, with its influence more justly distributed, and the checkers and balancers more diverse.

She was still at it, when they arrived at Paddington. All those times she'd been in other capital cities, seeing their museums, awed by their splendour and she'd hardly been back to London since she lived there. This summer it was unfurling, after all these years.

She hopped out, with her note book back in her sleek black cycle bag. She hadn't decided whether she was going to stay at a hostel. Last time, in Camden, there had been the triple bunk incident and her in the middle one. Sixteen in that mixed dorm. It had been a step too far. To date, her favourite London Back Packers had been in Pimlico. It was an old Victorian Pub, beside the Thames, with pretty flowers and bottle green tiles. From a top bunk you could look out of the window and see Battersea Power Station, and the No24 went from the bus stop directly outside. You could go to Hampstead via Charing Cross or get off anywhere in between. They served free teas, coffees or chocolate from the bar in the large communal area where you could enjoy them on large red sofas, watching people come and go or read.

Last time she had just fallen upon that street party with the Dolly Parton act belting it out for the deck-chaired in the Sussex Gardens. Walking to Marble Arch was easy as there were maps on every corner.

With rising excitement, Florence walked up Praed Street. Outside one of the Lebanese restaurants, a lone girl puffed on a water pipe. Florence loved the range of humanity you found in this spectacular city. There was beauty in the mix. Just as there had been with the cattle grazing the pastures adjacent to her long-since-sold smallholding. Those had been happy years, a tight twosome, a modern family, a time ago now. Crow's Nest, sold.

Florence sat on a park bench with the self-realization that she was in the September of her life, an Autumn chicken. She'd admired the elegance of Dorset and Manchester Street, the lovely Norfolk and Suffolk gardens and Oxford Street, with that Edwardian marvel, Selfridges. Pondering the innovations of the modern shopping world she felt 'the mall' and out of town complex to be dire and as for the meteoric rise of the soulless online shop, handy no doubt, but didn't it take more from society than it gave?

She remembered the overwhelming colour of abroad, the smells of spices and the vibrancy of the vendors in the market places. There the articles were in visual 3D. You could see a pyramid of large, yellow spheres or touch the waxy surface of a lemon, be mesmerized by the sheer hub of human interaction and be, at one, with the crowd. It was a more natural way of living, she supposed, not all shut up like an ant, in a glass, with a lid.

There had been fantastic new architecture and she was stunned by a domed, oval bus-shaped building. Would they have allowed it in Paris? It was a swish marvel of glass and steel but through what had it sprouted? Her memory was failing: her brain, no doubt, being eaten away by some mysterious disease. Fiction had Zombies eating brains. In real-life, modern-living enabled hungry little microbes, in gangs, to nibble away. Modern-living caused anxiety, too. So could age. She'd better make as much hay as possible before the sun went in.

By Hanover Square, were three little tents, by the ping pong table statue, and she wondered if they were inhabited by members of Extinction Rebellion and asked a couple of girls sitting on the benches but they'd shaken their heads and didn't really look the type. She thought of their latest tactic of wheeling food out of supermarkets and distributing it as they felt fit and how the media and the public would receive it.

Veering off into Mayfair she was pleased to find it much emptier and hardly anyone in the upmarket shops. Her eye caught one that appeared to just sell roses, white or red, but there was a mysterious staircase going up and she thought it strange.

The English Gardens had a divine display of flowers: beds of pale marigolds, exceptionally tall white Japanese Anemones and plenty more mixed with sculptures beautifully colourful, in a spiralling planted plan.

Those Flower-heads, Catherine and Rose, would know all the names. Florence remembered their trips to Hampton Court Flower Show and the Malvern Spring and Autumn Show. They would move so slowly, so intent they'd be on every bud and bloom. She had tried to stay with them as she delighted in hearing them throw off the Latin names with Rose following it up with its folk name, too, but she couldn't stand the slow pace, and would dart off diagonally and risk long separation, rather than just put one foot in front of the other in a straight line however beautiful, fragrant or friendly. She didn't take flight in fright but through an impatient skittishness, that seemed to be gaining traction, ever since she had cast off the steadying shackles of her job. She'd turned her back on Capitalism with its ridiculous metric of GDP, kicking up her heels, and would do many loops before rejoining them, on their circuit.

Outside, The Broad Walk Café, on a tin chair, with an Americano she wondered what bean it might be? Arabica or Rombusta and felt it more likely a blend including Liberica and Excelsa beans, too. She'd recently heard a podcast about the discovery of coffee. A shepherd had noticed how lively his goats had become after ingesting some of the berries so had, himself, tried eating the soft white berries and had appreciated how much easier it was to remain awake and watchful.

Two pigeons were mating on top of the table in front of her and a large young woman, blond with freshly cut hair, sporting a jaunty black porkpie hat, with a huge black fly emblazoned on her T-shirted ample bosom, politely asked Florence to mind her stuff as she disappeared back into the café. She wasn't gone long.

Florence remembered her travels when you did that sort of stuff for one another and that just a few spoken words might be all you had in a day unless you fired up a conversation as she did at times.

The girl had a delicious looking cream tea, scone, jam and cream. Florence loved cream allowing it once a week with a customary cream cake to be eaten alongside Tom on the old, brown leather sofa. Tom didn't much like cream so he had his own goodies which he would share. Looking over at the mouth-wateringly attractive, cream tea Florence was pleased that tomorrow was Friday and inwardly sighed. It would be lovely to be back next to Tom with a film. She could literally feel the texture of the doughnut in her hand and sense the delicious viscosity of its whitish filling. It might not be jam today, she looked at her coffee, but it would be jam and cream tomorrow. She alternated between chocolate éclair, Vanilla slice and cream doughnut and she bought them from Tesco's, after a couple of early drinks with Tom, in one of their local, cosy, dog-strewn Cotswold inns. They were back in their den, by nine.

Florence reflected on her day so far. She'd read Margaret Thatcher had once said how amazed she was at how little some people did in a day. Not her, here she had seen a vast swathe of London. Some of it for the first time, and all of it through the lens of a woman, this time, in the last half of her life not the first.

She was hoping to go to a comedy show that night and wondered if she could persuade Sara to come along too and then offer her a bed. They were meeting at three at the Hard Rock Café with loose plans to visit the British Museum. That was texting for you, thought Florence.

The T-shirted woman got up and fed the pigeons with her left-overs and then binned the plate. A man, in an adidas sweat shirt, spoke very loudly to his friend. Other than that Florence felt this, in new haunt, a perfect harmony; in this peaceful green swirl within the great metropolis: the mother city. Was the man being too loud or was she just culture-ignorant? Why was she jarred by it here when she was quite used to not understanding what people were saying, on her travels? It would take a while to rinse racism from society but things were looking up.

She was hopeful. It was something she considered frequently.

Florence asked the woman if she lived in London or was just visiting? She was from Archway and there, in the park, for a cream tea to mark the death of her mother a year ago to the day. Florence could see how important this was and said, "Happy Remembrances" and asked if they'd been close, already thinking that they had been. "There is an irony for those that get on well, on parting," she condoled.

The young woman with the black porkpie hat told her Queen Elizabeth had said, "The price of love is grief."

Sniffing frantically for crumbs, a small dog appeared and the porkpie-hatted girl engaged herself in a dog-based conversation. It was a sweet-looking chihuahua-cross and Florence remembered Mexico where her taxi driver had run over a dog. She thought this dog had a touch of dachshund or even beagle.

It took absolutely no notice of the smartly, dressed, "on-it" young woman. Porkpie woman asked, if she'd been to training with it, in a friendly, non-judgement manner. The girl replied that they had a personal dog trainer.

Florence guessed the young dog walker was Italian, and probably a banker's wife, and Florence was shamed by this swift judgement, and knew she'd not do too well, by some, under scrutiny. Did one always look at a stranger and eye up where you related to them on the pecking order? What was respect and why did you seem to need it?

Florence shook out her map and roughly decided on a course of action, a loose plan. She was meeting Sara at Hard Rock Café – well why not – it was superbly spacious and plush.

"See my tailor. He's called Simon." The solid beat of, 'Sex and Drugs and Rock and Roll' repeated itself over and over again. She settled on a Mocha.

Sara arrived on time. She had her dark hair in an air hostess bun and looked sleek. Florence, glad she was dressed up in her stripy blue and white trousers and cream silk shirt, got up and waved. "The loos are amazing," she said "I'll get us a Dom Peringnon, £385, shall I?"

"Coffee," said Sara, as flat as an Americano.

"What did you think of the loos?" said Florence eagerly when Sara returned.

"Well they were alright, I suppose. Not sure about the Joy Division plaque outside, a bit ignoble?" she said.

"Mmm, yes. Did you see the U2 guitar? It's signed by all four of them," said Florence. "Though I did lose a little patience with Bono, when on tour in Japan he sent his private plane back for his hat."

"Well according to what I'm reading in, 'Giant, O'Brian,' the Irish are very superstitious," said Sara.

The Spartans, too. Famously so." said Florence. "I love Hillary Mantel. That, 'Beyond Black' is a frightening book. Can you imagine the terror?" she said, "I did see Amy up on these hallowed walls. That 'Back to Black', a-maz-ing! I haven't seen Florence and The Machine anywhere."

"Yes, Amy Winehouse was special. Look you can get a Dead Rabbit here, for £13.00," said Sara.

"Not as pricey as a Suntory Hibiki Harmony," pointing to it on the Whisky menu "£18.50, no wonder they have negative interest rates," said Sara.

"I took Francesa, as a baby, to a Karaoke bar in Osaka. It's a wonder they could afford to get so pissed," said Florence.

"This new obsession with Fever Tree has swept the country. Look, it and Red Bull, are £3.50 and poor old Coca Cola and Pepsi are only £1," said Sara.

"The gentry are always rising and falling," said Florence. "We did have a loose plan to go to the British Museum?"

"Yes, yes. I haven't been for decades. I'm sure it's as boring as ever, but I'll give it a chance."

"How long have you got?" asked Florence, not yet with courage to ask her friend to the comedy show. Part of her thought, they ought to ditch the Museum and find a good old Victorian pub and get tipsy.

"I'm all yours, Florence," said Sara. "Shall we go?"

After an hour or so amongst the exhibits they left.

"Well at least we now know where the Etruscans lived?" said Sara, shaking herself off, as they stepped back into the fresh air.

"I think I would have done a lot better in Etruria than amid the Romans or Greeks. Though the Minoans, did seem to have a good time, in Crete. I certainly think dancing with bulls is preferable to stabbing them. Though I could see you as a Picador," said Florence, smiling.

"Shall we find a pub?" Sara suggested and Florence felt like linking arms with her, but knew better, smiled and shook her head.

They found one nearby.

"This has certainly escaped the Hard Rock Café treatment," hissed Sara.

"At least there are plenty of seats and no queuing. What are you having?" she asked her friend.

"I can see why. Dry white. I'm, to the loo."

Florence chatted to the young Australian barman and ascertained he had not even been born when she was dancing to, 'Joe Camilleri and the Black Sorrows' at a Melbourne night spot. A chap, on the next barstool, asked her what she was doing in town and Florence explained she was catching up with an old 'Roomie'. Alone, she would have stayed to chat, but knew Sara would consider him an undesirable, post pandemic or not, so she took the drinks over to a quiet corner and waited for her return.

"OMG you ought to see the 1960's linoleum in the loos! This place is a disgrace," said Sara, pulling a face at the wine, Florence had just bought her.

"Yes," agreed Florence who was heartily at home in the spit and sawdust atmosphere and enjoying her pint. She was preparing to suggest the Comedy Club. It was that and staying with Sara or catching the train home mid evening. It was too late now to bother with a Backpacker's Inn.

Chapter 10

Camden Comedy Club

Florence admired the perfect half-moon shining its right side against mottled sky. It was quarter to eight as they walked down Camden High Street to number 100, directly opposite The Blues Kitchen. "Do you remember

Diana Ross playing Eleanora Fagan as "Billie Holiday?" asked Florence.

"Yes, in 'Lady sings the blues.' I liked Diana Ross," said Sara.

They made their way to the bar.

"It's Noddy Holder," giggled Florence singing along

"Cum on feel the noise.

Girls grab the boys."

Sara rolled her eyes. "Poor Tom, I bet he rues the day you grabbed him," said Sara staring around in bemusement. "Are we the oldest in here?"

"Oh, I don't know. I'm blessed with age dismorphism. I went to a party the other week and I saw all these staid people and they looked so old and as if the fun had been sucked out of them but I realized I must logically be the same," said Florence.

"Preserve us. A mature Florence waiting to emerge?" said Sara.

"Demure sometimes, mature never! Though seriously, you know that song,' It's later than you think.' Do you ever worry that you are running out of time?" said Florence.

"To do what? I'm running out of wine. This wine, though not good, is better than in that last dive," said Sara who was beginning to regret agreeing to come to the comedy club in Camden and having Florence to stay the night. She never normally had house guests apart from Catherine who being like a sister didn't count. There were Anthony's children but then they were his 'guests.'

"I am getting more sensible. I'm thinking twice about the Congo. Ovid said, 'It's safer in the middle'.

"It is in the middle, the heart of Africa though I don't suppose it would be very safe on Blood River. Don't tell Catherine, she'll worry. Why don't you settle for Moon River and get married, don't tell me you think it's a bourgeois construct, maybe you could wear purple, instead," suggested Sara. "I didn't say it before, but I like what you're wearing today, for a change. You don't look bad for your age although I'm not sure if I agree with Catherine when she harps on about your Pre-Raphaelite good looks. I suppose it didn't help when Peter got that appalling crush on you."

"Oh, that was terrible," agreed Florence. "You do know I poured frozen water over that. I had to actually leave the country."

"Come off it! You leapt at the excuse to jaunt off to Sri Lanka, poor Francesca."

"Seemed to do the trick, with Peter though," smiled Florence. "They've got 'The Garden of Earthly Delights' on tonight. All for a fiver! I studied the symbolism of that painting for weeks, but not one question on Bosch or Brueghel came up in the exam. Fascinating triptych don't you think? It must have been scary to think where you might end up, after dying. They were obsessed with the Afterlife in the Middle Ages and going into the Renaissance, with Cranach and all that, Dance with the Maiden stuff."

"Hell, yes," said Sara taking a mouthful of wine.

"It's upstairs, the show," said Florence pointing to the rickety dark staircase.

"Erh! Purgatory." said Sara.

"Oh, come on! Sara it's really fun," said Florence, "It's sort of immersive. There will only be a handful of people and it will be the fun sort, especially, with alcohol in them. We'll probably be the only Brits there. Actually, I've been practising to have a go on Tuesday's Newcomer Spot but I'm not stage-ready. Tom bought me a mic."

"Just oven-ready. Has Tom been here?" asked Sara.

"No, but I've only just discovered it. Just been myself half a dozen times. How did I leave the joy of live comedy so late?" asked Florence.

"I need the loo before we go in and another drink," said Sara.

"You won't like them here," Florence warned.

Sara looked at her.

"They have no lids," said Florence, shrugging her shoulders.

"How rock'n'roll," said Sara, rolling her eyes.

Fleetwood Mac played as they took a seat, second row. Florence felt the excitement in her stomach as it lightened her heart. She loved the city and she loved the liveliness of this place. It had such energy and a soul. She was thrilled to have Sara next to her even though she looked po-faced and wouldn't return a fist bump or say, 'Boom.'

"You're not at the dentist's," whispered Florence loudly. Sara cringed.

"Where's Scottie, when you need him?" she whispered back and hoped more people would come. She made up her mind not to attempt any humour at all with The Stand-up, should he try to engage her, and sat with a partial frown. Again, she wondered why she had let Florence drag her to this point. They were all seeing one another next weekend anyway.

The audience was now six. In front of them, an older man sporting a grey, ponytail had two women hanging on his every word. Florence strained to catch them, too. His "Mrs," was one of the People's Peers, and setting up something to do with Modern slavery. She'd been on Question Time, a few times. Florence presumed on the panel.

Hearing this sparked Florence to disclose to Sara she felt ashamed of the way she'd dissipated her life and not contributed more, to the greater good. Sara had told her not to worry about it and that in 'Fable of the Bees' it explained all about the pitfalls to society by leading a virtuous life. She said it was a very useful book.

"Honeybees are responsible for a third of the food in the UK." Florence had said and Sara had said that on average people were around a third too fat so if the bees worked harder, they could have the monopoly.

The four rows of four or five chairs were now half occupied. People always sat by an aisle in order to escape to the loo, the bar, or humiliation under razor wit.

CAMDEN COMEDY CLUB in its familiar purple neon capitals shone out. The Comedian, even Florence found boring to begin with. It was a narrative involving the make-belief scenario of him being hired as a comedian for a houseboat party on the Thames. Jeremy Clarkson and then Jimmy Carr and "Shou Shou."

Within this ripping yarn, there included a fist fight between Brown and Blair with all sorts of references to blood and guts, including a charger retrieved from a rectum. Politics mixed with popular culture and the Jeremys died hard. Cameron was blown up when a hand grenade caught on his cufflinks. "No analogy there then," whispered Florence alluding to a certain political hot potato. Sara frowned at her.

In the interval the women got a drink downstairs.

"You know that Peter thing. I had the same thing, once, in Thailand, about a guy called Jack. Caught up, in a passion. Arrested by physical attraction. It was fierce.

Relentless. The power of looks, chemistry. Tom always says, "Nature's so clever." Put back my flight five times. And, also, I was sort of paying for him, his time anyway. I kept buying him presents. If I bought some jeans then I'd buy him some too. Paid for fancy restaurants. It seemed right. I mean I guess I had about twenty times the amount of money he had and I was on a budget. It was ridiculously cheap by western standards then."

"Interesting concept who pays for who or what and the power thing, though I can't really see you in a fancy restaurant," said Sara.

"The thing is. When I got back to England I just went completely off him. It was like turning the tap off. That's why Peter and I are so chilled about being around each other. It's like it never happened," said Florence.

"Well it did and I, for one, will never forget it. Catherine was distraught. You know he used to moan to her about the pain he was in," commented Sara.

"Plato said, 'Love is a serious mental illness.' It was a mid-life crisis. I should never have written that La Belle Sans Mercy stuff on the walls. I guess, I was having one too. He took it literally. Conflated it. Have you ever been driven to the edge by someone?"

"God yes," said Sara, picking up her wine. "Right into the ditch. I'll follow you up the stairs."

"Yes," thought Florence. "Sara's, 'Sam years,'" and making her way to the stairs thought of Jack and her time on elephant back in Northern Thailand. Once back in England, her passion, spent, she'd remembered him, without fondness. The romance remembered now was the exoticism, the wild location. She'd been in lust, she supposed, like the bull elephant that had thundered past them, bellowing and out of control, trunk and tail horizontal. She'd viewed that from the neck of an elephant whilst crossing a river. It had made her squeeze her thighs tight round the rough skin of its neck frightened it might bolt like a spooked horse. It hadn't, just waded on, knee-deep, behind the one in front. Her fling wasn't comparable to Sara and Sam, she felt. Marriage had never entered her mind, at the time. That thought came later, and was not driven by romance, but for the desire of a child, a nagging need that slowly took grip and steered her path. Nature is a clever thing.

Florence took the opportunity to tell Sara of the next installment of The Starchers. She had Clair winning the giant marrow competition but everyone knew that Simon had grown it. It was the talk of the village and had even been compared to Frankenstein when first being published, anonymously, with a forward by Percy Shelley to be his work. Plato said, 'Your silence gives consent.'

Part of the success of the enormous marrow – 32 lbs. – was that Simon had planted it in a corner of their garden that bordered onto cattle country so a good supply of cow dung had seeped through and generously fertilized the marrow. Florence told Sara it was meant to show good people being duplicitous and highlight the uneven playing field.

"You know when you had black hair, along with your straight features, I used to think you looked more like Francesca's mother than I did. Brown eyes too, and your olive complexion is nearer to her skin tone than mine. She wants to go and seek her father. I suppose it is very natural. I just wish I had more detail. She doesn't want me along. It's going to be tricky. Even at the time things were muddled. I was over on a Thai visa and yet she was conceived in Burma, Myanmar in one of the many villages along the hillside border. I did try and go back but they started patrolling the border with rifles and I could hardly say I'm pregnant I need to see the man with black hair and the red bandanna. All the Karen tribesmen wore them. It's the only time when language or lack of it has really caught me out. I didn't mind for myself, but for Francesca, the consequence has been endless. Probably why she's never had a boyfriend," said Florence after they'd returned to the bar when the show was over. "They were at war really, Burma and Thailand. And the tribes were in the middle with their own agenda. Then Westerners got frozen out of Burma altogether, for a decade or two."

"Well for a war baby she's doing very well. Own house, own car, responsible, futureproof job. I mean she could even come out of teaching with that Science degree. Catherine's 'well-jell' as you now so eloquently put it," said Sara not showing her amazement at Florence's revelation. She ordered more drinks.

"Francesca was a breeze, to mother. By the time she was seven she was more like a partner. We ate at Catherine's half the time. Both, Rose and Catherine were brilliant. My parents, too. You know that saying about it not being just the parents that raise a child, but a village. Well, Chadbury were very welcoming to their one and only mixed-race child. I mean, child with mixed ethnicity. I'm not sure how I would have coped if things had been different. Can I ask you something? said Florence.

"Yes," said Sara presuming it was going to be about Francesca.

"Have you had a boob job?" asked Florence. "You always had the biggest bosoms of us four, but 'The Ladies' look even bigger."

"No," said Sara.

Sara thought she ought to get Florence home. She wasn't used to seeing this vulnerability in her friend who was clearly struggling with concern, marbled with guilt, regarding her daughter. Was she afraid of losing her, or and quite possibly, of sharing her? She wanted to know if Catherine or Rose knew about this, but kept it back.

A cab dropped them home. Anthony had gone to bed but Florence was down to greet her hosts the next morning.

"Thought Korea was going to be the start of World War Three?" said Florence to Anthony, the next morning, while peeling a banana. "The comedian last night was on about sponsoring his Korean girlfriend, said you had to be on £18,600 or have £62k in the bank. Probably more by now as his act was a few years out of date."

"Politics at breakfast?" queried Sara.

"Lunch and tea, lunch and tea," sang Florence.

"Don't choke on that banana. We are probably already in one. Countries don't declare war anymore. Look at the Yemen. How many are wading in there? Though the third world war will be against pathagens of some description. The Fourth, that horrid nerve agent stuff. Tell Florence about that set of little fellas, the friendly ones, that hardly anyone's ever heard of. A type of bacteria."

"Archaea," replied Anthony, but he was more interested in discussing Geopolitics with Florence. Both of them, fascinated by how the direction of a rivers flow affected development, agreed that the sprouting of Central Europe was no accident. Anthony sited London and the Thames giving the South East of England an advantage. Florence went on to talk of the rich plains of Mesopotania.

"It's Greek for 'between the rivers', the Cradle of Civilisation between the Tigris and the Euphrates," she said.

"The Nile, too, and all that grew around that," agreed Anthony.

"I'm hoping Tom will come do that one with me, a cruise in our late seventies," said Florence.

The three sat for an unusually long breakfast, before sensing Sara had had quite enough of her, for the time being, so Florence took her leave.

On her meander back to Paddington Station, Florence stumbled across something that impressed her. Colour grabbed her attention, big bright pastels, and a sign Helen Beard "It's her factory" – U. Coaxed by intrigue, into the art exhibition, passed two smartly dressed young men at the foyer, she embarked on her journey around it, the only visitor. 'Action Button' and 'Her Corporeal Appetite," were two of her favourites. She read, in the glossy programme, along the bottom line, 'it starts with U'. Same topic different treatment she mused, thinking back to her Art History Degree. After climbing down the stairs, and walking along the empty herring-boned wooden floor into the body of the show she'd been brushed, very gently, by a large very clean, white-faced, Old English Sheepdog. Was it interactive with this particular show or some fluffy guard dog? What gave some, the strength of belief that they could represent the world, represent others? What might be the beginning for those, on the edge, leading the way in new thoughts? How did *grass roots* and *fringe* relate?

CHAPTER 11

The Moreton Show

Catherine and Rose had arrived early and parked themselves on the first available straw bale using Catherine's old, black, quilted Barbour jacket as cushioning against the prickliness of the straw. They were both disappointed that the ensuing act was from Broke FMX with aeronautical manoeuvres; noisy motorbikes. They'd come for the animals. The speaker was loud, calling out, "John, 32, got into BMX". The bikers were doing 'Evil Knievel' stuff, leaping off the ramp and performing a 'no-hander' or sticking out a leg out. One chap did a mid-air handstand on the bike's handlebars. Catherine and Rose were impressed, though they found none of it particularly enjoyable.

"Do you remember 'The Chaser' we normally watch – when one fence gets higher and higher?" asked Catherine fondly of her semi-horsey friend Rose.

"Yes, that's white-knuckle stuff to watch," Rose replied but neither wanted to see it as much as to give up their semi-comfortable bale for more traipsing, as they were gold dust now the grand finale drew nearer.

The bikers repeated their feats over and over again until they looked less spectacular each time they repeated the trick. The cliffhanger saw John standing on the handlebars mid-air where he performed a sideways turn. Catherine thought it improved their gig but at least with the horse stuff people fell off, horses slid into fences.

The crowd were loving it now, especially the children, and Catherine thought the show should move with the times. She recognized herself as old-fashioned, with an unrealistic idea of some bucolic ideal of Victorian country-living where everyone was happy, which she knew must have been far from the reality.

The sun came out and what a difference it made. No wonder it was so worshipped. The compère said the livestock were making their way into the main arena. A livestock auctioneer then took the mic and with an equally posh British-compère-market-town-show voice was talking about, "Livestock farming in England today". He spoke of grass growing and cattle bred over three hundred years.

"The vegans and the vegetarians haven't got all the answers. We are evolved to eat RED meat in a BALANCED diet – three times a day, seven days a week."

Rose pulled a face of disapproval. Catherine considered there was a collision of staunch beliefs. They would mimic him on the way home.

"Essential ingredients. We could not be as healthy without it," Catherine said in a deep voice.

"Important livestock farmers, essential to the nature of family in this country," postulated Rose.

Rose was eating less and less meat. Florence was a "flexitarian." Catherine and Peter remained traditional, though she was conflicted, loving the sight of animals grazing in the fields but hating to think too carefully about their lives – or specifically, how short they were, as there was no getting away from – most were bred for meat, most died very young. Once upon a time her ambition had been to have a herd of mixed heifers and steers, for store. She knew this to be head-in-the-sand hypocrisy. She was the Swiss banker to the narco-boss, both hands bloody. Whose hands are clean these days? She puzzled at the knotty problem of the guilt of western living. For every action there was a reaction. For every lack of action, a consequence.

"Don't you just love them?" Catherine said, elbowing Rose at the sight of the very tall Brown Friesian cows.

"I didn't know that they came in that colour. I thought they were all black and white – not glorious chestnut!" remarked Catherine.

"How Now Brown Cow," Rose returned, in a vowelly sound, even further away from what remained of her Yorkshire accent, mimicking the ring master's tone. She was more interested in the cute pygmy goats. She'd like to have one and teach it to pull a little cart. Take it around the village, she and Doug. Maybe Doug could ride in it or was that too cheesy?

Rose knew it was never going to happen, and didn't spend much time inhabiting idle dreams. She didn't want more duties at home. She was already nervous about the extra professional responsibility around the corner. She'd had an unofficial clue that the assistant head's job was hers, but for the formalities. She had not yet told anyone. It was not certain. She felt fraudulent when directly asked by Catherine, had told her 'nothing definite.' She had vindicated herself on the strength that 'definite' was indeed a very black or white word so her repose was appropriate. 'Appropriate' was one of her chief words and she often used it outside of professional contexts.

The main ring now had an impressive group of animals occupying it, all remarkably under control by their handlers, young and old, man, woman, girl and boy. A particularly confident four-year-old with a long, blonde plait and white coat was behind a huge bull with a cane, tapping on its rear, with the self-assuredness of a young landowner. In Rose's modest opinion, farmers who owned their land were sitting on mounds of money so why exactly did they get subsidized by the taxpayer? Rose had begun to question this after listening to a podcast on the history of England. Tradition could cover a multitude of sins. Catherine touched her on the shoulder and whispered loudly, "You know in the 1200's you could pick up 20 acres of land for ten shillings."

"OMG. That's 2p an acre," said Rose.

They continued to delight in the fun of the fare from the relative comfort of their yellow straw bales, under blue sky, locked in their mutual attraction to farmyard animals. Rose loved sheep as well as goats.

"I love the four-horned Jacobs, just look at those pointy horns!" Rose enthused.

After they'd watched the very last of the farm animals exit the ring, she suggested,

"Shall we go for a drink somewhere?"

"Yes, let's," agreed Catherine as she stood up rescuing the crumpled Barbour and freeing it from straw with a vigorous shake.

The show was busy and everybody seemed to be having a good time. The weather was pleasant as it neared five. It was the show's 70th anniversary and the biggest one day show of its kind throughout the nation. Catherine had always loved a country show and Rose did too.

"Tea, coffee or alcohol?" Catherine proposed. Rose, who wasn't a huge drinker, said she quite fancied half a cider, so off they went.

Rose had, as she had suspected, landed the job. Rose's parents were a long distance away so – physically – Catherine was her significant other. Catherine was thrilled for her dear Rose's achievement though it did highlight her own lack of professional success. However, she was relieved that Rose was there to stay. Catherine had had a real fear that Rose might have upped and relocated to Yorkshire as she might have applied anywhere in the country and no doubt would have soon been met with the same success.

Catherine knew Rose would work harder than ever making sure she was the very best assistant head she could be. She would have less time for Catherine but they'd still just be a mile away and with the dog walks and Catherine adjusting her expectations and building up a busier life of her own, things would be fine, just fine. She'd experienced the ebbing and flowing of Rose's working tides. Rose put in the hours, forever, taking new responsibilities: the pastoral care, the timetable, the school play, humanities, technology, English, science. Rose had been coordinator of practically everything at one time or another.

Teaching offered an enormous sphere she thought. Look at Florence, she'd gone up and down age groups like chords on a piano before finding her comfort zone amongst teenagers. Though unlike Rose, she couldn't give it 100% for long, and had given it all up.

Florence had complained to Catherine how the agencies made it difficult for supply teachers to obtain financial autonomy. Catherine was becoming ashamed of the shortness of her working life. Peter really didn't see why anyone who didn't have to should sweat it out, running around to service someone's needs. He hadn't felt Catherine capable of having her own business. She would find it too stressful and become bad-tempered. He'd seen it happen to wives. They were fine as they were, after all they had a large house, a smallholding to tend and one of the kids would no doubt soon get married and produce grandchildren. They would need support. His mother had never worked and thank heavens. Catherine hadn't had to tie herself up to a job. It had been marvelous, the right thing to do.

Catherine needed to wrestle her pride, and confess her envy to Rose. Maybe she could turn this into a positive thing. Rose would be inflated but Rose didn't need inflation, didn't seem to need anything. No, the simpler thing was to turn her own life around. She'd said it before. She'd been telling herself so for a decade. She'd felt too old to change then. *Pricy at a pound; cheap at two.* She simply must think of doing something of her own, outside of the home. It would probably have to be some kind of part-time voluntary work and that irked her. It irked her that in the later years of her life, her most developed years, she was no longer considered to be of any 'monetary' value. She had a price. She had been and remained, she felt, of significant economic worth. Hadn't she produced two workers and two consumers? A duty done with no respect. She was just a "just," and left with no hook to hang herself. She had love though, she had love and loved too. She had enjoyed much of her leisure time, enjoyed learning and been quite the autodidact for a few years now, even got a grip with quantum biology, fascinated by its 'for every action'.

She was a non-student, unemployed, economically inactive woman of learning. Maybe she'd catch a train to that city of Learning and Culture, Oxford, one day next week and educate herself with a museum and revisit the Ashmolean. She remembered going with Peter once. It had bored him though he did quite enjoy the Pre-Raphaelites which Catherine had first seen and fallen in love with on a school trip with Sara, the girls gooey over Ophelia. Sara, too, with her take it or leave it heart. Catherine still had a woodwork block of Lizzie Siddal with her head thrown back in some state – as Beatrice. Yes, and there had been the beautiful striking features of June, with her Pre-Raphaelite hair and all that rich colouring, that emerald green.

Florence had been so lucky, thought Catherine, to have received such striking looks. Puts one a yard away from the finish line surely in the 100 metres? Maybe she should change herself, update herself, but she wasn't comfortable with change. She'd make a rotten chameleon.

Chapter 12

Full House

Catherine had secured her guests and it was to be a full house. She had arranged for Gavin to drive them to Cheltenham, Montpellier with its abundant wine bars, for a night out. Florence had said she would only come if they went dancing so it would mean a taxi back.

Catherine was making a light supper: chicken with plenty of salad and new potatoes. There were no particular food issues so it was easy peasy. She and Christine had changed the beds, plumped up the pillows, put clean towels and upgraded the soaps and filled the house with flowers from the garden. Her lilies were out and their scent reigned supreme. The plan was to go to a wine bar Friday evening, to the Open Gardens on Saturday and on Sunday to chill and probably incorporate Sunday lunch.

Entering the wine bar, she was quite struck by the age of its inhabitants. They were with hardly an exception, mature and looked very much at home in the environment. Though anesthetized by a couple of wines Catherine felt unsure of herself. Her feet hurt. London had been different, it was a city, The City. This was fifteen miles down the road and quite frankly she hadn't realized that people over forty did this sort of thing. There was an energy that was most peculiar to her. She watched Florence who was face to face with Sara suddenly double up with laughter.

"What's so funny?" asked Rose before offering to go to the bar. Florence who loved a scout followed her offering to help.

"Shall we find somewhere to sit?" suggested Catherine who hated standing up even for short periods and didn't like being centre of a room. She felt too tall in her kitten heels but observed how brazen Florence was with hers.

"We can try," said Sara casting her eyes around and telling Catherine, "I see why the place was so popular."

Catherine knew she would have to put up with the situation and felt a long night coming on. She looked forward to a drink arriving.

"You can do all your chatting and tea drinking tomorrow at the Open gardens," said Sara with absolutely no sympathy and was enjoying the music recognizing a good deal of the mixture of Brit pop and old chart music and said how funny it was younger people listened to *their* music.

The band came on at nine-thirty and had a lead singer with a very strong voice. Rose thought she was amazing. They all did. By nine forty-five they were up near the front, their drinks on a nearby table being looked after by Bob and a friend in a blue jumper and they were dancing. Music and laughter flowed and the dancing became more self-expressive.

It was Florence who said they should call it a night. Catherine was wobbly on her feet and giggling, telling them, individually, how much she loved them. Sara took care to keep upright and helped Catherine to do the same.

Florence secured a taxi and Rose secured the price and helped Catherine into the back. The three of them sat and listened to Florence discuss immigration with the taxi driver. Florence liked to hear the opinions of others.

It was Saturday morning and three of the four women were not feeling their best.

"Why doesn't Florence get hung over?" asked Sara.

"Yes, she was putting it away last night," agreed Rose who herself had drunk more last night than in the last month put together.

Florence entered the kitchen in pale blue cotton pyjamas and said she never got head aches and drank water before bed. She also said that she slept it off and didn't know why everyone had to get up so goddamn early.

"Ha, you were so pissed last night Catherine," she said, looking around to see if Peter or Ben were in ear shot.

"They're out," said Sara chewing on her toast and marmalade.

"I can't believe we ended up dancing for hours," Catherine said, "It was such fun. I never usually get the chance especially now hardly anyone seems to get married."

She poured Florence some tea singing, "Build me up build me up butterfly baby," stating she couldn't really remember that song first time round.

"What's the story morning glories, didn't you just love it when all the guys got up to dance to 'A Town called Malice'?" said Florence "And you lot had such a good dance!"

"Well I loved the band. That singer was brilliant. She had such a range The Peppers, The Killers and Amy," said Rose.

"It's impossible not to dance to 'Valerie'," said Florence.

Florence said she had never stopped dancing at the weekend and that she and a couple of friends that she hung out with regularly danced on top of the bar at this one venue, The White Hart. Sara wasn't sure if Florence was embroidering and Rose mentioned something about, Health and Safety.

"Yes, last night it *was just another day in the office for me*," said Florence. "I go out every Friday and I'd say dance at least once a month, just love it."

"Meant to be very good for the mental health," stated Rose.

"I was just a little worried there might be some parents out. They are getting more judgemental about a teacher's behaviour these days."

"Puritanical kill-joys," growled Florence.

Sara put down her toast and asked her friends if they had experienced any problems lately with their mental health. Nobody spoke. Then Florence declared she had always had *spring fever* but that last year it had come with a fervour that some would say constituted a mental disorder. She explained that she was enveloped with a huge amount of energy and a wild array of possibilities, of ideas, that she wanted to see implemented. She had set her to do-list for the year, rather high. She thought it was three-quarter life crisis, realizing her hour glass had far more sand now in the bottom-half and the sand was whizzing through now, running out. She had so much to do and so little time. It had shocked her.

She explained that she could see in the eyes of others that they regarded her as eccentric or maybe more. She remembered thinking, homeless people who wanted to get off the street should be given shelter, immediately. She felt that money should be lent, without interest, to millions abroad for whom micro-financing would revolutionize their lives and if it meant printing money, to print it. She felt that the streets shouldn't always be grey but have colour and the houses too, as in Tenby or South America.

"You should see 'Tangerine'. It's a film that promotes colour," said Sara.

"I was one day away from Hypermania and three days from Hypomania. Or is it the other way around? One, is much more serious. Well I came down but it has left me a bit watchful. I guess I could have been in a mania of sorts. Of course, I rather liked it but it was worrying I guess for Francesca and Tom. Bless. Anyone else?"

"Did the Abyss stare back?" asked Sara.

"One must still have chaos in oneself to be able to give birth to a dancing star," Florence addressed the quotation to Sara.

"Well we need to start thinking about the gardens," said Catherine who had her own experiences, once or twice, in the last few years but hadn't considered telling anyone, let alone her friends.

"Hey that fourteen-year old was into you last night," said Florence to Rose changing the subject. "You were having a good long conversation," she continued.

"He wasn't fourteen. He was a gardener," said Rose.

"A gardener might be good with Roses," suggested Sara and Florence burst out laughing.

"He was pretty good looking," said Florence. "Bit like that guy from the diet coke ad."

"Oh, I loved him," said Rose. "Didn't we all."

"Is anyone going to have a croissant?" said Catherine who had especially gone to the Farmers market.

Florence told them of her book and said she was going to be able to glean some new material from this Open garden outing. Her play within a novel was called The Starchers.

They all obliged and tucked into the array of Waitrose fineries, including the Manuka honey. Loving having a captive audience, and overwhelmed with conviviality, Florence embraced the topic of her book.

"I'm writing a play within the novel called "The Starchers," and you are all in it," she laughed. "Don't worry you all have pseudonyms and all that."

Sara looked horrified and glared at Rose who also looked a little uncomfortable.

"I'm going to have to change it a bit," Florence continued "The dogs rather give it away,"

"I don't have a dog," said Sara.

"Well you're not in it. It's about the villagers," carried on Florence.

"It's a spoof based on 'The Archers' with farmers and councillors and a broad cross section and the village pub, fete, panto etc but I've crossed it with a Reformation Comedy so it's all very over the top.

"I hope you aren't going to be rude about the Councillors. They work hard and take it very seriously," said Catherine fearful that she would be compromised if Florence used something or some nickname she may have divulged.

"No, no I've mixed it up good and proper. It has a tinge of 'Lysistrata.'"

The other women looked at one another blankly.

"For those that aren't aware – the famous, bawdy satire of Ancient Greece. It's like an Aristophane's ribald anti-war fantasy but with mine there are two main tribes; the long-legged foxes and the short-legged foxes. The long-legged foxes want to make the village into a special village that takes in the homeless and sleeps and sponsors them in the school room."

"Anyone for more tea or coffee before we go to the gardens?" interrupted Catherine quietly.

Florence held out her mug. Rose offered to make them. Florence tried to pause until the others came back but couldn't and explained to Sara that the Long-legged foxes symbolised on another level the Whigs and on another the city states of Ancient Civilizations Tyre or Carthage or the later Florence. The Short-Legged Foxes were the Agrarian Martial shepherds that overran and conquered the city states as described by the revered Scottish Economist Adam Smith in the Wealth of Nations."

Sara had studied Economy at A level before her law degree and remembered the *revered* Adam Smith. Rose and Catherine returned with the drinks and settled to hear the rest of Florence's play within a novel.

"Have we missed anything?" said Catherine.

Florence looked at Sara quizzically.

"Not really," said Sara still rather impressed by Florence. She remembered Catherine had mentioned Florence, when passing through her Zen Buddhist phase, had taken self-improvement to heart. "Just the basic principle of Free Trade in the Modern world and whether it is in fact sustainable?" Sara summed it up and then added, "Without corrupting society with unfettered capitalism causing gross inequality."

"Oh, well what do the Foxes do, Florence?" asked Rose.

"I didn't really get what Sara just said about Free trade," questioned Catherine. "It sounds rather like a Russian doll. The book you have, a novel with a play in it, half farce, but within it an ethical and economical debate?"

"Yes," agreed Florence enthusiastically shaking her head delighted that someone had picked up the complexity of her endeavour.

"And there's lots of sexual intrigue, too, though very lame by Greek Myth standards. I mean there is no sister shagging or sibling shagging to be PC." she added looking at Rose. "Yes, Yes, Zeus done his sisters. They married; had children. Hera sounds ferocious. My play is just a romp. Everyone fancies everybody they shouldn't type thing. It's all going to work out happy, happy."

"How much have you written?" asked Sara.

"Just the end," admitted Florence but I've done heaps of characterization and it should be pretty easy to knock out. I've done at least eighty thousand words of the book so it's just the play that's not done."

"Being concise is a skill," said Rose.

"I'll tell you the cast," said Florence in fear that she was going to lose her audience. She reeled them off as dear friends.

Gerald and Rosemary, We-Know-Bests

Samantha and William On-its

Caroline and Matthew Shag-Arounds

Miss Prune

Rev Rake

Charmian de Vere

Candida and Henry Loon aka The Loonies

Kevin and Denise Moon aka The Moonies

Sir and Lady Duldrums

Chloe Passion and Jack Smack.

"Actually," said Florence proudly "The middle section of the play is very sexy as I've got Jack Smack and Chloe Passion down as a pair of American lovers that visit *Flatsbury*, as I call it. These lovers are caught up in the paradoxes of commitment and liberty, love and power." "Wasn't that rather like Shelley?" offered Catherine who had recently read the life of Mary Shelley and was quite pleased to let it be known.

"A tale of who porks who?" asked Sara.

"I don't care very much for that expression," said Catherine firmly as it jarred against her image of the Romantics even though she had been recently informed that Percy had been an Anarchist expecting his women to swallow free-love.

Florence continued over them, "They are kind of the Pied Pipers of Flatsbury. I was thinking of having that as the title or "Sex in the Village."

"So, Chloe Passion is Samantha?" chirped in Rose. "I wasn't very happy to be likened to Miranda."

"You're nothing like Miranda," said Sara.

"They go around engendering disharmony. Engorging all the women with sexual desire and all the men turn randy as satyrs. Gold and lead arrows fly around in all the wrong places as Chloe being complete sex-on-legs in true Psyche or Aphrodite style spins all the chaps around in circles and Jack does the same with the girls. He's diet-coke man handsome with just a tinge of menace, I mean Cillian not his brother, you know Peaky Blinders? It's Chaos in the village. They are all woken up and lively as this American couple meander through the village puffing potent pheromones."

"Is that a take on how Hollywood has sexualized and cheapened the British way of life?" asked Catherine.

"Well I guess it could be," said Florence. "I hadn't really thought about it like that."

"Oh," said Catherine rubbing her hands together rather pleased with herself.

"Wouldn't all the men just use porn," said Sara. "Thought that was the way. Sounds suspiciously like 'Midsummer Night's Dream'."

"Not in my book. If I was doing a rewrite, I'd give Hippolyta more than five lines." said Florence firmly.

"I wish I could write a book," said Sara.

"Well you could if you tried," said Rose. "There's a book in all of us," she continued and suggested one should begin with short stories.

"Yes, even those short on imagination," agreed Florence.

"Are we going around these gardens?" said Sara, whose interest in gardens was temporarily heightened by the fact she was landscaping a sixty-foot garden in a London buy-to-let.

"Are we taking the dogs?" asked Florence who was bent down practically rubbing noses with Hoover.

"Are you sure you weren't rescued by a wolf pack?" asked Sara in mild disapproval.

"You shouldn't stoop to a dog's level. It confuses the heirarchy," said Rose.

"Bla, bla, typical human-centric doctrine propounded over the airwaves by demi-god celebrities and TV moghuls. Anyway, Catherine, long ago, gave Hoover the crown and throne in her household. I wasn't up, but did she, by any chance, give the dogs a cooked breakfast and us lot toast?" enquired Florence still fussing Hoover and then Glove too.

"They only have a fry-up on Saturdays. It started as a family thing," said Catherine.

"Ah yes, and porridge through the week. Do you or do you not make them porridge every morning?" grilled Florence, jokingly.

"Yes, but I have it as well, and Peter sometimes."

"Whose car are we going in?" snapped Sara who felt hungover, and unused to communal living was beginning to have second thoughts about going away with these people, for a full week, though Florence had amused her greatly on their night out. She hadn't laughed so much for a long time. She remembered wiping the tears from her eyes at one stage but on the other hand, Florence was such an irritating know-all, constantly butting in, and making everything about herself. She must have had an awful childhood. Maybe she was raised by wolves, Sara thought and then turned her thoughts to Catherine's parents fondly. They had been an integral part of her childhood, her whole life when she considered it. Maybe she would pop in on the way back to visit Catherine's widowed mum. She wouldn't mention it to Catherine in case she ran out of steam and changed her mind. These days when it came to doing things she often overestimated her energy levels. Her morning eyes were too big for her afternoon stroke evening stomach. She liked Catherine's statement that she could only now do two parts of the three-part day.

"When we go away," Sara told the women on the way to the gardens, "I'm resting in the afternoon or won't make the evening."

"I agree," chipped in Catherine not at all pleased to be driving a car load of adults and partly worried whether she was still over the limit and also what to do with her guests after the gardens. "We could either have a lie in the morning or an afternoon to ourselves or an evening in."

As she said it she envisaged Rose would be up at dawn and Florence wanting to sleep in to eleven and those two sharing. How would that work?

"I'm happy to fit in with whatever you want," said Florence.

"We could play a game tonight," Catherine suggested.

"Poker!" said Florence. "I won quite a bit in Ecuador. There was an eruption or something and the volcano was on amber alert so the Coatapaxi National Park was closed."

"Poker would be fun. We have a set of chips," agreed Catherine relieved as she was beginning to feel she would have to invite the neighbours round or something. "And then maybe a film?"

"Yes," continued Florence in another flurry of excitement, "Poker at the pub. We could fleece those old boys. I could get more dialect for my play!"

"I'm not going to play Poker in our local, Florence," said Rose. "I teach their kids," she explained softly and added that she wasn't sure if she was up to another boozy night. She still had marking.

"Are we playing for money?" said Florence.

"No fingers," said Sara.

Catherine drove over the bumpy playing field to park. She would have preferred them all to have walked but was mindful that once stacked with purchases it would have been impractical.

"I do think it's admirable that you have managed a year without a car Florence. What do you do with your purchases?" she said as they disembarked.

"I carry them," Florence said.

"Florence doesn't buy anything anyway," joked Sara "She just barters,"

"You can pay for us all to get in for that," said Florence seriously with a large grin.

"I was going to anyway," smiled Sara with a playful cock of the head.

The sun was shining and the four women visited all twenty-three of the gardens. Midway, they stopped at one of the bigger houses that reminded Florence of a French Manor House. The glorious garden swept down to the Avon.

"You know we could go swimming," Florence said, sitting back absorbing the sun with her arms spread out, as she and Sara waited for Catherine and Rose to bring back the cream teas.

Once back in Catherine's garden, Florence brought up the suggestion once again.

"It's so hot Catherine. Why don't you have a swimming pool?" she said crossly.

"One, we haven't the weather and two, we don't want the fuss. I still can't forget the picture of my grandmother's Cavalier being drowned in the pool," said Catherine handing round tea in delightful china.

"Swimming pool, you'd be lucky. Peter won't even let her have a fountain," said Sara tugging her hair back.

"We could go to the river?" suggested Rose. "Why should the kids have all the fun?"

"OMG let's! It's on our doorstop! We could launch ourselves from the Paddle club," cried Florence with renewed excitement. Sara who had no intention of swimming in a river told them she didn't have a costume.

"I'll sort you one," offered Rose, failing to detect even a whiff of Sara's utmost disgust at the notion. "And Catherine can sort Florence."

"I don't need one," said Florence.

"Yes, you do," said Sara feeling that this somehow was now a question of damage control. She had been hoping for a touch of sunbathing, the blue sky was crying out for it, followed by some sort of snack supper and TV. This weekend, far from being relaxing, was becoming an obstacle course. One episode of Wild Swimming on Channel 4 and now everyone was jumping into filthy rivers. Annoyed, she thought maybe she should just go to the second part of the holiday, the city-break, and leave the others to the countryside bit. She would talk to Catherine and tell her to ask Rose to rebook her flight.

Once back at Bluebell Farm, Catherine left her guests on the terrace with a jug of minted lemonade, refusing any help in the kitchen. She returned with a plate of hamburgers, buns and a salad with notable amount of chopped ingredients mixed within it.

"There are eight," she said proudly.

"Two each?" said Sara.

"After that cream tea I'll struggle with one," Florence remarked. She would have preferred to go swimming there and then. What was it with people? Food. Food. Food.

"One and half maybe," suggested Catherine.

"Oh, are the menfolk joining us?" asked Florence with renewed interest.

"No, they are at the golf club. I meant for Hoover and Glove. They love a burger."

"Does Ben play golf usually or is it only that we're all here?" asked Sara.

Catherine explained that Ben had taken up golf a few weeks ago and father and son now played every Saturday.

"It's lovely, isn't it?" said Catherine who had struggled with it, in the beginning. She knew she and Jess had been joined by the stirrup for a decade during the horsey years. She knew that it was a brilliant thing that now, at last, Peter had time for his children, but a part of her missed having Ben, all to herself, and their Saturday trips food shopping. Where had Peter been when Ben struggled through exam years? Where was Peter when Ben's friendship group had been turned on its head, leaving him on the outside, looking in?

"Shall we walk down to the river?" Catherine suggested after they'd eaten. Rose complimented her on her delicious salad and offered to drive saying that it wouldn't be nice to walk back when they were all wet.

At the Paddle club, Catherine told them she wasn't sure if she'd go in if there were lots of people around and Rose said she didn't think the rowers met on Saturday. Sara was relieved to see a number of benches where she could quietly sit out this activity with the companionship of her phone.

The others had changed at the house where Sara had been given a navy-blue bathing costume with Madonna style rigid cups which she would not be seen dead in. She had accepted it gracefully disappeared into her bedroom and stuffed it in a drawer.

"I'll catch you later," she called over her shoulder as they disembarked from the car discussing footwear, and made her way over to a sunny bench.

"I knew she wouldn't come in," said Florence knowingly putting on flip flaps.

Sara even after positioning herself quite a distance from the banks could hear Florence's squeals. The three of them were making quite a racket.

They re-emerged twenty minutes later Catherine still dry and looking a bit sheepish but the other two were dripping and annoyingly full of themselves. Florence had mud all down her leg and her long hair draped around her like a mermaid. She was still shrieking.

Sara strode over to the car and was only too relieved that they were in Rose's. It would probably stink of river water for a fortnight. Florence was walking towards the car with her arm around Rose, chest out shamelessly oblivious to her exposed hardened nipples.

"Decorum," said Sara, under her breath, to Catherine who was explaining that she had dipped a toe in but the river bed was too squidgy to go in with bare feet and that next time she would take sandals.

"Oh, I do love a wild swim," said Florence telling her car-captive audience about the time when she had swum with Pink dolphins and heard the thud, thud, thud this giant fish made on the lake with its tail. Talk about River Monsters she'd scoffed adding, "Maybe I should get a Whale tail tattoo, signifies safe passage by water?"

"Florence keep still," said Rose half turning around to see what her friend was doing. You'd be mistaken, thought Catherine, if you'd surmised that of them Rose would be the safest driver. She was quite blase, when on familiar turf.

"I'm sorry," said Florence, "but I think I've got a river snail up my crotch."

"Arhhh!" said Sara, in despair.

"We're home soon. Can you hold on?" asked Rose turning around again to Florence.

Catherine closed her eyes.

"Did I ever tell you about the time I got leeched in Borneo?" said Florence and continued before giving anyone a chance to speak. "We were doing a lot of river wading and it was the wet season and I'd got my period. Anyway, went to bed exhausted and woke up and my sleeping bag was covered in blood. Bright red I was really worried until it dawned on me that it was leeches. That took a bit of management. My guide was a monk, not that that stopped him hitting on me come to that. What's your most embarrassing period story girls?"

"OMG!" said Sara and was surprised to hear Catherine quietly answer.

"Pony Club Camp," she said. "I was twelve and a half. Sara's mum took my jodhpurs back to wash and lent me a pair of Sara's and she came back with the washed pair and an array of sanitary provision. "It's always been a sort of secret between us. Strange how taboo it was. I mean I don't think I've heard my mother say the word 'period' to this day though I'd consider us very close."

They swung into Catherine's drive, a trifle fast, thought Catherine. Florence was first to get out, shaking her trouser leg vigorously and then putting her hand down her jeans. Everyone waited with baited breath, and then Florence relieved bought out a little twig and threw it into the flower bed.

Sara was looking forward to going home tomorrow and told Florence and Rose they smelt repulsive and should hose themselves off before being allowed back into Catherine's beautiful home. Florence lifted her upper lip pulling her bugs bunny face turned to Rose and blinked her eyes open and shut several times. Rose started to laugh.

"The terrible twins," complained Sara, as she opened the door, to let Catherine enter the house with a load of wet towels. "Tell Rose to wind down her windows to air the car," she told Catherine.

"I'm not sure. The cat might climb in and spray," explained Catherine.

"Erhhhh. The country," said Sara.

Chapter 13

The Council

Just as Catherine was leaving to attend a Parish council meeting, Peter stopped her to tell her that he felt it was time for them to move. The children were adults now and the place too big and expensive. Catherine said nothing. She didn't want to move. She loved that house. The children loved it, too, and Ben was still with them. Something odd had happened. He'd been at home all afternoon and usually if he wasn't at work he was on the golf course.

Catherine took her place at the top table at seven-thirty, that evening, on one of the folding tables that she'd carried out from the back belly of the schoolroom where they were stacked up in a neat row of twelve. As usual, she'd begun to unfold it, by working some annoying but efficient mechanism that involved squeezing a metal tube in a certain manner, when one of the men came, uninvited, to her aid.

In the five years or so that she'd been a Parish Councillor this always happened. They took it in turns, though this time it was the newly elected young middle-aged, snappy suited and fashionably bearded District Councillor, who though it was his first meeting, was explaining how the tables worked as he took it out of her hands. She stood aside smiling agreeably.

However, she was particularly verbal at that meeting. She was beginning to find her voice. *If not now, when?* Later that week, it occurred to her to question whether her words had been minuted.

The apologies for absence were received as were the declarations of interest. Then the reports from the County Councillor and District Councillor discussed. They had been put on-line earlier. The County Councillor was absent but the chief point she made was that early action would have to be taken if they were to fight the gravel pit Tarmac threatened. It would engulf the farmland that lay between the village and the river. A blot on the landscape that would certainly wreak many changes: unwelcome ones.

After this small bombshell the agenda moved back to a more usual flavour. The Footpath Warden reported 'a broken stile' off Boston Lane. Catherine was the go-between the Parish Council and the Schoolroom Trust, a body that looked after the building in which they were presently seated. She informed the council that after at least a decade of not doing so The Trust had decided to raise the hourly rate of hire.

The minutes of the Annual meeting held on the 16th July were confirmed and adopted. There followed discussion around planning permission at the Old Piggery. Questions were raised about the presence of an old caravan at the property.

Catherine's interest was finally awoken by two female police officers who had come to liase. One began by introducing the other as being from the "control room" who proceeded to monotonously read out from a report that from the 1st August there had been eleven incidents – involving just Chadbury. The woman had spoken quickly and used language that Catherine was unaccustomed to, but Catherine did pick out that there had been one for anti-social behaviour and six personals or domestics.

"How many?" Catherine asked.

It was explained that it might be six to the same house not six individual houses.

"I wouldn't worry too much," one of the young officers said.

Catherine answered, "Yes, well I do worry." Adding firmly, "Are they really calling the police without reason, possibly over and over again?"

The police officers defended their position, explaining that these matters were private and privacy had to be respected. The councillors seemed to agree. Catherine assured them that she wasn't disputing that, though later, she couldn't logically see the sense in it, if it only served to keep the status quo and asked what was the difference between anti-social behaviour and a domestic apart from the obvious "closed door". What happened if it occurred on the pavement outside the house or in the front garden? Would they think differently?

Her desire to increase her understanding of how a domestic situation was handled in their community by the police was appeased by the offer of a copy of the procedure followed by the West Mercia Police Department. Yes, she would, thank you very much.

The meeting went on to receive Receipts and Payment Accounts and approve the invoices for the Clerk's salary and for the Lengthman's painting of the railings and clearance for a wild flower area.

Finally, nearly two hours later Agenda 24 was reached and the Chair announced with authority the date of the next Parish Council. At 9.20 p.m. Catherine eyed the clock and as people started to shuffle papers and the chairs began to scrape her heart sank back to reality after a respite of humdrum village life.

When she was back out in the darkness of the street heading for her little grey car she felt the summer was over. Why did she care so much for the house? Why did the thought of living somewhere else so appal her and the thought of some other family taking over their house upset her so? She didn't think of herself as a jealous person though maybe she didn't know herself as well as she thought. When push came to shove, wasn't that when people showed their true colours?

At least if they moved she wouldn't have to do those meetings, though that one had been unusually interesting on account of the proposed gravel pit and the presence of police officers. If she didn't have so many of her own worries she might have looked further into the dealings of domestic abuse in villages instead of being expected to care about road safety and potholes? Drive more slowly was her view, and what madness was started when the country started paying out millions for car damage.

Maybe for the first time in her life she would stand up to Peter. He would be up. She would listen to him and then suggest they moved when the kids were more settled. Her children worried her. They never used to. Life had been so simple until they left school. Now it was fairly constant like a dull toothache, with no obvious remedy but just the vague understanding that the cause was up above the jawline so difficult to assess and if it wasn't too painful could be left alone.

She wanted advice. She wanted to speak to Sara. Thank goodness they were meeting on Tuesday. She would know what to do but she'd need to get the facts from Peter without talk of selling the house. What a beautiful place Catherine thought as she pulled into the drive and saw the double front of their façade; red bricked and lit up by Georgian styled lamps either side of the familiar green front door with its brass door furniture and the two stone pointers lying down either side of the bottom of the three granite steps.

Her first thought was where Peter might be and what would be his mood. Should she broach the subject or steer clear of it until she had formulated her own action plan? He was brooding in the kitchen which was not a sight she was used to. He wasn't usually so dark looking, so heavy. This captain of industry of Chadbury, reduced to this.

"Hi darling. I thought you'd be watching a documentary."

"I've been watching television since three," he volunteered not very cheerily, "and it's a load of rubbish."

Yes, that's right, thought Catherine, let him vent. Let him let the anger out, the disappointment and she must remember to agree, agree, agree.

"Yes, it is pretty awful, not that I switch on before five."

"Oh yes, because how you spend your day doesn't allow you a spare minute," he said viciously.

"Well the council meeting was quite interesting."

"Oh yes?" There was a silence then there rang out: "How so?"

"Well, there may be a turf war. Villagers against corporation. A gravel pit is threatening our sleepy village."

"What do you mean?" Peter retorted seriously and let Catherine half explain then interrupted angrily. "How can you make light of this?" he stared at her incredulously. "Don't you see? This is terrible news for us, and just when I thought things couldn't get worse. First my business, then my pension and now my house. We may not be able to sell the house easily, with this news hanging in the air. I mean why would people, in this bracket, buy a house with the threat of a gravel pit hanging over it?"

He left the kitchen before she had a chance to speak.

What could she say anyway? With the mood he was in he needed time to recover and she needed time to assimilate what was meant by "lost pension." The nightmare that kept on giving, "Sell the house." He was serious. Was there no waking up? Though it may have worked in her favour this possibility of a gravel pit? Things worked in a mysterious way indeed though the house didn't seem quite so rosy now that Peter had cast it in that sinister light. Could Bluebell Farm go from idyllic family home to cage in a space of a couple of days? To think she was ailing a few days ago for the want of being taken seriously, questioning whether she had enough, whether she was doing enough. She'd been softly agonizing whether to join the ten o'clock Yoga class at Great Rissington or the Tai Chi at 6pm at Snodsbury, and hadn't quite been able to commit to either in case she couldn't keep it up regularly, for what reason she asked herself now, perplexed. She'd been worried over her indecision about whether to update the tiles in the upstairs shower room because they looked tired and even by her unexacting standards out of date.

She'd been worried that the outside cat might have fleas or that the dogs were due for worming. She'd been worried that she wasn't seeing enough of her mother. Worry over her identity had slowly cloaked her with a seeping invisibility.

She saw now, why she felt this need to hold on to the house. It wasn't just an urge to keep the family nest; to not let go or to keep hold of something beautiful and precious. It was because it was her identity. The house was her identity, rightly or wrongly, and that is why the very thought of leaving it was so painful. She felt so inextricably linked to it, and when others had climbed the ladder or built up social capital, she had taken root in it so deeply. Oak roots not fir.

She didn't know how to move on out of it any better than she knew how to die. Was that normal? In the light of what the last couple of days had thrown up, was it even true?

She smiled to think just weeks earlier she'd been panicking that Rose might leave the village in search of career enhancement. Now it turned out it was she who might move away as she could never stay by and watch someone else drive up the lane through those iron gates to that front door. Unthinkable, and yet it was a looming reality. She imagined herself in a small executive home in the outskirts of a market town, a modern-sized, treeless garden with a neat panelled fence between neighbours; probably a newish house with four bedrooms possibly five though they'd be half the size of her current bedroom, in a street, neighbours everywhere, no views, no privacy and she'd be there all day long with Peter like two gloomy castaways when he realized that he didn't like estate living after all. Or maybe he'd take to it and not be gloomy at all; find himself a new golf club and bond with the neighbours and compare new household gadgets. These thoughts depressed her.

It depressed her how poorly she thought of Peter. Hadn't he worked hard all these years to support her and their children? Didn't he deserve sympathy in his pain and rejection? It must be soul destroying for him to have been ousted by his friends and colleagues, his life partners. She still hadn't understood what had happened and why they had got rid of him. Was it legal? Where was the morality in it? This winner takes all mentality was fine when you're on top of course, less fine when you've been stepped all over to facilitate someone's rise to it. She must avail herself to him. He must be hurting so and they must stay united, husband and wife near on twenty-seven years.

What could she do to keep her mind occupied and ease the pain of her thoughts and fear of losing the house? Everywhere she looked was something to remind her of her possible ensuing loss.

At this stage she was still sure something might turn up. There were schemes now that let you stay in your house.

"Their pension gone," she thought, "All of it. Their pension. Every last penny? That was terrible news. Even if they managed to hold on to the house how would they maintain it. How would they live? Did they have savings?"

Catherine had checked their joint account and nothing had changed much. It held about nine thousand. She was sure she had Premium Bonds but how many she couldn't remember. Only that she occasionally won twenty-five pounds though it hadn't happened for a while. A shot of panic ripped through her as she tried to remember their last win.

Chapter 14

Money

She'd have to talk to Peter. He'd been at that company over twenty-five years. Catherine's uncle had help him set it up with money from Catherine's parents, a loan though she couldn't remember if it was ever paid back and hadn't seemed to matter.

They'd had accountants, surely everything was not lost? The company had seemed to be thriving. She'd occasionally been into the office to sign something and it appeared busy if never very welcoming. They were dressed smartly and seemed abreast with modern practises and besides she had been frantically busy in the early days with that endless whirl of school runs and afterschool clubs not to mention The Pony Club.

They'd had a good lifestyle but if they didn't have a decent pension then how in reality would they maintain life at the farmhouse? Peter hardly lifted a finger. They had a gardener, a cleaner and a regular handyman. There were all those windows and doors, fences and gutters to keep on top of, not to mention the multiple roofs to maintain. The barn, the stables, the garage, tack room and store rooms, all needed a good sort out, cleaning, woodworm treatment and painting. It was an endless repair or renew circle. Always a list, hedge trimming, paddock-strimming, tree topping, drive maintenance, fencing, at least they had never got the pool, or even a fountain, Catherine mused. Always people to pay she thought. She looked out at the eucalyptus with a large thin branch extending right over the roof of the stables, pointing like a skinny finger. She needed to get the Tree Surgeons out again.

Already that year a lime-limb had crashed, one stormy night, blocking the driveway of her nearest neighbours. It had to be sorted very quickly and was expensive and stressful. At least they got some wood out of it. She loved a fire.

Catherine was beginning to cost out their current lifestyle and though she felt fairly frugal she realized the house ate money with its windows and doors, too numerous to count. Maybe it was impossible to stay? Maybe they just couldn't though, she still didn't really believe it?

It was 9.40pm so too late to speak to him about it now. She would have to wait to the morning and spend a night in the dark and maybe that was good as things might settle down.

An urge to be with Peter engulfed her and she entered his study. It was painted in grey. He sat at an Edwardian desk upholstered in green leather. Photos of the family and a small golf trophy, sat central on the window sill along with an art deco lady in pewter, and a potted Aloe Vera plant, both gifts from their children. He was pouring over paperwork, his laptop open and when he turned his head round by the light of his bottle table light his face looked ashen.

"Darling can I make you something or do anything?" she enquired gently.

"Yes," he said abruptly, "Half a million would do it. That's what those bastards at Rissington's have taken from us after all those years."

She lingered by the doorway and then quietly crept over to him and standing behind him she laid her hands on his shoulders and gently squeezed them.

"We'll be alright. Things will work out. I'm so sorry this has happened to you. It must be awful."

He put a hand on her hand and gently squeezed back and then shook her away.

"I need to look at these," he waved paper at her. "Do you mind, Catherine?"

He was irritated by her and she backed off and left the room. Her heart sank as she wouldn't be able to ask him anything that night but it was quite clear they were in a mess. A real mess. Half a million he had said. How much money did they need? How much money did they have? How much money were they spending?

By ten o'clock, the following morning, the sun was out warming the front garden and the set-up sunbed, within it. Catherine had done the rounds with the animals. She'd slung some fallen apples into the paddock for the horse and her dear pony companion, the chunky Strawberry roan, with his charming habit, of curling his top lip.

The dogs were, as ever, bursting with joy to see her and all over her, but for the brief minute that they wolfed down their light breakfast. She collected two fat eggs from the dilapidated hen-house. They bulged out of the spaces allowed by the supermarket egg box marked Large.

On the way back from her dog walk she decided she must talk of their finances with Peter. She would do her best to shut down any talk about selling the house until their situation was clear to her. Confrontation with Peter upset her, but she simply couldn't find it in herself to agree to selling Bluebell Farmhouse at least, not without other avenues thoroughly explored, and certainly not in a kneejerk reaction to sudden news, however frightful.

As her first attempt she made him a coffee and at eleven took it into his study. She suggested they had a little talk about their situation.

"Not now Catherine. Can't you see I'm busy?" he'd said, shuffling papers and not looking away from his computer screen. She retreated but at least she'd sown the seed. He couldn't ignore it. They would need to talk and now he knew it. Tomorrow was the day she had arranged to meet Sara who had seemed excited to be seeing her and Catherine was loathe to let down. She wanted to go anyway. As much as she adored the house right now she needed to escape as every step she took threw up a memory, reminding her of her attachment to the place and the transience of life and situations.

Besides, it was different now with Peter at home all day.

Again, in the afternoon she allowed herself the luxury of the sunbed after vigorously cutting back the border at last. She'd pruned fiercely and prematurely and thought, watching the rose heads tumble into the pink wheelbarrow, 'One small step.'

There had been another failed attempt at lunch with Peter, a meal hitherto she had not had to deal with, as she was happy to swipe a bowl of leftovers from the fridge and microwave them. It had been a small triumph when, Peter though a gadget lover, accepted a microwave into the kitchen.

No, it wasn't going to be easy having Peter around all the time. The answer to their prayers would be simple if he would get another job but at his age was it likely? Did he want one? She supposed as he'd been his own boss for decades, he wouldn't find it easy, but couldn't he start again? She was ignorant of the workings of this sort of thing and if he'd been his own boss then, why wasn't he still, and what had happened to their pension? She guessed all would reveal itself in time.

Back on her sunbed, as Peter had holed himself back in his study, she felt the rays and normally would have jumped up and splashed some factor whatever on, at least, to her face and chest. This time she didn't, she would absorb it all, the Vitamin D. She didn't rise to get her peaked hat either and wore no sunglasses. She saw the bright, reddish colour at the back of her eyelids and patterns form and felt quite peaceful.

Earlier in the afternoon she'd been reading a history book, the Hellenistic Period and concluded if Alexander the Great had embarked on an eleven-year plan that created the largest empire the world had ever seen. If he could invade Persia, sweep through Syria, destroy Tyre and conquer lands as far apart as Egypt and north-west India then surely Peter and she could find a way to keep their home.

It dawned on her it wouldn't happen with her on a sunbed. When did she get so lazy? The cement around the damp proof had chipped off and some weeds were getting in between it and the brickwork making it worse. This was part of the house and she needed to nip it in the bud before the damp set in. She would tell Gavin. How long were they going to be able to afford him?

She needed to do as much work on the house and grounds herself and get rid of all the tiny little annoyances that pressed down on her. Clear her decks, so to speak. She would finish the borders. Get them ship shape that very afternoon and formulate ideas while doing so.

She would blitz the place. She'd start to let go. A good clear out, she thought, to see what to hold on to, amid the piles produced by seventeen years of family living, and what to cut loose. Last summer she'd tried to empty the barn but they still had three, or was it four, old bicycles lying around. She'd have to be more ruthless about this. Have the bikes taken away. Nobody used them so they invoked guilt not *joy*.

She must explain to the children *their* reduced circumstances when she knew what they were. This catastrophe was going to create knock-on effects. They would be heartbroken by the sale of the house. 'Oh, this is awful. What a mess,' she thought and stirred herself to do something. Too hot for tea, she made two iced drinks, determined to extract some insight into their financial situation. She knocked at his door and immediately entered with the iced drinks. He was immersed in his business.

"Peter, can we talk now," she said in a low voice, softly placing the glass on a coaster bearing a long-eared, greyish brown hare.

Reluctantly he spilt the beans and then, shoeing her away, made her promise not to tell anyone. Catherine closed the door quietly. On balance the news had been even worse than she had anticipated. It would seem that life as they'd known it had ceased. She'd rather suspected as much. It was hard to face and the song "Yesterday" came to mind. She didn't really know what to do, so after a brief sit down at the kitchen table, she carried on with what she had been doing ten minutes earlier when she'd been in relative blissful ignorance. Wasn't that what you were encouraged to do as in the war days? *Keep calm and carry on*. Their pension was gone. All of it and it was irrecoverable and she'd received the unwelcome impression that any type of negotiation could risk getting them in worse trouble and that Peter hadn't been playing with a straight bat. 'Suing,' had been mentioned. A word that put the fear of God into her. Just when you think things couldn't get worse, hadn't Peter said when she'd announced glibly the possibility of the gravel pit miring their virginal countryside views? 'Peter looked dreadful,' she thought, 'he was taking it harder than her. Well it was his identity really,' she supposed 'Big cheese at the office, he'd grown that business.'

The dogs wandered behind her panting in the gloriously hot mid-afternoon sun. This planet was warming. It was now September but felt like June. She mentally added the month of September to be included to her own version of British Summertime. A podcast had said that during the medieval period around the 1200's it had been warm enough in England to enable the making of very drinkable wine.

Her objective that afternoon was to clear the smallest of the barns, the one next to the row of brick stables. Back and forth she went dragging things out; making piles. She was determined not just to shuffle items from place to place as had been a habit. Things had moved from the little barn to the big barn, from the cellar to the garage from one bedroom to another. Only a fraction of the articles would ever leave the premises. Food getting shoved round the plate. That wasn't going to happen this time. It would be an empty plate and no throwing up.

She'd categorize them into piles Burn, Tip, Charity, Gift or Store. One stable alone would be allocated to store the beauty being even if she hadn't been able to part with the item it would be out of sight, neatly until it could be further appropriately dealt with.

Wild ideas started to circulate in her head as she gathered ten years of old dog-beds and stacked them in the burn pile. Why had she kept them so long? They already had beds in two places and there was their old brown Chesterfield sofa they used as a daybed.

She was surprised at how soon an area could be cleared but it was still an enormous job and would take more time or more people and more people cost money. Money, money, money that's all it would be about now she felt sadly. Could they afford this? Could they afford that?

'Keeping the wolf for the door,' now seemed what life was all about. She was clearing the barn but how could she clear a mortgage? Debts? How could she make a good living?

CHAPTER 15

Catherine The Great

They met at the British Museum. On her way in, Catherine passed by, a small table set up on the street, by a Chinese Civil-Rights Movement. She didn't stop to see what they were saying as she mistook them for a religious organisation. Besides, she was in a *me first* frame of mind.

She saw Sara who was dressed in a smart navy suit and open toed kitten heels hovering by the queue, apparently undecided whether or not to get in it. It was two o'clock and due to the swollen numbers of after lunch museum-goers was already building up.

Catherine waving her arm called, "Sara" and Sara promptly stepped into the line and waited for her old schoolfriend to join her as in days of yore. They stood, side by side, and then shuffled along as the queue threaded up and down, neatly cordoned by metal railings, slowed to snail pace due to the rigorous bag searching procedure.

Catherine turned her head to Sara and whispered, "I don't think they do this at the National Gallery and certainly not at the Portrait Gallery."

"Well at least there aren't any of those annoying bomb scares where everyone has to evacuate," said Sara and Catherine pulled a face in agreement adding with a distant smile "Do you remember I told you   Donkey Dale set me up on a blind date? The boys were pretty awful and mine, well it was never going to work, was a foot shorter than me. It was mutual repulsion at first sight. We were in the days where one regarded the opposite sex as yes or no and no one wanted to waste their time on a no. There we all were, in an Olympic pool, at fifteen, Diana exposing her mature physique. I've never been less annoyed to hear sirens. I was delighted by the bomb-scare and snuck off home."

"You were allowed to change then?"

"Yes, we must have been. That would have been funny, the swimming pool empty, and everyone outside on the pavement shivering away in their bathers."

They shuffled on some more and Catherine couldn't hold it in any longer.

"Sara, I need your advice. I know this couple and it turns out that they haven't the money they thought. Their situation is really quite precarious and their house isn't paid for and they're getting on. Their pension has disappeared and what's more the husband's lost his job. Well   his business really."

"Does his wife earn?" enquired Sara.

"No," Catherine shook her head.

They stopped talking as they exposed their bags for inspection. Sara reached out and brushed her arm across Catherine's back.

"Come on I'll buy us a coffee. I love talking money. Let's get to the bottom of this. It sounds very serious so don't expect a miracle cure, but these things can spiral from bad to worse unless measures are taken. There is always a way forward and money troubles are usually much simpler than illnesses or love agonies and need not always lead to drastic endings. You grab a table. Americano?"

Catherine knew how much Sara loathed counter service, and felt a rush of affection.

"I'll need to know a rough estimate of assets, flexible and inflexible, debts including mortgage provider and terms and current expenditure. Got a pen?" Sara added and then left.

Catherine slowly brought out a black biro and an envelope and did as much as she could but realized she was shamefully ignorant of her own affairs and for the first time, sitting on the wooden chair, at the café at the British Museum it dawned on her that she had no idea of what Peter had earned or used to earn.

When Sara returned with the coffees Catherine implored her not to tell anyone, as there were children involved and because the husband had insisted.

"Discretion's my middl' name m'lady," replied Sara in an accent intended to amuse Catherine or at least to put her more at ease.

Sara saw Catherine's deadpan expression and glanced at the figures on the envelope and grimaced.

"If it was a question of a bit of money I'm sure a friend would help out but I can see this is past that. We're talking many tens of thousands. Hundreds," said Sara.

Catherine looked into her coffee cup. She didn't like the affirmation. Sara looked at her friend and thought how fragile she looked. Catherine, who was always so together, so matter of fact, so everything's well, so "Can I help you. Can I get you anything?" So nicey, nicey. Well she was floored now.

The figures only gave a vague grasp on 'the couple's' situation but she'd focused on the mortgage and knowing the property's rough worth and ages of the couple she could see it wasn't at this stage too much of an emergency but they'd need to produce an income if they wanted to keep it. She picked up her coffee and stroking it caught Catherine's eye.

"How much do you want to keep the house?" she asked.

"I can't sell it. I love it,"

"Well, make it work for you or get Peter back at mill," said Sara adding, "and fairly quickly too. You've always said you'd like to do riding holidays? You could accommodate and cater?"

"There's no money in horses, but do you think I could run a Bed and Breakfast?"

"On your head, Catherine. Isn't that what you've been doing for years anyway?"

Sara meant what she said though hell would have to freeze over before she'd change a sheet or cook an egg for money or love these days.

"Your house is perfect and so well placed for Stratford upon Avon and the Cotswolds."

"I don't think Peter would like it," said Catherine realistically.

"Well he'll have to get another job then and the faster the better. Seriously Catherine don't be worrying about him. He's lucky you're being so nice about this. Some would not be. I mean he's ruined your retirement, nearly lost you your home; kept you in the dark. Whether or not you stay or move things aren't likely to be the same. No, Catherine if you want to keep the house you'll have to fight for it and stay in the picture. You like history, don't you? Well here, you'll have to pull out your inner Catherine the Great."

"Ha, now she had a go at effecting change, tried to abolish capital punishment and torture. You mustn't tell anyone about this. The children don't know, nor does Mum. I hate keeping people in the dark," said Catherine and added, "I know how Florence must feel now."

"Look, you still have plenty of money really. Your house is worth a fortune! Besides Florence is having a whale of a time. She swans here. She swans there. Feeling sorry for yourself is one thing but feeling sorry for Florence. Please. If she's had to struggle to readjust she's done it with a cocktail in one hand and a good novel or travel guide in the other, in any number of attractive locations, none of which she has to lift a finger to maintain. Feeling sorry for Florence, now that is a waste of one's sympathies," Sara insisted vehemently.

"I feel badly for not telling Rose though I haven't seen her so much with the approach of the new school year, up to her eyeballs, in Assistant Headship," answered Catherine.

"About time too. She's always been too talented for just a classroom teacher at Primary school," said Sara scathingly. "It shocks me when people can't realize their true worth."

Catherine frowned. "Perhaps she enjoyed being 'just' a classroom teacher. Goodness knows, what you've thought about me over the years."

"I've nothing but the utmost respect for the way you've rallied round your family. Those children of yours are fine young people and a credit to you. This adversity might mature Peter from toddler to ten-year old and make him more a befitting life partner for you. This could actually improve your relationship, if you get it right," suggested Sara. "If you can look it holistically."

Catherine muttered a thanks but thought Sara sounded patronizing and annoying and she wasn't used to being annoyed; especially not by her best friend, whom she knew was trying to be a comfort as well as a brick.

Sara let out a sigh. "Things will get better. You've had a shock. Things seem terrible now and then weeks later it will be, "What was all that about?" "

"My life isn't like this though, usually," moaned Catherine.

"Oh please, Catherine. I've read your diary. Remember 1982?"

Catherine looked at her blankly.

"The false alarm!" shrieked Sara and sniggered without mercy. "You were bricking it."

"Not quite as much as Todd," commented Catherine smiling again.

"A plan will unfurl," assured Sara, "I can see you are all over this and that's why you are feeling tired. Be careful of exhaustion, mental exhaustion. I'll help you, though I'm not changing any sheets, but I'll help you. So, will Peter once he's mourned the loss of his ergonomic chair and look- I'm- better -than- you- suit."

They finished their coffees and discussed Catherine's expenditure and she promised to find out the details of their current mortgage. That was of vital importance as far as Sara was concerned and they were to strategize how Catherine could build an income.

Catherine pointed to a picture on her £2 museum guide.

"Ram in a thicket," she laughed. "It's Peter."

"You wish," said Sara who was never one to miss a double entendre when the chance presented itself adding, "Room 56. Do you want to see the Elgin Marbles first?"

"Oh yes," said Catherine, "That horse's head one of you put on What's App looked superb. You must be feeling quite au fait with the British Museum?"

"Yes. Twice in the last fortnight. Like my sex life!" chortled Sara.

Catherine didn't comment.

The pair made their way slowly past the marbles to the Pantheon horsehead. Catherine's attention was riveted for several minutes until at last she felt quite calm and that indeed all was not lost. She hoped she and Sara would have time to reminisce about their pony days, so dear to her heart.

On the request of Catherine, they viewed the room entitled Medieval Europe AD1050-1500 where Sara was genuinely taken by surprize at how knowledgeable her friend was on the subject. It went far beyond which monarch reigned. Furthermore, she appeared to have a good understanding of the prior build up to this period and mentioned things like the Anglo-Saxon Chronicles and Danelaw distinguishing between the Swedish and Danish Vikings.

"Well the Black Death was a particularly virulent and terrifying form of pneumonic and bubonic plague," carried on Catherine.

"Terrible. Must have been terrifying," said Sara.

"Yes, it just swept through countries – Asia, Europe, the Middle East. Around 25 million dead in Asia and around the same in Europe and countless more in the Middle East and if you think fifty years earlier at 1300 or so the population of London which was by far the biggest city was only fifty thousand or so."

"I wonder where it started?" asked Sara who had muddled it up with plague around the Great Fire of 1666.

"Well I believe it was in the 1330's in China. Yunnan Provence.

She further explained that the Black Death first reached Europe mid 1300's with the Mongol armies besieging the port of Caffa, and part of the attack, involved throwing infected body-parts in. On the bright side, it did improve worker's rights due to labour shortage."

"Shocking this low wage and gig economy we have now," said Sara.

"Yes, and I did hear, somewhere, that it continued to break out, every twenty years, for the next three hundred odd years, right up to 1665 or 6 or whenever the, 'Fire of London' broke out."

"Pudding Lane," concluded Sara.

Chapter 16

FALLEN APPLES

Florence sat in the bright morning sunshine looking out at the grass and the fallen apples in a paler shade of green. There was a wondrous sun-dappling that patterned Catherine and Peter's well-maintained lawn.

She remembered, nostalgically, how she and Franny had often collected their own fallers and made a crumble, picking blackberries to stew alongside the apples. She'd liked the feeling they came from her garden, and when too pushed for time, was glad to sling them to the nearby ponies and pigs. Doing the rounds, recycling, living off the land had felt good.

Florence remembered how cosy they had been in their cottage surrounded by little paddocks enclosing various animals. To the three apple trees they'd added two plums and a pear tree to make a little orchard. It was rather nice here not having that guilt of leaving fallen apples to rot on the spot. These apples were Catherine's and Peter's worry. They could pick them up or pay someone else to do. Florence felt she might help herself to a few, sure Lady Bountiful would be only too grateful.

Catherine bought a tray of tea in china mugs, bone-thin not wafer. Florence was cross that Catherine had bought out biscuits. She resigned herself to having one as she might need to "chub up" for her Amazon trip as she had no idea of the food situation on the boat.

"When do you go?"

"November 11th."

"Oh, that's soon. I hate November here. November and February, I could do without. Two months of winter is quite enough. One for Christmas and the other to recover. I must admit I quite like January now that the kids have left school and all that. I just hole up in the snug with the dogs by day until Peter comes back." Catherine confessed. "So, details then Flo?"

"Well I fly to Bogota and then straight to Leticia. I did think about a city break but frankly I've spent long enough in Bogota, so its straight to the Amazon. I have to book into that lovely mother and daughter guest house. It has a gorgeous outside part with hammocks and a little swimming pool. I love it. I must find out about the weather. Leticia is amazing but I've only ever been in June. I'm getting a boat from Leticia, Colombia to Manaus, the city in the Amazon, Brazil. I'm not sure how long it takes but a few days and you have to bring your own hammock," she finished proudly.

"Have you got a ticket for the boat?"

"No, no I'm going to hang out at the guest house until some like-minded travellers turn up. European, Antipodean, North American, anyone with some English really. You string up your hammocks but you only have this tiny area so you have to grab your space in the early hours before the boat sets off. It sounds a bit harrowing so I'd rather do it with someone. It would be much easier if they were female but not essential. I mean I'm sure the locals would help but I don't want to be a burden. It's not as if I haven't spent plenty of time being the only Westerner somewhere or other for better or for worse," Florence confided.

"You're so brave," said Catherine looking at Florence with pride, affection and a tiny smidgeon of incredulity.

"I'll be fine," stated Florence shaking the crumbs off her fingers.

"Fine?"

"No really. If I lose my nerve I'll just have a lovely time in Leticia and do some more of the jungle. Go piranha fishing and canoeing. There's plenty to explore there though I don't suppose it will ever beat the first time I went when I met that crazy old timer Harry at that Ayawaska House on stilts in Puerta Narina."

"Is that Colombia?"

"Mm, I think so but you go through Peru and Brazil to get there, I think. One half of the river belongs to one country and the other to another. There's a stretch of land and rivers called No Man's Land and I think it was there, but I'm not sure. Sans frontiers."

"Goodness, Florence is that wise? I mean isn't it drug country?"

"Hmm," Florence dismissed the comment. "That was the least of my worries. Talk about living in the moment. I had one of my top three adventures ever."

Florence glowed and continued as she sensed a rare and genuine interest from her friend.

"Harry this old guy, white beard, 70's, asked me if I'd like to see an indigenous family house. He said there was no road. Well there were no cars on the island anyway. He said it was a bit tricky to get there and not to bring anything to carry. We set off and after a mile or so heading inland, I found myself behind Harry walking along or rather balancing on a series of semi floating logs. Those endless logs! They were submerged in the thickest of mire. Who knows how deep that mud was? My walking stick never made ground contact when I poked it down to get some sense of security. Walking or rather shuffling along with sideways feet and tiny little steps when you can't see dry land in front and then not behind either and with absolutely no one about apart from this chap in front of you who is fully engaged with his own safety on this precarious journey, knowing there are abundant poison dart frogs, the bright yellow ones, living either side let alone the odd Black Caiman or snake. The mud in the swamp was several feet deep. It was perilous. You had to concentrate so hard to stay up right. One false move and you're in. Rather like those metal buzzer things that you have at village fairs or in pubs before computers, that you had to manually negotiate that circle of metal which would instantly buzz if metal touches metal.

It was like that. I had to give it all my concentration. We carried nothing but our stick, not even water, and in that humidity. We shuffled along, for log after log, half sideways. All made more terrifying as I suspected we'd have to come back again on it. The terror of it. Never known anything like it before or since. I'd have never have gone if I'd known. It was an amazing place though when we arrived."

"Arrived where? What was it?" Catherine asked craning her head very slightly towards Florence.

"Oh, just a family home though rather a beautiful one. Very, very basic; sort of stone age, with a poor baby monkey strung up. I had to do it back, that walk. Harry must have been into his seventies. I'd had no idea he'd be so fit and balanced. One of the sweetest things I've ever seen was Harry with that captive infant monkey. It was tied up by a piece of string around its neck attached to a beam in the rafters. Apparently, it's illegal now to make them pets but the tribes have been doing it for countless generations. They keep the monkey tied up when it's very, very young so it only gets used to those surroundings and won't leave and eventually becomes a much-loved, untethered family pet.

It was pitiful when Harry stretched his hand out to it and it just clung to his fingers with its tiny delicate hands. I've never seen such fragility and such an obvious connection between species. That baby had such an urgent need to touch or be touched. It was a moment of tenderness and one of my most enduring memories. There was an exchange between them, a jolt, like the Michaelangelo scene of God and Adam on the ceiling of the Sistene Chapel you get on greeting cards," Florence stopped.

"It sounds incredible. Will you go back?" asked Catherine.

"Highly unlikely. I'd never find it again in a million years not to mention the log walk. I will go back to the Guest House. There's this great woman, Luisa, who runs it. I think she owns it. She's about our age. She runs it with her daughter, who had the most gorgeous, silky black, down-the-back hair, then just the day before I left, she comes back on duty with a sleek Cleopatra. She still looked beautiful but I felt a sadness, a passing on," Florence recalled.

"Yes, I remember when I had mine cut shorter. I think I was about eighteen," recollected Catherine. "Mind you it was never ever that long. Don't ever cut yours Florence."

"Oh, I suppose I will one day," sighed Florence and continued to tell her friend about this lovely, friendly Back Packers Inn with its little pool and hammock area and honesty bar, where among other things travellers told tales, sewing seeds. "It had a really chilled vibe and they were so helpful," she continued. "She linked me up with Lucio, well I think that's what his name was, a right old character. Though I have to say that when they said he had a bit of English they were not exaggerating. "BEEG animal," were two of them and he'd repeat them very excitedly when the opportunity arose. I knew more Spanish care of a single Johny Spanish podcast. Off I went with him on a three-night adventure. Public transport took us up the Amazon. I bought a torch in Brazil and a coffee in Peru and saw this awesome fish market with a dead caiman hung up with one of its front legs sliced off. I read somewhere that there was a community of Caiman Eaters; the "Israelites." All that in one morning and then it was up the Yavari to our basic accommodation next to a Ticuna village."

"What were they like?" asked Catherine helping herself to a chocolate biscuit. She was a good listener and Florence realised how little she repeated her adventures to anybody. Who is ever interested, she felt?

"No idea. I didn't want to disturb them. Thought they'd be sick to death of foreigners gawping and snapping away. Besides, I'd be wary of unleashing pathogens. We took no notice of each other though I remember the women washing clothes in the river and the children on the banks with a kite, running. It was an enchanting river. Lucio took me out on the boat again and again. He and this young teenager from the village who had no English and I can't remember if he had any Spanish or Portuguese but we got by. The boy on the motor-board and Lucio up at the front with a long pole and me in the middle. We'd motor, then float, motor then float. It was sooo beautiful with the river covered with lily-pads and the trees overhanging either side. No one else in sight and the sounds of the jungle everywhere and then a flash of a bird or fluttering of butterflies. So many butterflies, oranges, yellows, sort of saffron. They'd waft over the boat in masses. It was like going through a coloured cloud."

"It sounds heavenly,"

"Once," Florence exclaimed, "this yellow frog jumped on board about an inch away from my foot."

"Was it dangerous?" Catherine asked.

"Lucio showed it some respect," reminisced Florence reminded of how he had carefully scooped it out calmly with a sawn-off empty two- litre water bottle with the air of a bomb disposal expert.

Florence explained that she'd found out later about the South American Poisonous Dart Frog and how its toxicity was off the scale. A touch of the skin of that dear little frog could kill you though she pointed out as it obtained its poison through what it ate, once in captivity on a different diet was quite harmless.

"Was he "Beeg animal?" Florence mimicked raising her voice and Catherine gathered she was back on the boat in the jungle with Lucio and the boy.

"Beeg animal. Very beeg," he'd say when he spotted a caiman with its eyes peering out above the densely lily-coated river. Then I'd enquire what it fed on or whether the males and females differed or if they were group animals and he'd reply "Yes IS colour." We'd communicate, have a laugh, but understood very little of what each other said. We got by though it did annoy me, at first, when he'd point to the sky and say "parrot" and sound as though he should get a medal when I had around twenty-five species of macaws, parrots and parakeets flapping around in my head to trawl through and tie up with the bird high above, so high that you couldn't distinguish its colour. Not like when you go to a proper organised tour like I did at the Saltlicks with an expert guide, powerful binoculars, tripods, waterproofed field guides with all the parrots of the region in size order in brilliant colour so you could see the orange cheeks of the orange cheeked parrot. It was a wonderful wildlife experience though you did have to get up at 4.30am and cost quite a bit and there were, though not hordes certainly a throng of viewers, all polite but a few on the annoying side."

"Where was that?" asked Catherine still nibbling on a biscuit showing no signs of second-hand travel fatigue.

"Can't remember the name but somewhere off the Tarranpota. Near its confluence with the Rio Madre de Dios."

"Which country?"

"Peru."

"And where were you this last time with this fellow Lucio?" asked Catherine.

"No Man's Land I think. There are around eighty kilometres where Peru, Colombia and Brazil converge and no country checks you. Well that is what I heard. It came up on my phone as where I'd taken photos or sent something, "No Man's Land," so must be."

Florence swung her hair over her shoulder with her left hand and thought she ought to talk to Catherine about something more domestic but Catherine asked her which trip had been her favourite so far and she was flooded with memories that had filtered out the lonely, worrying and duller parts and squeezed and enhanced them so that she was bursting with glee at the recollections and felt given a chance she was more than happy to share them especially with her dearest friend of whom she thought the world.

"This Lucio, he may have had hardly any English but he had character and was very daring and there was this one boat trip that really sticks in my mind. We were on a tributary which may have been the Yavari and it was covered with lily-pads and pretty choked by general rain forest. It wasn't that deep where we were and branches and odd tree trunk had fallen in. Every so often he'd leap up and machete the undergrowth. You had to take a bit of care not to be in the way.

The boy on the motor was safe enough but I was quite near. It wasn't a big boat. The boat would ground itself on some underwater debris and one or both of them would leap out and pull and push the boat free and leap back in usually grinning. They were pretty agile, those guys," commented Florence.

"How old was he Lucio?" enquired Catherine.

"Hmm," paused Florence.

"Not married?" Catherine asked.

"Mmm. Don't know?" Florence said shrugging her shoulders.

"What did he look like?" Catherine asked.

"Like a piranha. Really like one. He had that Hapsburg underbite. Very pronounced just like a piranha. He took me fishing once in a creek in a smaller boat and I got to see Piranhas. They come in three colours and I caught a slimy Dogfish and something really weird happened. This Dogfish that I caught started talking or calling. It was calling out in distress. I can't remember what it sounded like but it happened. I You Tubed it when I got back."

"It made noises," Catherine stated.

"Yes, and very plaintive ones," assured Florence, "Though I can't remember what they sounded like. I'm pretty sure it was a slimy Dog fish and it's the first and last time I've heard a fish-call. These things happen. The ape, in a metal cage, smoking cigarettes in Java; the burning tyres in Sri Lanka; the road blocks in India; the crack house in Downtown Miami; the Volcano erupting in Ecuador. I don't go around recording them."

Catherine looked at Florence's petulant face and saw an underlying vulnerability, maybe caused by the realization that her friend knew that one day she might stray too far to get back.

"Oh, we're all different. Thank Goodness. More tea Vicar?" smoothed Catherine.

Florence followed Catherine into the kitchen and made some admiring comments about its sparkle and asked Catherine how her children were doing and said Frankie was doing very well in her new teaching job.

Catherine listened, worried internally about her own, but verbalised just a fraction of it as she'd heard the suggestions mixed with platitudes before, and didn't feel up to having yet another discussion about it, that particular morning. Tales from the exotic, embroidered or not, were a welcome change from her half-worried world.

When they were settled again, on plumped up cushions on pretty white metal Victoriana chairs, with fresh tea, Florence started spurting out about her recent Amazonian adventure.

"Once there was this tree log blocking the entire width of the river," exclaimed Florence.

"What did you do?" asked Catherine.

"Well Lucio had pointed over to a, "Beeg caimam. Very,very beeg." He reckoned it was between four and five or was it five or six metres long. You can estimate their length, you know, by the distance between their eyes."

"Oooh," Catherine went, holding her mug with two hands, and leaning towards her friend affectionately engaged with the tale.

"He was very excited," Florence recalled with great enthusiasm. "It was about ten metres from the boat and they tried to get over the log but our boat grounded on it. We were stuck. Lucio and the boy hopped off and waist deep wrenched it free and leapt back on quickly. The boy on the motor and Lucio with the long pole steered it back a good few yards and then, again, we went for it, full throttle. Again, there was this awful jolt and scraping as the boat grounded itself. What a noise it made crunching on the tree trunk. They got out and this time it was harder to dislodge but they managed it. At this stage I was wondering if I should get out to make the boat lighter but I didn't fancy it as you couldn't see anything beneath the darkish water, just the lily pads floating on top. The menfolk seemed all over it anyway. They got the boat free again and did the circle and the young man opened it up and we roared at it and again it crashed and grounded."

Catherine interrupted at that point to say that it sounded like her early, show-jumping days with her first pony, a distinctly individual Welsh cob that hadn't taken to the ring and least of all to brashly painted walls. She explained how fearless she'd been at twelve and after it had refused the jump, she'd hauled her pony around and pelted towards the wall again but Billy had dug his hooves in and slid into it. This had happened three times, though on the last try he'd slid in and scattered it. The bell had rung out notifying all of her elimination and she had left the ring ignominiously.

"Oh, Sara told me it was your horse that was always covered with rosettes and that your bedroom was stuffed with cups," Florence remarked.

"That was later. My parents upgraded me when I grew out of Billy. Go on with the story, please Florence," answered Catherine.

"Well it was fourth time lucky for us. It was one of the most exciting times in my entire life," sighed Florence. "You had to cling on with your life. Bit like the motorbiking days with The Filthy Few. Doing the ton on the back of a Gold Wing."

Catherine hadn't known Florence during that teenage year when Florence had hung out with a Motorbike Gang and wasn't interested in it, so asked her what the next leg of her journey would be. But Florence was still too caught up in her Crocodilian experience and explained that it had been a Black Caiman lurking in the water and that they were the aggressive branch of the Alligator family. She took it upon herself yet again to explain the "4th tooth" rule to Catherine informing her how to tell the difference between an alligator and a crocodile.

"With the crocodile," Florence taught, "you see the fourth tooth on the bottom jaw. It is conspicuous when the jaw is closed, whereas with the alligator which includes the caiman, the fourth tooth, bottom jaw slots into a hole in the top jaw so is not conspicuous."

"The fourth tooth. It sounds like a cult or a title of something. Maybe you ought to write a book with it as a title, The Fourth Tooth. How is your book going anyway?" asked Catherine feeling maybe she'd heard enough about crocodiles for one day. She didn't really share Florence's passion for the wild. Her heart would lift if she saw the spread of a majestic oak or a deer soar the hedge dividing brown from gold or green. A nature-lover, but not with the burning passion that would send her friend into arm flapping rapture. Florence was so excited by life, Catherine didn't have the heart to burden her with sorrow.

CHAPTER 17

A Handful of Water

They assembled at Bluebell Farm, at Sara's request, for a working supper. Florence considered that Sara was overdressed for the occasion. She bent over the kitchen island to kiss her host Catherine who was wearing jeans and a pale blue lambswool sweater.

"Well there's the name to start with. Bluebell Farm," Rose said. "It sounds so idyllic."

"Yes," agreed Sara "People pay now to see fields of flowers. I saw signposts for Lavender Fields on the way over here,"

"That's a housing estate," clarified Catherine, who, though she was touched that her friends had rallied around her with the express purpose to save her home, was weary. Maybe for the very first time in her life, was weary of life. Suddenly the fact that she only had between ten and thirty odd years left, seemed a positive thing. It felt a good thing that, within two decades, she would not be expected, or maybe even capable of, sensible decision making.

"You could have a wild flower meadow!" suggested Florence, "and hedgehog homes."

"They've all been eaten by badgers," Rose stated.

"Well, all the more reason for hedgehog homes and maybe a Stoat and Weasel Sanctuary."

Catherine poured the wine. Sara had caught her in the kitchen and ranted that she couldn't believe that Peter had racked up another two hundred and fifty thousand on the mortgage without Catherine knowing. Had she signed? She had said that she wasn't aware of it and that it had been done in chunks over the last two or three years.

"Where is he now?" enquired Sara.

"Golf club," said Catherine so tearful that Sara changed her approach.

"Well, we are here to help you take immediate and energetic measures. You have support now and there will be a solution. There will be a way forward. You will feel better. At the worst you sell and move and start afresh in something you both like."

Catherine started walking back to the others with wine glasses and nibbles and stated,

"I know. I know, but I don't want to sell."

"Change can be hard," sighed Sara.

"Yes, my Uncle David said if you can get used to change you can get used to anything," said Rose who had taken over the cooking and was pressing the spaghetti down into boiling water and made it cascade out in a near perfect sphere. In her head the solution was simple. Reduced financial circumstances meant reduced housing. 'Simples'. She knew better than to say it but what did the three of them need with such a big house anyway?

Sara who seemed to be chairing the meeting asked Rose if she'd bought flip chart and pens.

Rose left off Bolognese duty, bustled and produced four fat felts in black, red, blue and green.

"What is our time frame?" she asked.

"Looks about ready," said Catherine stirring the sauce. "Oh, you mean the money," she observed and questioned whether they should eat first.

Sara explained, as she took a seat and was going to let the food come to her, that there were two main points to consider in the crisis, revenue stream and gearing. They needed to produce an income to pay the bills and mortgage and also to pay off debts. Sara said that paying off the mortgage would have to wait though any reduction in the amount owed would help.

She told them she would put twenty thousand into a fund to pay for a modest start up and that there might be some grants available.

Rose started the Spider chart with 'Income Revenue' from Bluebell Farm in the middle. The three women brainstormed and Rose wrote down the ideas crisply. Catherine explained they didn't have enough land to do anything agricultural or equine based and poopooed the idea of having a yard of any sort, though they did have stables.

"It's very, very hard to make a living from horses. It's more usual to lose money," Catherine said and this crossed out many of Florence's suggestions as they were animal based and included a cattery, a dog kennel, a luxury dog house kennel and accommodated riding holidays.

"You could have a range of jewel encrusted dog collars," she laughed.

Sara looked at her crossly but admitted that it was that sort of radicalism that might get Catherine out of the mire. She suggested everyone pledged a month of their time to the project and that Ben and Peter would help, too.

"You could have a small animal theme," suggested Florence. "The Hamster Hotel with every room having a small mammal within it; a rabbit room, a gerbil room, a chinchilla suite. It would be relatively easy," she concluded.

"Wasn't there a Hamster hotel in France for Furries with a giant wheel," laughed Sara.

"OMG I forgot about that!" shrieked Florence collapsing into laughter. "Do people actually do that. Run around in a wheel?"

Catherine and Rose looked at each mutually perplexed but didn't pursue what was meant by Furries, considering ignorance bliss.

"As Mahatma, once said. I don't let people walk through my head with dirty shoes or something," said Catherine.

"I thought he went around barefoot any way," said Rose.

"Have you heard of Annie Besant? She paved the way for some of that, you know Indian independence," said Florence.

Sara, resuming her position as chair, appealed to her friends for their support in the mission to save Bluebell Farm. Florence mentioned something about helping but it might have to be partly from the Amazon, and Catherine asked everyone to sit for supper.

"I can help set up the place for Hen Parties when I get back from South America. Stag ones, too," added Florence.

"But where would we live?" asked Catherine perplexed.

"You could get a caravan," chirped Florence, "On the paddock, out of sight, obviously."

Catherine didn't look happy.

"Yes, I suppose we could go over and live at my mother's, though Peter wouldn't like it," Catherine said, wondering what her mother would say if she suggested it.

"Well let's eat," said Rose. "I've just popped the garlic bread in so it will be ready by the time we've helped ourselves," she said as she helped Catherine put the dishes in the centre of the table ready to be passed round.

"There is loads and I've already kept some back for the menfolk," Catherine implored. She added that getting the house up to standard to "House party let" would be very expensive and that she was sure there wouldn't be enough hot water for eighteen hens, or the place would fuse if everyone had hair driers or showers at once. Who would do the linen?" she queried.

"A firm," Sara assured her telling her that would be the least of their problems.

Catherine looked at Sara and could see that if she was going to get anywhere she would have to adopt a can-do mentality, and also discipline herself enough to share the work ethic of her two working friends.

"I don't know what's wrong with me?" she complained. "I don't seem to have a work ethic?"

"Oh, it's just you are out of practice. You are a very competent person and here is an opportunity to show it," said Florence though she added that in her opinion hard work was rather overrated and since the advent of farming around twelve thousand years ago, there were some definite winners and losers. She added, "In the words of our dear Eleanor Roosevelt "Nobody can make you feel inferior without your consent," or just as fitting, "A woman is like a tea bag; you never know how strong it is until it's in hot water."

Catherine winced.

Over supper they discussed whether she ought to cut her teeth on Air B n B, all agreeing that she would make a perfect host and could still live at the house and that they, in some capacity, could be there to help, and that Christine could do the beds and Gavin could be on hand in case of any maintenance issues.

Sara, after stating that the Coriander pesto was shockingly fresh, was very keen to make a business plan immediately after supper and most importantly set up an anticipated start date to inject some urgency into the project.

Sara also suggested they advertised Jess's old room as The Studio and thought it better to have it as a Short stay. She thought that it might be very arduous keeping an old farm house up to the standards of cleanliness that people now required according to, 'Four in a Bed'.

Florence, feverish with new ideas, was still wanting to explore the rustic theme and was pushing Shepherd Huts. She was daydreaming about one of her favourite fictional characters Bathsheba Everdene.

"You might think of Hobbit Houses," suggested Rose. "He drank at The Bell you know and Oxford's just a spit away by train. They all hung out there. Lewis, Tolkein and another one?"

"You could have a 'Rings' theme and landscape it with different backdrops and run Lord of the Rings movies on the wall that backs the stables," she added.

"Oh, there would be all that planning," groaned Catherine.

"You will have to muster some enthusiasm, Catherine," urged Sara.

"How about high-end Homestays?" she suggested.

Catherine slipped off her chair and left the room. The others continued bandying back and forth suggestions and Catherine returned with white pepper but Sara thought she might have been crying.

"Yes," said Rose standing up with enthusiasm. "I could help give some English lessons and you have Ben and Peter with their native tongues and you would be a great teacher. I've always thought that."

"I'll help," joined in Florence, "if I'm here."

"You could get Peter to drive them into Stratford or Cheltenham for day trips," continued Rose.

"Or to the train station for excursions to Oxford or London!" Sara added.

"Go for the Chinese, Catherine. The rich ones. Rich children with their guardians. You could cook for them. Run them to Bicester Village. Sort out a package with so many hours of English. Trips. This thing has legs. I really do think it could work," she said with jubilation.

Catherine smiled under a furrowed brow.

"I feel this is the most suitable plan to meet the situation. I'll talk to Peter," she said flatly.

"No, no, no – not yet!" huffed Sara crossly. "We need to get the business plan drawn up and proto cards and prospectuses. It will need pitching or rather presented as half up and running."

"Yes," agreed Florence "And you could trendy it up as the Film Hotel like the one Fran and I stayed in Bratislava. We stayed in 'The Julia Roberts' and all it was, was a couple of blown up photos of her on the wall. Quite effective when you're miles away from home. Of course, I'd suggest more modern stars than Bruce Willis and the lot they had."

"You could do 'Cities,'" suggested Rose. "European or plain British. Rome, Berlin, Paris or Birmingham, Bristol or The Manchester?"

"Or Painting holidays with the rooms called Monet, Van Gogh, Frida Kahlo or Artemisia Gentileschi. Or writing courses with Du Maurier, Bronte or Hardy rooms?" said Florence excitedly. "I'd help with the courses. It would be great and we could meet all sorts of nice people!"

"Yes," said Catherine distinctly luke-warm. "They are very nice sounding ideas, but that sort can be a pain to deal with. I prefer Chinese children with their carer. I'd feel more comfortable dealing with children and their …. their guardians. I wonder if you can do it without masses of Red Tape. I mean I don't mind a bit of checking but it can go too far and make you pave over your entire drive if there is a whiff of a cranny. Do you mind if we forget all this stuff now? You all have been so helpful and I do think there is hope after all. The Chinese one appeals to me very much, so thank you. Let's talk Lithuania now. It's only a whisker away now and I, for one, can't wait."

"Yes, I'm really looking forward to it, too," agreed Rose. "I'll know by then whether I've got the Assistant Head post."

"Well if you don't get it they are mad," said Catherine.

"Vilnius, by all accounts, is an enchanting city," said Rose, "Fantastic architecture and lots of café and street life."

"But first, we chill for four nights at a chalet hotel in the deepest countryside by a lake. What could be better?" asked Catherine.

Florence raised her glass and said how strange it was that a speck of its contents had once been in the Lithuanian Lakes. Catherine thought for a moment, realizing everything on earth was just all one big recycle, energy as well.

"So, there is a finite amount of water, of liquid and it just goes around and around the planet and up the centuries?" Catherine said picking up her glass.

"Yes," said Florence waving her lager, "This could have been in the Yellow River during the Ming Dynasty."

"Ming means "brightening," said Rose. "I think they tried to abolish slavery."

"This could have been part of Niagra Falls," said Sara, staring at her white wine.

"Or Napoleonic sperm," suggested Florence.

"Argh, I'm not sharing a room with you on holiday," said Sara.

"We haven't decided," said Florence. "I said sperm, not spunk," she added.

"Can you just filter it a little more or you'll put Sara off her Rice Pudding," suggested Rose, guessing it would be she who shared with Florence.

"Ok then, how about milk from Cleopatra's Bath?" continued Florence pursing her lips with satisfaction.

"Blood of Boudica," she added quickly or, "sweat from Rosa Parks?"

"Enough, Florence! Besides I get the impression Rosa Parks was very cool," warned Catherine and added that her wine had been in the Trevi fountain. Florence said it was cool for ladies to sweat now and that her garlic bread could be part of Bracken. Sara looked at Catherine who whispered Bracken had been Florence's much adored and now deceased Springer spaniel.

Catherine collected up the plates and Rose filled up the water glasses and topped up the wine and fetched Florence another can.

"Where is Lithuania?" asked Sara looking at Rose.

"Baltics. Russia, Poland and Belarus are neighbours and then of course the sea, The Baltic Sea. You have Latvia on the other border and Estonia is next to Latvia," she added. "Both pretty lovely in their own way too, apparently. Next to Estonia the Ukraine with Kiev as its capital."

"Do you think they'll have tea and coffee in the rooms?" asked Catherine. "Peter and I went to Paris for our honeymoon and there was no kettle."

"Oh, how terrible," agreed Rose.

Florence burst out laughing. Sara told her to shut up.

"How did the Eiffel tower measure up?" Florence blurted, now beside herself with laughter.

"There was a magnificent view," remembered Catherine impervious to Florence and her tone-lowering. "At night, Paris is so pretty with all that original architecture, the Seine and the lovely lights twinkling against the evening sky."

"Ah it sounds gorgeous," said Rose.

Florence shook her head in agreement, but with too much mirth.

"Elle est chiant," remarked Sara.

"What does that mean?" asked Rose who prided herself on knowing some French.

"'She is a pain in the arse,'" said Sara eyeing Florence, "Or more literally, 'She is shitting'."

"No, I'm not," said Florence assuredly still finding a great deal of humour in the situation.

Rose who like Catherine was able to rise above things said, "Steven and I went to Marrakesh for ours. We were in the Kasbah and he kept on about the smell. It did a bit. We got lost and had to pay a boy to guide us home. Got the feeling it happened a lot. Alcohol free too. Though Steven and I weren't big drinkers we hadn't realized it would be a dry honeymoon."

"Not like Sam and I. We used to get stupid drunk together. It wasn't 'til decades later I realized that we weren't a fortunate match, at all," Sara said frankly.

"Oh Sara, Sam and you adored each other. You were so suited, so in tune with one another. It was magical."

"We're getting off the point here," said Sara. "Catherine remember the mantra: I will, I shall and in the future, I will have saved Bluebell Farm. Mission Possible!"

"Here, here, to that," added Rose.

"Faint heart never won fair Farmhouse," joined in Florence.

They talked more about their venture and their forth-coming trip before they wound up the night and made their way home. Sara made sure she got Catherine's ear before they left and told her friend that they would get the house thing under control if it was possible, and that on no account was she going to share with Florence. Catherine told her, "Of course we're sharing."

Sara relaxed and with a hand on Catherine's forearm thanked her for a lovely evening. Catherine went back to the kitchen slightly cheered, but as she stacked the dish washer she worried. She finished clearing and then washed her hands filling them with water and watching it slip through her fingers.

Back in her room Florence flicked through her novel. Where was the intrigue? No page turning, no feisty female detective, hardly any action, what had her book though it had so absorbed her, have to offer?

Collecting a can of lager from her stash she tore off the top. She was looking forward to shortly being away with the girls and would force them to go dancing in Vilnius and listen to strangers.

PART TWO

"It's me again.

I told you at the beginning *one* was going to die."

So on with the story; the four women on their holiday in the land of Lithuania. The sun is out and they are set fair.

CHAPTER 18

The Pied Wagtail

"Here we are in the heart of the Lithuanian Lake District and it is gorgeous. The Pied Wagtail seems ubiquitous," said Catherine eyeing the garden beneath the balcony of their hotel room where the green lawn was dappled by more shade than light. She was reminded of home and a shock, she had been dealt just before leaving, was playing on her mind.

"Had you no idea?" asked Sara softly as she already knew the answer and just wanted to give Catherine a chance to rid herself of plaguing thoughts, to speak them out-loud.

"After our talk in London," started Catherine sat on the broad twin bed with her arm stretched behind her and her head bent forward, "I found out our mortgage was for the £180,000 with Birmingham Midshires. However, I also find out there is a subsequent bank loan with the house as collateral of a further £280,000. I was so angry Sara. How could he have done it? I confronted him and he shut me down in a tirade of anger telling me I had no idea of what he suffered trying to keep me in a lifestyle I was accustomed to."

"Oh yes, you so love that eighty-thousand-pound Audi," Sara quipped and then wish she hadn't, though luckily it didn't seem to have derailed Catherine's outpouring.

Peter had taken yet two other loans. He owed the firm money and the taxman too. Peter had said they had needed to take out secured debt to pay off high interest debt. He said he'd done it, time to time, to support the family, to pay for school fees, family holidays, the horses, their lifestyle.

"The new kitchen?" said Sara, again, wishing she hadn't.

"I know," said Catherine angrily. "Sara, we have nothing. Less than nothing. We owe. I still can't believe it. We've been living a lie. It's classic magazine stuff. Oh, and the car was on finance. They repossessed it the day after I found out about all this. Just before we came out, the day before yesterday."

"You have certainly been through it," said Sara sympathetically.

"Yes, he was so upset. And so not Peter. Poor Peter, I wasn't sure whether to leave him, but he had some golf games planned so I guessed it to be alright."

"Probably won't harm, to have a little space. Ben's there. This is fairly major stuff, though I'm certainly not suggesting that there won't be a path through it. I'm not convinced that he can do what he did legally with regards the house. I mean it is in joint names?"

"Yes, it is."

"It used to be the case where both signatures were required but things have changed so much but it is definitely worth checking when we get back."

"Oh, it's a nightmare, Sara," turning her back on her friend so she could gaze out the window. "I am worried we are stuck in something from where there is no conceivable way out. Debt. Being sued. It's such a mess," said Catherine.

"I wish you'd said something earlier, I thought you were a little quiet. I just assumed you were a bit homesick, or that Florence was just dominating the scene as she tends to."

"She is funny," Catherine smiled. "I wish I could be more like her. She doesn't seem to care about staying in one place, though, I know she misses Fern Cottage."

"Well, we're all different," said Sara knowing that she could only offer platitudes.

"She does have a good lifestyle," said Catherine, "but she still has money from her sale."

"Shouldn't think that could last for ever but I'm pretty sure that woman could enjoy herself anywhere," said Sara.

"Oh yes, happiness is a state of mind, largely, but try telling my reptilian core that!" laughed Catherine.

"Do you still have your shares?" asked Sara

"Yes, about ten thousand," said Catherine.

"Well that's a start," said Sara.

"I know I'm in debt but I don't even know who with," said Catherine.

"We can find all that out later. Catherine, there will be a way through all this. I have a friend in London, he'll know which are the correct steps and in which order. Don't forget you have your mother's house too, not wishing for anything to happen to Dorothy, of course. Does she know any of this?" said Sara who wanted to give Catherine some Euros there and then. She wanted to tell her friend that she had money that she could help to a degree.

"No one does. As I said in London. The kids don't know. Only you."

"Do you think Peter's told people?"

"I don't think so."

"I wish we'd had that Financial adviser chap you put us on to. We did get life insurance though at least."

"Now there's an idea. Did I read they had hemlock out here?"

A loud and rapid knock against their wooden door jolted them and Sara rose to answer it. It was Florence with a bottle of wine and Rose smiling with two glasses.

"Isn't it perfect?" Rose beamed looking positively girlish compared to her end of year look.

"It was until you two barged in," budging up so Rose could sit down, although she had disappeared into their ensuite to pick up two more glasses.

She returned still brimming with enthusiasm, "Don't you just love a bidet."

Catherine was standing by the window with her back to them and Sara could see her quietly wiping her eyes.

"I've never really known how a bidet works?" she managed.

"Well I put my leg on it when I'm shaving it. Oh, and I wash my pants in it sometimes," claimed Florence and started to open the wine and then stopped and produced a bottle of beer and opened it with a handy brass bottle opener in the shape of Bolivia with a llama-shaped metal handle.

"I believe it's to wash your bits in," said Sara.

"Yes," agreed Rose, "you sit facing the taps."

"Oh gross!" Florence said, pulling a face.

The wine was poured and distributed. Sara proposed a toast.

"To the Lithuanian Lake District," said the women, in unison.

"Yes, and to my best friend Catherine," added Sara.

"To all my friends," said Florence

"Friendship," toasted Rose, in fond agreement.

"To us," Catherine raised her glass half smiling. "How long have we known each other?"

"Well, you and I, have passed our Golden," stated Sara proudly.

"We've all done Silver," said Rose. "We are heading for Ruby!"

"Here's to many more, then," said Catherine and went on to ask the others where the wine had come from and they all agreed the hotel was simply marvellous and so quiet.

"It makes Chadbury seem busy," said Rose and Sara giggled.

Rose gave them a potted lesson on the surrounding countryside. "There are between six thousand and two thousand eight hundred lakes depending on how you classify them. They could be ponds." explained Rose. "The one I have my eye on, as a starter walk, is a 5.8 km, a short taxi away. A circular one, like the one outside our hotel." She explained further, "Some were formed with just surface water, others not."

Florence who had heard some of this already suggested they went down to the terrace and said there was no one down there. "We should do this more often guys!" she said with such enthusiasm that it couldn't fail to uplift. "We could go to Buenos Aires and drink Martini on the rooftops!" she sighed and span in a circle towards the door, nursing her bottle of lager in her long fingered left hand.

Sara rolled her eyes as Rose tutted, "I don't know about that!"

"Just over thirty years ago, we were roomies! Well Catherine, not you, a visitor, we were all roomies." said Rose, as they made their way out of the bedroom towards the terrace "58 Bedford Road."

"I can still see it with those big stone pineapples framing the front entrance," said Florence, "and the white house next door with those two boys. That prim one with the posh job in the city and a TR5."

"Oh, and that lovely gentle Scottish one, Malcolm, who sold clocks in Camden market," said Rose.

"He made them," continued Florence, but no one could recall from what.

They sat round a table and wondered if they should ask at reception if the restaurant was indeed open as stated. Sara went to enquire and came back with the apologetic receptionist who looked strained and slightly red-faced and Rose hoped Sara wasn't being too demanding.

"I think it was pottery," said Rose, after their order for a bottle of wine and a bottle of lager had been taken.

"Oh yes," agreed Florence. "Didn't it have a stamp of a frog, a fat, smiling frog?"

Rose told them that she was pretty sure that he got the frog thing from her as he'd come over sometimes for tea before the others got home from work, when she was spread out with her marking and using all sorts of encouraging stamps and stickers, one of them, which was a frog, stating that, you had come on, 'in leaps and bounds'.

"I could never understand a word that boy said," said Sara.

"I think we should make this an annual event," said Florence.

"I wouldn't mind," said Rose.

"Neither would I," added Catherine, raising her glass.

"I suppose," said Sara glancing at Catherine fondly.

"Goody, goody the motion is carried. It is therefore decreed that from this day forth, a year must never again pass, without we four, meet again, in thunder, rain or brilliant sunshine. I'm so happy," Florence said, swigging from her bottle.

Sara wondered if she should pass on to the others what had befallen Catherine and that she, currently, wasn't up to being everyone's personal fan club or rock, as she was busy trying to find balance on the slippery sea-bed of her own life.

Catherine hadn't told her not to say anything, but Sara sensed it was not for her, to tell them. What could they do anyway, at this point, but give her sympathy?

"I suggest a round of coffee," said Sara. "We don't want to be falling off our chairs by tea -time. What are we doing for supper? Have you enquired on Trip Advisor?" she directed the question at Rose, knowing that it wasn't the sort of thing Florence or Catherine used.

The coffee arrived. Sara took hers black and Florence told her she wished she could dispense with milk, as quite often they didn't have it abroad, or used condensed milk.

"Do you ever get homesick?" asked Rose.

"Oh yes I do. The strange thing is sometimes I remember the worst part as the best bit. Somehow, the loneliness parts are inversely proportionate to how much I relish the memory of a trip, once back. It sounds strange but I'm beginning to think there's some truth in it. I mean, it's as though even though I'm really, really enjoying this trip and this is the prettiest of pretty places and I so, so much enjoy hanging out with you guys, when I get home it will just be filed in my bank of lovely times away with my buddies and I'll define it with a snapshot taken of us, maybe here by the lake. Us four, by the side of the lake, and it won't stick out more much than that," said

Florence, drawing circles with her hand along the woodwork of the table where they were seated.

"So, what you are saying is that it is good, being homesick, as you reap the dividends later," checked Rose.

"No pain, no gain," Sara said.

"No cross, no crown," Florence agreed.

"Someone's got a high opinion of themselves," said Sara.

"It's true, the rougher the ride the sweeter the harbour. It's like the smile on an ugly baby. Or woman." Florence modified her answer and smiled at Sara, who was beginning to scowl.

"Oh, I just want an easy life. No sheer cliffs or deep harbours, just green rolling hills. Middle distant views," Catherine joined in.

"When you've been alone for just a few days, meals, nights, journeys however stunning the scenery or bustling the city, it's just so lovely to link up with a stranger, a fellow traveller or two or form your own little group. A little travel-family, and find the possibilities opening out again, as you saunter down the street, with your new gang, wondering nonchalantly, which restaurant to eat at or which bar to hit," Florence sighed.

"Oh, I'd like to travel more," Rose said. "I'll do it one day. Machu Pichu, Anchor Wat, The Great Wall. They are all on the horizon. I'd like to tour Scotland, too."

"I'm more for city breaks," said Sara.

"Do you think Peter would like it?" Rose asked.

Catherine went to answer her but there were no words. She picked up her cup and stared at it as if mesmerised. Time slowed, Rose looked at Florence waiting and then Sara rang through the silence with a "P-P-Peter. Think he'd be happier in Scotland or the Algave, with a golf club in his hand."

Later Rose asked Sara if Peter was ill or something. Sara refrained from answering, "Not yet" and mentioned that he might be stressed at work which was enough for Rose to back off with a, "Oh."

It wasn't as if Florence had not picked up on anything. It was just that she thought they should override it, as there was a group of them, and they were on their holiday. "Hang on girls," she smiled. "Let's get some music. I'll bring down the cards too," she added as she raced away.

"They've got board games," added Rose. "Scrabble!"

"Oh God. Kill me now," moaned Sara "I'm not playing that game with Rose ever again with her arsenal of two letter words with X and Z in them and her linear hunger for victory. Have they got Monopoly?"

"Haven't you got enough houses?" said Florence as she pushed passed her returning in a miraculously short amount of time with her phone and a little, red plastic speaker the size of a cup; in shorts with a loose, azure T-shirt and waving her arms around, triumphantly, displaying newly adorned silver bangles.

Seconds later, they were listening to Bob Dylan and Florence had four beers brought over by the girl on reception, who was stylishly supporting a circular, green tray above shoulder height with one hand.

Florence fetched a pack of cards from her drawstring bag.

"Grief! Where do you think we are, the OK Coral?" muttered Sarah "I am not playing Poker."

"21 then?" said Florence.

"Is that Pontoon?" said Sara.

"Yes," said Catherine. "We play it sometimes, in the Lake District."

"Shame I didn't bring UNO," remarked Florence and started dealing.

By five, the women were quite merry and had ordered a bottle of wine though Florence had stuck to beer. Florence was telling everyone how "sorted" her daughter was but that she'd never seemed to have a boyfriend.

"I mean what is that about?" she said, holding her bottle out in front of her as she hadn't used the glass provided for her.

Sara had noted this trait in her. To begin with she'd drink it from a glass and then after maybe two she would drink straight from the bottle. Did she know that's what she did? Sara was still reeling from Catherine's disclosure and wondered how best she could protect her financially from Peter. She wouldn't want to give them money to be swallowed up by ill-advised loans but wanted to help Catherine and would do so but they'd need advice.

Rose, who had a reasonable voice, started singing and looked as if she ought to have a guitar on her lap. She'd tried to learn it, more than once, and envied the occasional highly gifted musical member of staff that had passed through her teaching career. It was a gift but then with instruments you had to hone it. Rose gently sung.

"Play my favourite," said Catherine. "Play Sara." And when it was finished, she commented, "That is such a beautiful song."

They played another hand and Sara dealt, eyeing Catherine who looked to be enjoying herself, relaxing and winning the odd game. She had even suggested visiting some castle before the next day's intended hike.

"Not too many miles, I hope," said Sara curling her nose up at Catherine and making her smile.

"Or too many hills or slippery stones," added Florence.

"On no account any slippery stones," checked Sara.

"I'm not a hill climber," expanded Florence, "I overdid it on the hills in Northern Thailand. Oh, that was a time in my life," she said fondly exhaling "but it has left me with limited capacity for hillwalking and then that four day walk to Machu Pichu, a couple of years ago, well that made me want to die. Thank god for the mule. It saved my life. I called it Mary. There's a pun there if you get it. Mare-y but now I'm allergic to hills," she insisted casually.

"I don't mind a climb, of course no ropes or crampons, but a hill is quite satisfying once you've got to the top and can see the view and that you have made it to the top," said Rose.

"Like the Abbey Fields," chirped Florence, "or Bredon Hill? They could be much bigger. It's a question of pace not size, and for me the slower the better, and without many people around, so you are free to go at your own speed and rest when you want to. I'd like to make a toast to walking the beautiful lakes of Lithuania and may most of the walking be mainly flat but may all our ascents be manageable and all our descents not too painful," joked Florence and Rose commented that they were not going on an obstacle race but for a walk round a lake.

Florence had changed the music to Amy Winehouse and *Back to Black* was echoing round the terrace and still they were the only guests.

"Oh, wouldn't it be fun if Terence the Tapir, suddenly turned up," said Florence "and serenaded Rose under the blue-black sky?"

"Extraordinary," said Sara.

"Yes, could you envisage it, a Thomas Hardy-like plot where, set in the Wessex of Lithuania, Rose and the Tapir elope into the moonlit horizon," spluttered Florence.

"Yes, but I don't even fancy him," said Rose.

"In time Rose, in time," said Florence giggling so much her eyes were watering, pouring her friends more wine.

"That was never going to happen. Now that young man at the train station," Rose warmed to the topic.

"Rose," Sarah interrupted, "He was about twelve."

"Rubbish. He was in his thirties," corrected Rose.

"Sometimes I just want to stuff everything in," groaned Florence swirling her curling locks around dramatically, "If I were single, Rose, I'd go for Mi-guel. Use it or lose it. Time and tide. 'And at my back I hear times winged chariot drawing near.'"

Rose stiffened. She didn't like too much advise or scrutiny and said, "Some of us have lives outside our genatalia."

Catherine, who never normally divulged anything of a "bedroom" nature felt for Rose and realized it was always Florence that was behind the subject.

Sensing that the women were not in the mood for 'bedroom' talk Florence launched into the theory that free style dancing had no pegs to hang achievements on. Rose and Catherine were confused as to her meaning, but strangely Sara picked up on it explaining that if one had been in a school or uni-band or even learnt an instrument there would be societal recognition for the achievement, but for dancing to contemporary music there was no such thing, and yet it was skill and expressed passion, and usually improved with practise. In its way, it was as skilful as the cut and thrust of fencing, and the language of dancing appeared in the modern vernacular positively with noteworthy people being referred to, 'movers and shakers'. A paradox.

Florence wriggled forward, in her seat, shaking her head in agreement and said her body just *knew* the classics; the rhythms. It was if she could lose herself, let the music work through her and she begged them to find a nightclub on their last night and attack the dance floor claiming it would be such fun.

Rose asked when they were going to eat? It was decided that as it was now five and they'd had a few drinks that a walk round the lake would be a good idea to straighten them out before dinner.

Florence sauntered over to talk with the receptionist who appeared to be the only other person, outside the kitchen, at the hotel. Florence discovered her to be studying English and engaged her in a language lesson. Very soon hoots of laughter were ringing around the foyer, as Florence and Rosalind embarked on a meeting of minds.

Chapter 19

The Stroll

Once shoe-ready, the ladies embarked on a stroll around the lake. "Isn't it beautiful," sighed Rose as they walked along the pine clad path, under the shade of the tall trees.

"Are there really bears?" asked Florence, knowing that though rarely sighted, they could be lurking in the woods.

"Bears!" arched Catherine.

"Oh, they won't come on the site. They loathe humans," assured Sara.

"Well in Canada," went Florence, "You had to go around in groups of four, or more, and if faced with a bear you spread out your arms and make yourself as big as possible," she leapt in front of them with her legs and arms outstretched and pulled a face.

"You could be very annoying, if you didn't make us laugh," said Sara.

"Oh, and the good news is, ladies," Florence said, "no grizzlies. We've all seen what damage they can do. I take it you all saw the delightful DiCaprio and his dust up, in 'The Revenant'. However, just in case you find yourself in the great Canadian Wilderness, looking up at the magnificence of a grizzly you do Not on any account try that 'bigging up' stuff with the out-flung extremities. Instead, curl yourself into a tight TIGHT ball, and roll away to safety."

Florence linked arms with Catherine and asked after her children. Catherine said that Ben was gardening and that Jess had found an internship, in Bristol. Florence enthused about Bristol and the post which was marketing a magazine, aimed at African women.

"OMG, that is so cool!" Florence shrieked and Catherine felt a tremor that maybe things would be alright after all, as the image of Jess with her long fair hair, succeeding as the fashion editor of a Glossy, flitted across her imagination until she remembered the rent was due on Jess's home-share in Clifton, a hefty five hundred a month. Then, her monthly allowance too, going out by standing order.

"What do you fancy for supper?" Florence enquired, stroking her shoulders gently, and reiterating how much she thought of Jess's achievement. "So exciting, I wish I'd been born with a social conscience or an iota of ambition! I think I was nearly fifty, before I took stock of anything at all."

They had walked to the other side of the lake and stopped to look at their hotel.

"It looks like something out of a fairy-tale!" said Florence.

"Yes, all that wood is lovely," agreed Rose.

"And the pretty shutters," said Catherine.

"They should lose all those orange, plastic chairs from the terrace. It makes it thirty years behind Britain. Horrid," said Sara, flicking some pine needles from her shoe.

Rose took a picture of her three friends telling them she'd got the lake and the hotel in. Then, they took a group-selfie.

Back from the circular walk they stopped at the jetty. It struck forth into the lake and small rowing boats were moored on either side.

"Oh yes! We are going boating!" cried Florence. "Look how the sun casts a golden light across the lake!"

"Yes, hiking and boating, tomorrow," agreed Rose. "The great outdoors."

"I feel ablaze with the possibilities," Florence answered her.

"I think I'll give them a miss," sighed Sara "In fact, I'm ablaze with the great indoors, in particularly, my hotel room's rather comfortable bed. I'm hoping for Netflix. How about you Catherine?"

"I think we should have a go, Sara. It sounds nice and it's not as though we have to go out for long. It's on our door-step"

Sara shrugged non-committedly.

The weather seemed set fair, cloudless but just chilly enough for a sweater and they decided that they would take the boats out the next morning and then go on one of the longer hikes in the afternoon. Rose would orienteer.

Sara insisted that it would be no more than three hours, largely flat and they would have transport back prearranged as she was on holiday to relax, not wear her body out to the point of exhaustion. Florence told her the hotel could arrange massages.

With a teacher's natural experience and diplomacy Rose suggested that they split up and Sara could do all the relaxing she needed. Those that wanted could do a more challenging hike. Florence felt it would be more fun if they all stuck together. She had been a little concerned that in Catherine's fragile state of mind she might back out, too, leaving her in Rose's capable hands. The other two were needed to slow the pace.

Though Florence loved the great outdoors and considered herself to be as fleet of foot as the next person and welcomed a chance to gambol and frisk amidst the lakes and mountains with the chance to spot a tufted squirrel, she was not in favour of any test of endurance and certainly not up to one of Rose's.

Rose who had once been in the habit of famously cycling eight miles there and back to the swimming baths, to swim thirty lengths, before getting into school, refreshed, and as one of the first there. So wrong on so many levels, thought Florence, torn by fear and admiration, in equal measures.

While Florence, enjoyed comfort in her own skin, viewing Rose's self-discipline close-up, made her aware of her laxidaisical approach and personal weakness. She thought if she'd had the gift of persistence, she might have achieved something worth-while, run for political office, worked changing lives in the charitable sector, translated a forgotten masterpiece or indeed finished her novel, her play, her boardgame, her comedy sketch.

"Oh, do come, you two. Please come. We can do anything you want on the last day," Florence pleaded.

Rose who didn't like confrontation was already feeling the dimming of life as she knew it. The protection from her everyday life, that the start of their holiday had afforded, was waning. Her world of comfort and security was coming to an end. She would be in her new post by the end of the week.

She was nervous and wished she hadn't taken it on. It was one thing that little Charlie Thornton be sure to have his epi pen out with him on a school trip or that everyone knew of Jamima's peanut allergy but to be in charge of it, to be fully responsible for it all. And there was so much of it, each year the list of dangers and allergies grew and grew. Amongst the new intake she'd spotted Edie, poor child, was apparently allergic to water. What happened if it rained? She warned herself not to catastrophise.

What had she been thinking of when she'd applied? And it would only get worse if they were to be Ofsteded. She told herself the children were still children and they would make everything worthwhile. They had the charm, the love of life, the playfulness, the humour and she wouldn't let her new responsibilities prevent her focus on that.

She looked at Sara who was pulling at her trousers, unsuitable, Rose felt, for the trip to the lakes. Was it for herself, or other people, she'd struck out of her comfort zone?

She was left with fruit-loop Flo, while Sara and Catherine were spending hours in their room together no doubt chewing over the old days and remembering school puddings or discussing family members or talking old family pets as they did with Catherine saying do you remember Bandit and Sara replying do you remember Caveman Billy, as if neither one of them could forget those childhood memories forged in the steel of youth and bonded over and over with the ravages of time.

"Caveman Billy," thought Rose who felt unusually sour and out of sorts, "What sort of a name was that for a pony?" Sara had said that he was named after a pop record and that one day she'd arrived back from school and there he was tied up in the garage, at the bottom of her garden, in the heart of a market town. No one had a pony in her class, she thought. In the whole school there was only the Robsons who kept them, and they were farmers.

At least Florence hadn't really ridden much although she did claim to have had free use of 'Aladdin Sane' another pretentious name, felt Rose. What was wrong with, 'Daisy' or 'Chester'? They weren't racehorses, although she had heard Florence boast that Laddy, part Arab, could beat anyone hands down on the flat at Stoneleigh Deer park.

They had a pleasant supper that night at Martha's, recommended by Trip Advisor, the one of the only two, open in the small town. It was a ten-minute stroll from the hotel and had pretty, chequered table cloths and hearty traditional food, served by a waitress with a beautiful Slavic face.

The restaurant was empty except for the couple who sat by the window. The women took the centre table although it was laid for six so they could spread out. Catherine once again remarked on how much she enjoyed this fringe season and Rose said it was strange as the schools, at least in Britain, were still out unless she'd made a terrible mistake and they'd started without her and that she hoped she wasn't going to get some low-level anxiety dream about them all assembled at Staunton Primary, waiting and she never showing up.

Sara said that they'd still all be rammed into French Campsites or on the Costas or still just at home getting under everyone's feet with the parents, counting down the days, until the start of school again.

By the time they had eaten their way through the substantial main meals, no one plumped for dessert. Florence made numerous toasts waving her bottle of lager around and asking if their wine was cheeky enough. Sara told her to put a cork in it and waved for the bill, insisting on paying for them. Catherine and Rose put up weak protests. Florence, both eyes closed, stuck out both arms and said "You're pushing through an open door here."

A cat sauntered up, white wall-eyed with a tabby tail and partial tabby face and a torn ear and Catherine remarked on what an unusual and beautiful cat it was as she bent down to stroke it.

Florence told of the abundance of dogs loose on the streets in South America and Rose mentioned the cat haven she had once come across near the Colosseum in

239

Rome. Florence said that she was getting to like cats more and more with each passing year and if Tom didn't live so near a main road she'd encourage him to get one, maybe an Abyssian, Burmese or even Siamese.

"I could see you as a cat lady," Sara chuckled. "Yes, one of those ladies with a dozen cats. They'd be nesting in the bath. One hanging round your neck, as a scarf."

"As long as we all use the litter tray I'm looking forward to it. A welcome change to be surrounded by grace and independence of spirit. The cats and I will be very happy. And they won't forget me when they inherit the earth along with Japanese Knotweed and viruses."

"Dogs, every time for me," maintained Rose. "Cats are aloof and I'm getting fond of the birds in my garden."

"What do you call a Magician's dog?" said Florence. "Labracadabra!"

"Such a sense of humour," said Sara.

"Not as bad as yours. Yours, like the trots, must run in you 'jeans.'" said Florence.

"Watch out Florence, for those packs of street dogs, you so love. Look what happened to Jezabel?" said Sara.

"Oh, Kitty has claws," said Florence, then quickly turned the conversation to bird-watching.

The women discussed squirrel proof bird feeders and marvelled how ignorant they had been, for decades, of the pleasures of bird observation.

"I guess I have that joy in store for me," said Sara. "I shall attempt to curb my enthusiasm."

Florence enlightened them to the fact that female songbirds did sing in the Amazon as she'd heard them and that Darwin had been quite wrong.

"Oh, that's right Florence, we are not descended from apes at all, are we?" said Sara.

"Bears actually. Quite, quite possible, a friend told me on good authority," she was laughing, "his name was Yogi." Further words followed but disappeared into her giggling.

They left the restaurant in good humour and ambled back to their pretty hotel, two by two under a cloudless, twilit sky deciding as it was still not too late they would have a nightcap.

Chapter 20

The Night Cap

Once back from Martha's, Rose went to her room, to be alone. It was not that she wasn't accustomed to being in a group, but this was relentless, and she realized she was no longer used to it. She wasn't really worried about having had a mild anxiety-dream, was she? Where had it come from? Usually she was always woken up by her alarm before the short dash to school, with school matters to remember and a swift walk with Doug, rain or shine,

Maybe it was Florence's influence. Florence had enthused that morning about an exquisite dream she had had. As a highway man and, at some personal risk, she had rescued two children from a burning building and then galloped them to safety. Rose never had dreams like that. Not that she could remember anyway. Florence appeared to have any number of wild stories and fantastic dreams. Lucid, even?

She could recollect the Steven break up, the fallout on those mornings when she'd woken comfortably and then been struck by a rush of confusion, a jolt, and then the reality would creep, first as a suspicion, shortly held, and then the reality soon afterwards cruelly confirmed.

Rose could still feel that jolt. Why was she letting herself go there? She felt her confidence waning. Her grip seemed to slip as she indulged in remembering those mornings many years back. Those mornings she'd woken in a cosy cocoon of sleep and been banged with the facts, by the empty side of their bed, on awakening. It wasn't that she'd had nightmares. Just one long day-mare.

Yes, he had gone.

Yes, he wasn't next to her.

Yes, there was still the tartan duvet that he had picked.

Yes, he had been having an affair for months.

Yes, she was alone.

Yes, she was a "one", in the world of "twos."

Yes, she would have to double her mortgage and pay all of it.

Yes, she would have no husband to share having no children.

Yes, she had loved him so.

Yes, he'd been the best friend she'd ever known.

Yes, he had duped her.

Robbed her.

Left her.

The punch that had come from nowhere.

At the time she had had a few of these morning terrors but taken the knock pretty well. Maybe she did have a glass chin to take *the slings and arrows of outrageous fortune.* Then she remembered the depression.

Everyone said at the time, good old Rose taking it so well, back at school the following Monday and so good with the children, so cheerful, so upright and with that lovely smile, to greet anyone she passed in the corridor, whether cleaner or county council high ranker.

Rose returned to the group to hear Florence eulogising about dumplings and making Catherine promise to teach her how to make them as it would be such fun. They could have a dumpling party and invite some of the villagers round so she could study them for her new play, 'The Starchers'. When was that play ever going to materialize? Had anyone ever seen one single page and what about that novel she had reportedly returned to, based on the travels of her youth?

"How is your play progressing?" she asked Florence.

"Tops, thank you. I've got the opening lines," Florence said.

"Oh, let's hear them, then," said Catherine, making way for Rose.

Florence got up and with an exaggerated sway of the hips walked a half circle and faced them and in a deepened voice recited proudly:

"Be afeared, tis the eye snatcher.

Remember what happened to Eros.

Anger me further

And you'll be on the Ferry, one-way,"

"Oh, is it set in Newcastle?" asked Sara straight-faced, eyeing Catherine and for back up.

"Yes Sara, Newcastle-on-Styx," said Florence undeterred.

Changing the subject Florence remarked that if they had been in Spain, some troubadour would have come to serenade us.

"Oh, I do like a bit of Spanish guitar," said Rose. "Do you remember us playing, 'The Gypsy Kings'? Florence would put it on relentlessly in the kitchen. Do you remember playing Bolero and dancing on the kitchen table when we got back from Down Mexico Way?"

"God yes," laughed Sara, "I think I left marks on the table with my heels. In fact, I know I did though I couldn't admit at the time cos of that Gestapo Stephanie. I was so mortified."

"We used to stay up so late," said Rose. "Florence you were such a night-owl. I never figured out how you could still go into work the next day."

"Yes," Sara agreed. "I could only do weekends but you Florence were out nearly every night."

"Do you remember that house party in Whitstable? We drank the house dry and you and half of them went out on a fishing boat to sea," said Rose.

"I do remember that. There were all these ropes aboard. I think I threw some pots in. Very naughty of me. It was somebody's boat, somebody's livelihood," said Florence ashamedly. "You don't think at that age. I'm so looking forward to going out in the boats tomorrow. I love a row!"

"God, being in my twenties was such fun. Which decade would you choose if you could live one over?"

"Could you change it?" asked Sara.

"No, it would be the same," insisted Florence.

"I think ten to twenty," she replied.

"Me too," said Catherine.

Rose said she might just repeat the last ten years.

"Do you think you will go on to be a head?" Sara asked.

"Sara, I haven't even seen what it's like being an Assistant head yet," she said lifting her glass to her mouth.

"It's just around the corner," said Catherine and continued, "give it a week and you'll be thinking I've been doing this for years and you have! It will be second nature to you."

"Well that's not strictly true," Rose said but didn't qualify it instead asking Catherine which of her children might have children first. Catherine thought it would be a long time off and Florence piped up to say she was despairing of anyone making a dishonest woman of Frankie.

"It doesn't seem to be a priority. I mean at her age I just went through them," said Florence.

They all agreed Catherine would make a lovely grandmother.

Sara lifted her eyes and admired the iron work of the terrace and then turned directing her gaze at Florence and with lips slighty pursed, coated with high quality deep red lipstick asked, "How many? How many men?"

"God knows, do I detect some judgement in your voice?" Florence laughed, "Hundreds, I mean, I didn't sleep with them all. I was quite a prude. Well to begin with," she chuckled.

"How many?" repeated Sara twitching her jowels. "How many, 'all the way', as we used to say?"

"Oh, hold on let me think. Tell you what, I'll write out a list and give you it the morning. Place. Age. Name, if I can remember it. Anything else?" said Florence.

Rose couldn't tell if she was joking or not but said that if someone had set that for her homework it wouldn't have taken her too long. She paused momentarily lent forward and added she had let her guard down on a girl's holiday to Corfu. There didn't seem a good reason not to, and she went on to describe a rather touching holiday affair. She said that in that fortnight lay half her score, but the first week was very different to the second. Catherine wanted to hear more on the second week romance, and was amazed Rose had never told her about Konstantinos. Florence asked if she was at it 'constant'-ly with Konstantinos. Sara told her off for being rude.

Rose concluded, "It was a little love affair, now I think of it. We said goodbye the night before I was due to leave. Well it was in the small hours. I still remember the moonbeams. The next day I had that feeling in the pit of my stomach, couldn't eat breakfast, packed, checked out and Julie, Vanessa, Penny, Fiona, Jane, all of us, went with Christine our tour rep. to the coach and we were all standing in a line quietly. It was early, and then Konstantinos slid down this dry bank and came running over to me and asked me to stay: to stay and be his wife!"

"Oh, that is so romantic," enthused Florence, now totally captivated with the story and the others agreed.

"He was very handsome," added Rose. "I still have a photo. The two of us, on the beach, with the sea and sand, holding hands. I think I'd have my twenties back," she laughed. "You know that, "which decade would you repeat." I mean I was on a high and for the next year, I sailed through life."

"On the wings of a dove," said Catherine with her hands clasped, looking at Rose.

"Oh, I love that song," interrupted Florence "I'll play it later. Patti Smith. I'm trying to add to the repertoire Abba and Boyzone."

"Shut up Florence, I want to hear more about this romance," said Sara sharply.

"We wrote. I was at uni. It meant that while other girls were getting their hearts ripped to shreds and feeling under par about it or spent inordinate time and energy chasing boys," and she looked at Florence and smiled. "I had it in the bag. Gorgeous, adoring boyfriend in hand, and I could just get on and study. I think that's why I did so well in the first year. Got a first, you know in Year One. The *only* one in our year, to do so. One of my proudest moments. Partly down to Konstaninos. He raised me up."

"Oh, 'a radiator' not 'a drain'. Did you seriously think of marrying him?" asked Catherine.

"Well, yes. Yes and no. My family wouldn't have liked it. Not because of the waiter thing, and don't forget waiter status in Greece is different to the waiter status in Britain, but my family were simple, working class. I was the first to go abroad," Rose explained.

"Did you see him again?" asked Sara.

Rose explained that they had planned to but somehow it didn't happen in the first few months and then she was less and less moved by his letters that due to the lack of his English and non-existence of her Greek proved to be an insurmountable barrier. She guessed it was, after all, just a holiday romance and he'd probably had dozens, some intense, some not. I do wonder, very occasionally, how he remembers it?"

It was quite unlike Rose, to speak to them quite so openly about something of that nature. Florence felt there was a general dropping off of screening. She felt an intimacy, an honesty growing between them, interweaving on the existing edifice of their friendship. It was a mossing up of the walls on a structure that had already weathered a great deal of time, trial and shared experience.

"Of course, everyone keeps some secrets, secret," thought Florence, "But maybe we keep too many."

She wanted to tell them something, how much they meant, but didn't want to spoil the moment. They sat in silence, out on the terrace, and looked out at the lake. Then, became fidgety, and asked Catherine if she had ever had a foreign romance.

"No," Catherine answered.

"So, it's only English for you?" said Sara.

"No, I've *been* to Scotland too. Duncan, the chemistry student," Catherine said.

"Oh yes, the one with those thick glasses," said Sara and tried not to snigger but didn't manage it which sent Florence off into raptures.

"I'm going to have a spasm on the floor!" she shrieked in hysteria.

"Which Walton would you have shagged. Open question?" said Sara.

"Erin!" said Florence "but I would probably have run off to work in the Dewdrop Inn rather than live in that family. Or shot Daddy Walton with his hunting rifle."

Catherine disclosed that she entirely loved every member of the Walton family and had watched every episode.

"Though if it came to bedroom stuff," she said. "I'd have opted for Charles Ingalls."

"Me too," Rose and Sara agreed, unanimously.

Rose said, "So Catherine's been to Scotland. Ohhh. Isn't that how Arthur put it to his chums after his wedding night with Catherine of Aragon? 'Tonight, I've been in Spain,' or something to that effect. Now there is a 'he said, she said.' Eat your heart out Weinstein."

"Yes, and the stakes were even higher at court, in Tudor times," said Sara. "'High risk, high reward,' as my dad used to say."

"Heads rolled, in those days," agreed Rose. "Catherine of Aragon was arguing that her wedding to Arthur who was aged fifteen, hadn't been consummated, therefore her marriage to Henry couldn't be annulled on the grounds of incest."

"Well if she was using the fact that he was fifteen and therefore unable to roger her, she was on thin ice. I can vouch for that. I like the idea of being at court. I would ride a milk-white mare, the prettiest Palfrey in court, and wear a Wimpole with a lavender silk. My knight would be called Godfrey, and he would have to ride with a knot in it, for many a long decade," said Florence.

"Does she ever shut up?" said Sara.

"Oh, do you remember Godfrey, on Dad's Army?" said Rose.

"My sister loves God, best," said Sara.

"Whilst not on horseback, I'd be in my turret, doing needlepoint. I would give Godfrey, quests," said Florence.

"Needlepoint leaves little scope for the imagination," said Catherine.

"Not necessarily," contradicted Florence.

"Maybe you were no lady, but a servant," said Sara "A plain servant, with a very, very disfigured face, no teeth, foul breath, generally very stinky and not a chance of getting laid, even by a donkey,"

"We ought to go to Benidorm next, for a laugh, girls," suggested Florence and then under her breath to Catherine that there were plenty of donkeys, if that's what Sarah was into, and Catherine reeled her head back, in repulsed discomfort.

"Did you know that Henry VIII ordered for all the Welsh ponies to be culled? I think he made it law," said Rose.

"Oh, how cruel, and just because he was too fat to ride them," said Sara crossly.

"So, I think Elizabeth 1st repealed the law," remembered Rose.

"Oh well even if it's not true, let's just spread it anyway, as apparently, the truth is old-fashioned and is irrelevant. Not even remotely desirable these days. Undemocratic, even," Sara said.

"It is a fact. I've just googled it. The official act passed was The Breed of Horses Act 1535. He wanted any horse not up to carrying a soldier killed. Talk about equine eugenics," Rose reported.

"An example of the abuse of power," said Florence.

"In 1540 he ordered that no mares under 13hh were allowed on Common ground," added Rose.

"Mmmm, several analogies spring to mind," said Florence, fiddling with her hair.

"Well that's Dartmoors, out," said Catherine.

"Oh, and Shetlands!" said Sara.

"No, I don't think that follows. Scotland was a different country. After Elizabeth 1st came James 6th of Scotland aka James 1st of England. The red cross of St

George combined with the blue cross of St Andrew to make the Union Jack in 1606, however, the "Acts of Union" weren't for a hundred years. 1706 and 1707, passed by England first and Scotland second producing Great Britain," said Rose thumbing her phone.

"I'll miss our Queen, I won't like a king," said Catherine. "I suppose it's because I've only known a queen but she is a good one."

They all agreed. Florence and Rose didn't feel like arguing for a republic that night, though Rose mentioned she would have been with the Roundheads in the Civil War. Florence said it was a tricky one and although she agreed with some principals of Oliver Cromwell she preferred the lifestyle and dress of the Cavaliers. "All men should have long hair," she said followed by, "I mean who would ban Christmas? Yes, and what was that Oliver Crowell as Lord Protectorate, governing a Republic, doing appointing as successor, his son Tricky Dicky."

"The abuse of power," said Rose shaking her head while getting out her map and told them a little of surrounding countryside to get a consensus on what walk they might do the next day. Infact, she gave them two main choices and suggested that Florence and she might do a longer, more challenging one, the day after.

Once back upstairs in the privacy of their own room Sara asked Catherine whether or not she thought Florence was getting sillier.

"I thought with age came stoicism and repose. It's like she has to whirl everything up. She can't apprehend a single thought or hear a single sentence without feeling driven to incorporate it into some fanciful grand scheme and share it with whoever's present," complained Sara.

"I wonder if she actually does that list?" smiled Catherine.

"It will take her all night. Poor Rose. She has been good about sharing with her. Poor lamb," said Sara.

Catherine was going to say she wouldn't have minded but then realized how it might sound and refrained.

"She's not that bad. Don't you just love her zest? You know Sara, I just don't know what I'm going to do when I get back? I just can't see a path through. I can't see a way to cut us, my family, out of this tangle. I'm felted up in it."

"There is always a path Catherine. I'll help, I promise. I have resources. We both have. You know what I'll do, what I can," assured Sara.

Catherine knew it but internalized the, "what I can," as an unwelcomed proviso and thought Sara was a good friend but she wasn't a wizard. She thanked Sara and asked her not to tell the others. Sara mimed the sealing of her lips.

Catherine told her that Rose was full of schemes to turn Bluebell Farm into a language school and Florence has been googling Party House sights and reckons they charge five thousand a weekend.

"I'm not used to having to be guarded, to speak with omissions or half-truths. I'd have made a terrible spy."

"Oh god you're talking like Florence now. You have a couple of days left here, Catherine. Lighten up and enjoy them. When we get back before we unpack or do the washing, we'll unpick this mess and start to fix it. It will be hard but I'm quite sure we are up to the task. I'll come and stay if you like and help you get the whole truth of the matter."

Catherine sighed and felt a little lighter and went to brush her teeth and change and thanked Sara again and pulled out her Apple and What's App'd her family.

Chapter 21

Breakfast at Tiki Inn

At the hotel by the lake, near the sleepy town of Ignalina, that fine morning, breakfast was being served on the terrace. Florence appeared, looking outlandishly bohemian, in a garment, half coat, half gown. It had birds of paradise embroidered on the yellow silk. She advanced along the terrace to join Sara and Rose. They didn't comment on it.

"Morning Bitches," Florence greeted them.

Sara turned to Rose and said, "Oh dear god. Please shield me, here comes the solar flare."

Florence took her place between her friends who had already made a start and were sipping coffee with their cereal.

"Hey gang, what's the action?" she said.

"No action, we are just waiting for Catherine," said Rose. "She's probably on the phone to all her significant others."

Shortly after Catherine appeared in creamy white culottes and a Pirates of the Caribbean frilled shirt. Her hair, lit up gold, by the sun.

"Catherine. You look different, so elegant. Like Mephistopheles. The White Devil!" Florence remarked clapping her hands excitedly. "It is the most glorious morning. I watched the sun rise from our balcony, and felt such joy to be alive."

"She didn't," said Rose shaking her head then tilted her head and closed her eyes.

"I did. I went out onto the balcony, lent on it and cried out, 'What's the story, Morning Glory?'" said Florence.

"Oh god. She's going to put us off our cornflakes," said Sara staring at Florence with an all-round pained expression and feigned squint.

"You do look very nice," Rose said, smiling at Catherine.

"Oh, someone call the Gallagher brothers," said Sara, "The White Devil? I thought they were meant to be dark with little horns."

"'The White Devil' was one of my all-time favourite plays. Webster's such a genius with those exquisite lines:

"Lilies that fester smell far worse than weeds," I mean, how true is that? Just totally!" cried Florence. "You know that is in a Shakespeare sonnet, too."

"Totally," echoed Sara, regarding Florence with a degree of tolerance and giving her a quick false smile.

"I guess the sweetest things can turn the sourest," said Catherine, quietly.

"Doesn't it just evoke the brutal pungent scent of a lily; the cloying burden of true-love imploding," said

Florence. "Oh, oh, oh and then there was those other lines:

"Those that lie down with dogs, Get up with fleas," Isn't that just marvellous?" Florence implored.

"Don't let Hoover hear you say that," laughed Catherine.

"Or Doug," joined Rose.

"Yes, she has managed it" said Sara pushing away a bowl of half eaten soggy cornflakes.

"Watch yourself girls. No smiling or laughing!" warned Florence, "it's the joy police!"

Rose grinned and looked at Sara, quickly adding, "Oh I did love Joy Division. That song."

Florence pounced on this, "I didn't know you liked Joy Division. 'Love will tear us apart'. What a TUNE."

Catherine said "I'll be rather relieved when my kids get passed twenty-seven."

"Yes," said Rose "it seems to be the Beechers Brook of Rock stars. Jimi Hendrix, Amy Winehouse, Janis Joplin, Brian Jones, Kurt Cobain."

Florence rattled something in her hand. It was an A4 sheet of paper folded into quarters displaying a fair amount of scrawl and wry smile swaggered across her rather weary looking face.

"I've done my homework, Miss," she said waving it very near to Sara's face.

"Oh god," said Sara looking sideways at Catherine and said, "Hand it over."

"No, I won't. You are being rude," Florence shrugged and flicked her locks behind her shoulders displaying the full allure of her red-blond abundant waves that tumbled over the silk of her robe that dazzled in the sun.

"Pass the jam," said Rose.

"Skid the grease," joked Catherine.

"Pass the peanut butter," said Sara.

Florence sat bolt up-right and scurried into her bag for a zebra stripped biro, unfolded her piece of paper, looked down a list of names and details and mouthed Peanut Butter as she wrote it by one of them and smiled and folded up the page again and breathed, 'Memories girls' with a gentle smile. Aware that they were all looking at her went, "Good grief, we've all done it surely. Remember that chocolate body spread faze in the naughty nineties? It was all the rage."

"Oh yes. I was given a pot at Christmas from the staffroom Santa!"

"How about you Catherine?" joked Sara.

Catherine dropped her brow a fraction and pursed her lips dismissively.

"Marmalade?" offered Florence.

"The mind reels," said Sara sounding very slightly alarmed.

"Marmalade?" said Catherine makes me think of Paddington Bear.

"Oh, by Michael Bondage?" giggled Florence.

"Leaving Paddington safely out of it. Marmalade on private parts?" asked Florence. "Maybe a raspberry nipple?" she continued and even Rose started tittering.

Sara turned her eyes up to the skies and muttered shaking her head "Beyond saving." to Catherine.

Catherine's lips opened and looked bemused as she nibbled on a marmite soldier and biting into it hard and speaking with her mouth still full, told them all that SOME people liked to keep their private lives private.

"Yes, that's enough you lot. Un oeufs enough," intervened Rose. "Cereal, anyone?" and thought she might as well be at school as it seemed incumbent on her to prevent Florence from spinning out of control, wreaking havoc and causing Sara to cross over from sharp to unpleasant. She couldn't remember Florence being such a tease.

Florence flipped the conversation to say she'd once seen a row of fleas, dissecated and dressed up. It was in a Museum for Minatures in Mijas on the Costa del Sol and had some extremely tiny things in it like the Seven Wonders of the World ingrained on a toothpick.

"Yeah, yeah," interrupted Sara, "and people have written the declaration of independence on a grain of rice."

Florence, after realizing her friends did not share her exuberant mood and might want a quiet breakfast, settled and listened to Rose tell them about The Lakes.

Rose has produced a map and told them to concentrate. They listened quietly while finishing their breakfast. Sara despite her talk would have preferred to have gone through Florence's list in some details. However, it would probably better to bring it back in the evening and she would be sure to ask Florence for her list later on.

"Could you ask the March Hare if she could pass the marmalade?" said Sara to Rose but looking at Florence.

"In the warm afterglow of that delightful breakfast I will leave you three to it," Florence said and left.

Rose hardly noticed and had found a place called Ice Hill on the map that had intrigued her but she doubted these two women would be up for its exploration.

"It's the obital variations about the sun, more than our emissions, that determine global warming," she remarked.

"Global snoring?" said Sara deadpan.

Catherine laughed.

"And increased carbon put out by volcanoes," Rose continued.

"Global yawning," said Sara putting her hand over her mouth provocatively. "'Plastic Fantastic', the Charlatans, great tune, bring back Snowball Earth, all is forgiven!" snapped Sara, cross that Florence had taken leave of them. A phone went. Rose was the only one with one pounced on it and listened.

Rose put it down and then said.

"It's Florence. We are invited to, 'a story by the lake in an hour.'"

"It will be her book," said Catherine.

Chapter 22

By the Side of the Lake

"Storytime by the Lake," announced Florence.

The women gathered around the table with its umbrella not yet up, with their drinks, and Florence produced her manuscript.

"Oh my God it's typed," said Rose, "and on that old paper too."

They all crinkled the paper with interest trying to negotiate the time in their lives when it was common place. Sara broke the spell.

"There's quite a lot of it," she said defensively.

"It's just an extract. A chapter in *"The all-true Adventures of Florence Fortune; Torch-bearer and Pioneer."*

Sara turned her head to Rose and rolled her eyes.

"I hope you're all sitting comfortably and have everything you need. I don't want any, 'Brigits the figits' here detracting from story-time," said Florence looking at Sara.

"Just get on with it," she snapped, lifting her coffee. "If it's longer than five minutes I suggest a break," she added.

"Let her start," Catherine said "I'm really looking forward to this. It's about your travels in America? How old were you?"

"I was twenty- two. Just after University. I'd got a useless degree in The History of Art and Architecture so went out to make my fortune."

"And how had you envisaged doing that?" asked Sara with more interest.

"I thought I could be a mud wrestler," answered Florence sincerely. "I guess I was naïve. Shall I begin? This extract is from New Orleans. I'd just arrived I think from Florida on the Greyhound bus or it might have been Trailways actually."

"Do start," encouraged Rose sitting fully facing Florence, head bent in clear intention of hearing every word. "And probably best if you read it all in one go."

"Yes, like having a tooth pulled," remarked Sara quietly.

Florence rattled her paper and read the title.

The Birthday Boy

I had said my good-byes to the Plaza Hotel and the dear old lady on reception and was once again on Adventure's Road.

Florence looked a bit rattled, "Oh sorry Ladies I'm still in Florida. It does sound a bit corny but remember I was only 22 and travelling alone."

"That's fine Florence," said Catherine "We're happy to listen. Probably better if you keep going and comment on it at the end."

Rose nodded in agreement.

"Yes, just get on with it!" urged Sara impatiently.

"I had said my good-byes", started Florence

"You've said that bit," said Sara.

"Sara why don't you go and listen to a podcast or go for a walk," suggested Rose.

"Because I want to listen to the all-true adventures of Flo-jo," retorted Sara quickly.

"I had said my good-byes to the Plaza Hotel and the dear little old lady on reception and was once again on Adventure's Road. I carried my bags to the bus-stop. I had decided to take one last look at the harbour before saying a farewell to Miami completely. I suppose in the back of my mind I hoped Michael would, somehow, still be there. I was excited as the bus crossed the drawbridge back to Downtown Miami and was practically first off it. I made a bee-line for the harbour across impossibly busy roads and felt myself scorched under the mid-day rays. I could see the harbour now. My footsteps quickened and with them my heart beats.

"Please be there. Please be there," I whispered to myself in frantic hope. He had gone though. My bird had flown. A sinking feeling swept through me and I dropped

my bags down on the ground and stared out to sea- as Mad Kate and the French Lieutenant's Woman had done before me.

I knew my path was simple now. I had to leave Miami. I decided to catch the next Greyhound Bus to New Orleans. I had an aunt there. I took a last look at the harbour. Many of the boats had grown to be familiar sights to me. "Miz Lou", "Fairwinds 2", "The Family" stood there as tall and as proud as ever, gently rocking with the motion of the water.

I was slowly making my way back across the harbour when I saw this figure sunning himself on a wall. He was stretched out, cat-like, and seemed dead to the world.

However, as I made my way quietly past him he looked up, sat up and called out, "Hi Lady."

I stopped and greeted him and he jumped up to kiss my hand.

"How debonair," I thought and ran my fingers through my hair as I had seen film-stars do. Miami had given me a laughable feeling of grandeur.

He seemed a very pleasant guy and we stood chatting for a while by the side of the wall. It turned out that it was his birthday and he insisted that I should join him for a drink before I boarded the bus. I agreed. He took my bags and I followed him. He kept turning around to say that he could not believe how pretty I was and that meeting me was the best present he could have hoped for.

I was as pleased as Punch with all the compliments he was paying me.

"Flattery will get you nowhere." I laughed and he informed me that I had a sexy laugh which made me laugh again. He walked in front of me positively bouncing along. We cut through past the back of shops, dodging dustbin cans, at a speedy gait.

"We're nearly here, we're nearly here," he kept saying swinging back on his tracks and smiling as he spoke.

A few minutes later we arrived at the Barbary Bar. We seated ourselves on bar stools and sipped cold beer. It was only 11.30 am and Jerry and I were the only two there.

It was a long thin bar decked out as a ship and behind the counter was a large wooden ship's wheel.

Jerry explained that every hour on the hour the barmaid spun the wheel and if it landed on your number you won a drink of whatever you fancied. He hastened to add that we had arrived just in time for the Happy Hour.

Excited by the prospect of a few drinks I disappeared to the Rest Room to freshen up.

"This is fun," I thought while putting a comb through my hair.

The bar filled up slowly during the course of the morning until a party of foreign business men entered the premises. They drank shorts in large measures and laughed loudly – patting each other on the back every so often. Everyone made full use of the Happy Hour and, for a Tuesday lunch-time, things were certainly swinging. I put some very old records on a very cheap Juke Box and the businessmen sang along.

I tried to buy Jerry a drink but he refused fiercely. Although I felt no physical attraction towards him he was good company and I was glad that I had met him. He was slight in build, almost delicate. His blond, curly hair fell around his young face in the same way that artist's portrayed Cupid in the 18th Century. Jerry's mouth was his downfall. His yellowed teeth overlapped in a very crowded jaw yet his eyes were remarkable. They were so blue. They were certainly the bluest eyes I had ever seen this side of the screen. They had a habit of staring at you for a little longer than was polite. It made you wriggle and change the subject. I think he was aware of this.

Jerry was obviously warming to the effect of the alcohol. He began to tell me his life story.

He had been born and raised in Colorado. There, he described the mountains were so beautiful that you could hardly draw breath for their splendour and when you did it was pure and fresh like the waters in its pools. He had left home at fifteen when his mother remarried and not been back since.

He had done everything to keep food in his belly and clothes on his back – washed dishes, pumped petrol, worked in shops, factories and on building sites. You name it and he had done it. It was eight years now since he had arrived in the Sunshine State and boy did he hate it.

The people were mean and cold and the city a concrete jungle. He dreamed of going back to the wide, open spaces of Colorado, Sky country. He told me that he had saved up a lot of money in the bank and soon he would be off – back to the land he loved and family he had deserted many years ago.

There was a far-away look in his eyes and he spoke dreamily. But in a matter of seconds his tune had changed. A wide smile had sprung to his lips, he sat bolt upwards and slapped me on the knee and told me that my wish was his command.

That afternoon we ate Wimpy, nipped on a little bus which sped us back over the Causeway to the beaches. We sunbathed for fifteen minutes, sweated profusely and decided to go to the pictures.

There was no queue for the matinee and Jerry bought our tickets with ease. I bought some chocolate in true cinema-going style and the usherette ushered us in.

It was only a few seconds after we had sat down when I felt Jerry's arm slither round me but I did not mind. I remembered the numerous warnings I had received never to trust a stranger and I laughed to myself at the pessimism of such dreary advice. It was a nice feeling to snuggle up to a new-found friend.

"Blow Out" turned out to be a very exciting film indeed. It was certainly no sloppy romance but fast-moving and hard-hitting. It basically dealt with the corruptness of the government and the utter danger of the streets. John Travolta paired with a prostitute turned good and there is a spectacular scene when a sinister hitman is out to murder the girl. Travolta, a sound mixer, has been able to monitor the movement of the girl and can hear the chase but not see it.

At last he catches on, jumps on the trail and charges through a whole carnival, up a great flight of steps just in time to see the knife plunge into his girl's body. This crescendo was brilliant and gripped the audience to their seats. That early evening a good number of us left the cinema somewhat shaken up. Now if I had watched the film in Bonny Britain it would certainly have affected me a little but here the film had loosed some bolt in my system and fear flowed through me. The violence I had seen on the screen I could now witness on the street and breathe in the air. I was pleased I had Jerry for protection.

Jerry suggested that we go to visit one of his friends. He wanted to show me off he said. I was quite happy to but I explained that I would like to check into a hotel soon. He nodded his head and linked arms with me.

Already little gangs of youths had emptied onto the streets. They stood around in threes and fours, smoking joints. There was a large Cuban community in Miami and many of them worked in the numerous hotels. Each time I walked past a group I felt their glare burning into my skin.

Unperturbed, Jerry led me down alley-ways until we entered a run-down housing estate full of small wooden hut-like dwellings. Cats roamed the paths everywhere. Finally, we arrived at Chris' abode. It was miles away from anywhere I could remember and my heart sank as the sky opened and the rains fell and when it rains in Miami it pours.

I huddled myself into my flimsy summer jacket and stamped my feet as Jerry knocked on the door. He was greeted, with little enthusiasm, by a large bare-chested youth who dwarfed Jerry and made him appear sickly and weak. The guy invited us in. He had cheered up on noticing female company.

Jerry introduced us and we sat down on his mattress. Apparently, the electricity had failed and the only available light flickered from a couple of old yellow candles.

"Don't tell me you had a threesome," burst in Sara in disgust.

Rose started laughing.

"Stop it you guys. Go on, Florence. It's really good. I want to know what happens next," urged Catherine frowning at Sara.

"Please don't tell me that buck toothed Hill Billy is Francesca's father," Sara continued.

"He wasn't buck toothed. His teeth were overcrowded and yellow," observed Rose, "and you are a decade out with the father bit," she added.

"Can we get on with the story please?" Catherine urged as she was seeing a despondency growing in Florence and wanted it checked.

Florence sighed and then continued.

Chris's place was simple. The whole structure consisted of just one room with a loo sectioned off in the corner. He explained that he only needed it for somewhere to crash at night, then winked at Jerry. He lit the joint he had been rolling with one of the candles and took a few deep drags.

By this time, I was beginning to get anxious for somewhere to stay. I was imprisoned in discomfort by three main reasons; number one I did not know where I was, number two it was pouring with rain and I had bags and number three the memory of the recent film had undermined my courage and I was too scared to venture out onto the streets alone. I hinted to Jerry that I should make a move soon but he seemed more intent on his joint than on my plight. He told me to sit back and relax – a most agitating remark at the best of times.

"Yes, cool it chick," drawled Chris and smiled lecherously.

"You know you can stay here with me tonight. Jerry wouldn't mind if I borrowed you. I'd give you back in the morning."

I rapidly decided that this Chris was not a nice boy and that I definitely wanted to vacate the premises – fast.

I looked at Jerry with pleading puppy dog eyes and he sensed my discomfort. Doubtless he fancied himself as the gallant knight in shining armour and protectively shot an arm around me. It was quite funny really. Chris chuckled and popped next door.

It was then that Jerry explained to me his dire straights. "This guy" that Jerry had been sharing a flat with had disappeared that morning with three hundred dollars of Jerry's plus his old guitar, as well as some of their landlord's valuables.

Consequently, Jerry had been thrown out of his digs by the Landlord who believed it to be a set up. My heart began to sink as Jerry continued his sob, sob story.

"You can't trust anyone, these days," he said bitterly. "I don't have any friends I can trust. Miami is a mean town," he went on.

He suggested tomorrow we should visit the Beautiful Parrot and Monkey Jungle, the next day the Florida Keys and then leave the God-forsaken place and make for Colorado together.

We departed from Chris's in the dying rain and treaded our way back to the beach. Jerry told me that he knew a manager of a hotel who would give us a couple of rooms. We arrived at the Paradise. It seemed to me to be a sleezy joint infact the Dog-hole would have been a more suitable name. Jerry sat me down in the foyer and approached the reception desk. He greeted his friend and I heard them discussing something in low tones.

I could see that Jerry was agitated, he kept shifting from one leg to the other and then gesturing with his hands. I could see that his friend was not having any of it. I decided to intervene and made my way to the desk to inquire what the trouble was. The man apologetically explained that he could not just give rooms out for the night. He worked at the Paradise, not owned it. I told him that I quite understood and that I would be very willing to pay for a room.

Jerry pulled me aside and suggested we share a double room as it would be cheaper. He insisted he wouldn't touch me. I hesitated, I did not want to share a room with him at all, but he had spent all his money on me and now was nearly broke and he had had a rough time so I agreed.

We paid seven dollars each and went up to see our room. I was relieved to see two large separate beds and chose the one nearest the door. It was a shabby room and the balcony looked out over the kitchens. I did not mind though I was only there for the night.

The evening was relatively young. It was around nine-thirty and Jerry strode around the room apologising for running out of cash. He kept saying he would have loved to take me to this restaurant and that night club. I told him that it was fun just being with him. He seemed moved and bantered on about the importance of friendship. He said I was the first decent person that he had met in Miami and that I was to be very careful and not to trust anyone however nice they seemed.

"This is a sea full of sharks," he warned. "The big fish eat the little fish. They just swallow you up and spit you out."

Proudly I told him that I had met nobody who had done me any harm. I told him about the Cuban family and the Boy's House that I had stayed at and how these sweet old men in ragged clothes and burnt out bodies had clubbed together to give me bus-fare because they thought I was broke. I told him of the guys I had met in hamburger joints and how interesting I found them. He smiled, momentarily, and called me "Lady Luck."

However, he still thought that I was crazy but I argued back that I had faith in human nature.

"You don't understand the way it is with people round here," he warned. "You're sweet meat at the zoo. Sweet meat at the Zoo."

I thought he had stopped but he had not.

"When I think of you wandering around out there amongst all those wino's, weirdo's and creeps it makes me want to get up and shake some sense into you."

"Listen to me," I protested "I'm alright.

Chapter 23

Jerry

Sara shuffled about and picked up the empty wine bottle and waved it at Catherine. Catherine mimicked a, "Shush" but to no avail. Florence had stopped, put down her paper and looked crestfallen.

"Oh, Florence don't stop. It's really exciting!" said Catherine.

Sara waved an empty glass.

Rose stood up and told them she would go to reception and organize drinks. "I'll go to the bar. So strange that we're the only people here. I'm loving the story Florence."

"But as students of the human psyche. Does my character ring true?" enquired Florence, earnestly. "And are you following the subtext?"

Rose hovered looking a little blank and said she thought the character rang true but wasn't sure about the subtext.

Florence gushed, "Well it's obviously about the struggle between good and evil, on the lowest level, but sub strata it concerns a person's capacity for optimism or pessimism and faith in human nature. I mean, I don't know the detail of Giselle or Madame Butterfly but they seem strewn with victims and gloomy. My protagonist……"

"Shut up Florence. You'll spoil the plot," cried out Sara. "Just wait til the drinks come and read the rest but I bet she wouldn't go back with Jerry again. Am I right? No, don't tell us."

"Well that's what you know," joked Florence, enjoying the attention. "Actually, she leads him out of the valley of doom into the light and they move to Sussex, England. She takes him to her dentist and her parents buy them a pub and then they frolic and gambol in the South Downs with their two golden retrievers and twins Henry and Tatiana or Tats for short," replied Florence at speed.

"I don't think so," said Sara wagging a finger at Florence. "More likely, they go to Bolton Mountain where she gets dumped with Auntie Darlene and Uncle Buck, an ugly drunk, and is up for a life of servitude, dungarees and squirrel pie. Oh, and corn and lots of babies who scream and have names ending with "ene." On the bright side she will inject some fresh genes into the rather narrow selection on Bolton Mountain and from there on in their teeth won't be quite so overcrowded."

"You can tell a lot about anthropology through teeth," said Rose. "Apparently we don't need our Wisdom teeth anymore because of the change in diet. No one has to grind stalks down anymore."

Rose returned and soon after the receptionist served the drinks and Florence took a welcome gulp from her pint and waited to be asked to reconvene with her story. It was not only her work but her young self they were trampling. It hurt to be a writer she reflected, you expose yourself how ever hard you try and wrap it up. You needed to accept the side-effects of the cathartic vehicle of expression.

"Maybe we should have part two tomorrow," she heard herself say.

"You started, so you finish," declared Sara firmly. "Very foolishly you had got yourself mixed up with a guy with yellow teeth and were in hotel room all be it with twin beds. Always a silver lining as they say."

Florence continued:

"OK," he butted in, "Take one of these guys you meet at MacDonald's. He might be cool but more than likely he's on the pick-up. He'd see you alone, a stranger in town. He might be as nice as pie, say good-bye then wait for you to come out, follow you, beat you, rob you, rape you. It happens every day. Wouldn't even make the press.

Sweetheart, do you know how a murder is written up in Miami, a few words in a long column like the Car Sales ads. Then again you might get a pimp who slips a Micky Finn in you drink when your head is half-turned. He bundles you out into his car. No-one would bat an eyelid. They'd think you'd fainted or had too much to drink. Those who knew the score, well, they'd look the other way. Then it would be back to his apartment and before you'd half come around he'd have screwed you and jacked you sky-high full of some drug you were probably warned about at school. You'd come around and he'd fix you up again. You wouldn't know what had hit you, little girl. After a few days, BANG you're just another of his hooked-up hookers. And don't say it could never happen to you because you're dreaming. You reckon you could get back to your dear old family in green and grassy England after that? England, ha, where they slap your wrists if you're caught smoking a cigarette under sixteen! You'd be too messed up to find the bathroom. America is a big country. No-one would find you. Do you know how many people go missing every year? Well – let- me- tell-you!"

He stared at me, shaking in his own excitement.

"People have been sweet to me," I insisted stubbornly. In quick jerks he tore off his shirt to reveal two deep scars across his back.

"So, this is sweet is it," he spat accusingly.

"Gosh, how did you get those?" I managed, somewhat taken back.

He explained that he had been ambushed coming home one night and that two big Cubans had attacked him.

"All they got was thirty and a gold chain," he spoke, in lighter tones. "Dangerous people around; stop a guy coming out of work, come pay day with a "I want ya money." Stop you for a cigarette in the street and if you don't give them one they'll take the packet."

I asked if it had hurt when they stabbed him. He explained it was like a quick thump and then a burning sensation. Later on, he admitted that there were a lot of good people around and that today he had met the best of them. I smiled, got up and kissed him lightly on the cheek and wished him a happy birthday. He seemed chuffed and his face glowed.

"You're right, you're right," he enthused bouncing up and down on the bed like a ten-year-old. If you never spoke to strangers we would never have met. There are a lot of good things happening, a lot of good people and friends are real, precious. The trouble is," he reflected "that in big towns everyone just rushes around and no-one stops to smell the roses on the way."

We talked on and on about everything and nothing. It was the sort of, which comes first the chicken or the egg conversation, that new acquaintances, who feel some empathy, often embark on as common if somewhat shaky ground. The conversation swang from religion to superstition to Star signs. I told him he must be Leo. He shook his head and told me Aquarius. I said nothing, resuming the conversation and we both agreed that he best things in life were either illegal, immoral or fattening.

Jerry disappeared to buy some cigarettes from the foyer and I saw this as an excellent moment to get ready and into bed so I washed, changed and leapt into bed as fast as a ding bat. Jerry returned and told me that I'd been quick and lit a cigarette. We smoked a while and then Jerry came over bent down and pecked me. I reached and gave him a good night kiss and then he trotted off to his own bed and switched off the light. I was relieved and happily drifted off into an easy sleep reflecting how lucky I had been in the people I had met. Lady Luck, Jerry had called me. I liked that.

Chapter 24

Daybreak through Tattered Curtains

The dawn was breaking through the red tattered curtains as I woke to the awful sight of Jerry perched on my bed piercing his blue eyes into me like a knife through butter. I jerked and asked him how long he had been there. He did not answer my question but instead started;

"You look so pretty and innocent lying there I just thought I'd come over and get a closer look. I still like what I see."

This time it was Catherine who interrupted.

"Oh goodness Florence! What were you thinking? Why didn't you call reception when you had the chance?"

"Oh yes, reception where his mate was, remember? Remember?" said Sara.

"Or the police?" continued Catherine.

"Oh yes and say, well, I went Dutch with this guy after a drinking and drug taking session though I couldn't for the life of it tell you where or who with and ended up with him at this hotel and gave him a kiss goodnight, as you do, but now he's on the end of my bed and I don't fancy him. Can you take him away please?"

"Yes," said Catherine. "It's a bit of a pickle. Before the "Me, too movement," too."

"If you ask me, Florence was thoroughly enjoying this Cat and Mouse stuff. I mean not tackling him about lying about his birthday was a lost opportunity. Quite clearly a case of a pilot fish swimming with a shark. I mean just look at her, she hasn't changed. Doesn't even need to hunt in pairs. Jerry being the Pilot fish, of course."

"No, no," she did right not to call him out then. "Male ego," Rose reminded them, shaking her head.

"Well what actually happened?" said Sara. "Florence this is all-true story isn't it?" she asked.

"Ye-es," said Florence unconvincingly.

"You're so lucky to have such a detailed account of your young self," commented Catherine.

"Yes," agreed Rose I kept a diary but it didn't go into much detail. I've only got a few photographs. Not like nowadays, and they're so staged. All on holiday or birthday parties and none of everyday life. An unbalanced account."

"I wrote a diary from a young, young age," said Catherine and as a thirteen-year-old I had one of those five-year diaries that had a little gold lock and key but there wasn't enough room to write so I ditched it as I was a page-a-day-er."

"Yes, I had one of those, too," said Sara.

"I know I gave it to you," reminded Catherine.

"Oh yes, I forgot you two have known each other since you were six- year olds."

"She was seven. I was six," corrected Sara.

"We should have a diary party!" shrieked Florence. "When we get back to England we could get a piece of card, make a quick board games with our names round the side repeated in order all the way round. Fill the drinks, throw the dice. Hey Presto you have an entertaining evening. When you land on your name you could read your own or elect some-one else, with a specific day too!"

"Mine wouldn't be that interesting?" said Rose.

"Well no-one would choose you then?" said Sara.

Catherine gave Florence a worried look and suggested she should read the next bit, right to the end. She could see that there were only three or maybe four of the crinkly sheets left.

"Oh yes let's hear if Florence is raped by the Hill Billy," said Sara clapping her hands.

"That is wrong on so many levels," said Rose. "It may predate Politcal Correctness, but I hope we don't."

"It's WOKE now, teach," said Sara, not in the least bit sorry, adding, "Well you can see she's gone on to fight another day. Look at her."

"We can't see internal scars," reminded Rose.

"I didn't mean that nasty sort of rape, more Geogette-Heaving- Bosom-Heyer or was it, Barbara Cartland? Neither were my thing."

"I meant emotional scarring, Sara. What is your own experience of rape?" asked Rose seriously.

"None of your beeswax," stated Sara.

"The wolf doesn't know how the sheep feels," Rose muttered but made sure they all heard.

"That's deep, Rose," Catherine said.

"Machiavelli. I do have feelings, you know," she said and reached for her orange juice. "It's not always been bright and breezy for me," she concluded.

There was an awkward silence so she filled it, "Oh my diary would just be full of entrances like, 'Had Spaghetti Bolognese' or 'I had a bath' or 'I did my homework.'"

"Crikey do you remember the days when people didn't shower every five minutes or take a bath every single day?" said Catherine

"Yes, and a world before the internet, smart phone and e-mail?" added Sara.

"Did you have that hair style with the side flicks produced by those curling tongs everyone had?"

"Certainly not. I travelled light. No tongs or even hairbrush just a comb. My hair was the same as it is now. Just a bit longer I guess."

"Lone Dog," said Florence. "You know, by Irene Rutherford McLeod."

They looked at her.

"I'm a lean dog, a keen dog, a wild dog and alone," she quoted back at them.

"Finish your story now, Florence. He was on your bed staring down on you," said Catherine.

Florence winced. "I'm not sure if I'm in the mood anymore," and folded up the paper and opened up her string bag to put it away.

"Just as I thought – a tease," said Sara in a sharp and matter of fact manner.

"Take that back," said Florence, by way of an emotionally-ridden order.

"Sara!" exclaimed Rose in horrified judgement.

"Oh sorreeee," said Sara "I wouldn't want to offend the bouncing ball of justice."

Florence turned her head away from Sara and asked the others if her work felt immediate?

"It's meant to have a faint whiff of "red in tooth in claw," but the main bit is to convey "Confused anger," well, maybe not confused, but someone knowing that the blood he sheds will eventually drown him."

"Yes," said Catherine, "I see that and it conjures the past with such clarity I forgot where I was."

"It's really good, Florence," said Rose. "I know teachers, like modern parents, are very liberal with their praise, but I really mean it. I, for one, want to know what happens next. It's a page turner."

Florence grinned and agreed to finish it.

"I did not like the way he was looking at me and told him that I thought he ought to go back to his own bed.

"Are you scared?" he leered,

"No. I'm not scared. I'm just a bit tired and I want to get back to sleep," she answered defiantly.

"You ain't going to get no more sleep tonight, lady."

"Oh, come on Jerry stop pratting about. It's too early to make movies."

"This ain't going to be make believe," Jerry assured me.

"Oh, stop messing around Jerry and give me a cigarette,"

"Sorry I can't do that. You see I smoked them all when you were asleep and I was laid awake thinking of what I could do with you."

"Oh, I see. Well in that case you don't mind if I just quickly nip downstairs and buy some more. I'm sure you feel like one now?"

"You ain't leaving this room the way you came in it."

"Will you please stop looking at me like that," I said with pleading eyes and shaking voice.

Make them feel big I heard the advice of my self-defence instructor run through my head. I did not have to try.

"Don't look at me like that Jerry," I softly begged in whinging tones.

"You, YOU, shouldn't have kissed me last night," Jerry broke in excitedly, "You've brung it on yourself. It's your fault. You don't know what that does to a man."

"Oh, for God's sake that was a friendly good night peck I returned to you six hours ago. Jerry can't you remember last night we talked for hours. You said that you were glad you met me and that you wanted to be my friend. You said that I had made your birthday complete."

"It wasn't my birthday last night. Remember I'm Aquarius- the ever- changing water sign?"

"Jerry, I don't care if it was your birthday or not. We made friends."

"I don't want no friends," he sneered, sinking those eyes deep into my flesh.

"We're going to make love," he casually explained and then mechanically in a higher pitch repeated the statement.

I rolled my eye as if he spoke in jest and told him not to be so silly. Not a flicker of a smile passed his lips.

"We're going to make love," he repeated for a third time as though it was a foregone conclusion, some inevitable occurrence that would take place in the near future.

He reached down with his hands to remove the bed covers that I had huddled around myself in protection. I pulled them closer to and told him to cut it out. He lent forward and stroked my head.

"Honey, don't struggle. It's going to happen. Let it be."

This had gone quite far enough in my book and I leapt out of bed and walked to the other side of the room. Jerry's voice followed me over telling me that I was only making things difficult for myself. I told him in my most confident school matron voice that if he pulled himself together now we would not mention it again, but a cat can sense a frightened bird.

He walked to the door and as he slowly clicked the key round and removed it safely from the lock, he inquired

"When did you last have a man?"

It began to dawn on me that I was locked in the same room as an absolute nut and that it wasn't the safest place to be. I hopped over one bed and around the other and grabbed the phone picking it up to get reception. Jerry laughed and said, "There's only old Bob down there and he ain't going to help you because he's my friend. In fact, if you go on doing that then he might just come up and join the party, but that would spoil things wouldn't it, Lady Luck."

I put the phone down as I decided that one was quite enough to cope with.

"Oh, Jerry please try to remember yesterday," I started.

"Listen, I don't like to hear a nice lady like you begging. All I want is to give you a good time. I know you want to really, you just too much of a lady to admit it. Maybe you is a little shy now but I reckon you could be a wildcat once you got going."

He advanced towards me. In fresh spirits and in firm voice I broke out, "My God if you come closer I'll scream this place down. I swear it."

Jerry's smile dropped a second. Good, good I thought and urged Jerry if we stopped now I would consider it just one big joke and we could go to the Parrot and Monkey Jungle as we had planned. It would be my treat.

"Don't patronize me," hissed Jerry savagely.

He wiped the sweat back off his brow with one hand and with the other he reached in his jacket pocket. He pulled something out from this pocket and regained his smile as he watched my face as he flicked the switch.

"Now them pimps might not want to have scar faces but then I'm not so fussy. You ain't no business to me, just a little bit of fun."

I stood there petrified for a few seconds as Jerry walked towards me singing Pretty Baby.

I saw the bathroom door and he saw where my eyes had darted but I ran. I flew. I slammed, locked and lent against that bathroom door.

CAME THRO THE JAWS OF DEATH

Furious, he'd leapt after me, now kicking the bathroom door. I filled my lungs with air and I screamed. Screamed as I had never done before. Screamed as if there were no tomorrow. Screamed as if he were plunging the knife into my cheek. Screamed until help came.

Florence put down the finished page on the table in front of her but her eyes followed it downwards. Rose clapped and they all took a sip of their drinks.

Chapter 25

The National Park

After the story by the lake, they decided to go out on their walk. Rose told them they would be entering the Aukstitija National Park and embarking on an 8.5 km walk of an easy nature and she had arranged a packed lunch from reception and transport there and back. Everyone should meet at reception at noon, ready to go.

Once in the Park, it became clear that the walk was going to be more a pleasant stroll than a hike, and the women remarking on its beauty, relaxed, although Rose did talk of doing one of the more arduous walks, the next day, with Florence.

Not long into to the walk, Sara had made a point of being alone with Florence, and had it out with her.

"Did he really have a knife?" she asked.

Florence flung her head back and laughed. "Oh I can't remember. It may have been a gun. I think it was a gun."

She told Sara that she would tell a different ending to each of them, though only one of them would be true.

"Ridiculous," Sara had huffed, as though her suspicions had been confirmed. Silliness was not to be confused with innocence, and could be divisive, she felt.

"Catherine, is this like the Lake District in Cumbria?" asked Florence skipping ahead between Rose and Catherine. "Does the water shine like that? Glittering as though there are thousands of mirrors or fairy lights on the water!"

"Yes, it is lovely there, quite similar though you don't get quite the promise of such exotic wildlife. What is there here, Rose?"

Rose said she would investigate the matter but was pretty sure there were elk, deer, and wild boar as well as storks and Golden Eagles.

"This is wonderful. I would so like to see an Elk," Florence sighed looking through the spruce and pine, deep into the forest. "I am so, so glad we came! I am enraptured!"

"I think we are all having a very nice time," agreed Catherine warmly, and then wondering whether to disclose to her friend her own new very straightened circumstances but decided against it as she didn't want to spoil things.

"Frankie is doing so well!" she said, instead.

Sara breezed up beside them on the wider strip of sandy path and enquired about Jess stating her Goddaughter was more than welcome to stay in London if the Bristol thing didn't work out, and then after a sideways look at Catherine added, "London is stuffed full of opportunities for such a bright young thing. I think this interning thing has gone too far. Exploitative! But it's here to stay and as I say we would love to keep her and give her the London break, so please tell her when you get back, that is if you want to."

Florence had fallen back with Rose who told her, "Lithuania used to be the largest European State and once stretched from the Baltic to the Black Sea. It was the Lithuanian Grand Princedom. So, it contained areas of the present Poland, Belorussia, and Ukraine."

"I hope your reading is up to date. I've never heard of Belorussia and I can't remember it being on the Eurovision Song Contest," Florence said but secretly made a note that she must come back and travel throughout this previously unenjoyed area as it had so much to offer. She warmed even more to it, when Rose started to inform her of the country's religious history. It had been the last Pagan stronghold. Florence liked Pagans, at least, liked the idea of them. She harboured a desire to immerse herself in it one day and said, "I'd like to be a crone."

"Be careful what you wish for," said Rose. "We'll all be crones, one day."

"I'm glad I bought these walking boots," said Sara. "They really do support the ankles. Walking is SO much easier."

"Rose converted me, from court shoe to trainer, during our jogging years," said Catherine looking down at her feet. She was back in jeans and trainers.

"A dash to freedom, indeed," congratulated Sara and told her she'd once been fully paid up member of the

Converse coloured canvas brigade, but that they lacked the robustness of the boot. Style over substance. Of course, some shoes have neither," she said looking at Florence darting along in little more than pumps.

Florence claimed to have worn Doc Martins and dresses. Catherine reminisced about Laura Ashley and an Edwardian-styled, white Sailor-dress with a hip waist. Florence claimed to be a punk rocker and said her 'best strides ever' had been pink and black striped ones from the King's Road. Rose said that she hadn't been fussed about fashion and admitted she was often rather jealous of the kids having a uniform as it meant none of that palaver of deciding what to wear. "I don't much care for skirts. They are restricting but I like a nice dress at times," she said.

Florence said she was totally, totally in love with the skirt suits of the 1940's, as of the Bette Davis and Lauren drop down beautiful Baccall, and that "Gilda" glamour of Rita Heyworth and then even more so, though she did note that it was for the overprivileged rich, that luxurious, ostrich feathered silky, damask opulence and knock out style of the 1890's and the Georgians. The Georgians dressed well too. Great hats. She couldn't abide the Victorian style, at least for women. Dreadful hair. Dreadful dresses. No wonder they wanted the vote. She asked them which style they would choose if they had been born into the ruling classes of any era.

"Not this again, Florence!" complained Sara.

"Can't we just enjoy the scenery without some fanciful scenario to work on. How does Tom put up with it?"

"Tom loves it. He has a fertile imagination and is probably very much missing the stimulation," said Florence.

Once back at the hotel they split up as previously agreed and Sara, once unbooted, threw herself on the bed claiming exhaustion.

"Oh, I didn't find it, too bad, really, though it might be too early to tell," said Catherine slapping her left hip.

"Not the walk! I meant Florence. I can't believe how much she goes on!" Sara corrected rubbing her knees.

"Oh, I quite like that. It's what I most like about her. She gets so inspired about things. It can rub off on you. I still don't know whether to tell them about Peter and I, our finance crisis. I suppose not, as we only have tomorrow here and then it's high jinxes in the city and then back to face the music."

Sara told her that she couldn't see another few days of keeping it to themselves, mattering much. Once they knew, Florence would have all sorts of fanciful ideas and it was not as though they didn't partially know the situation, and were working on possible schemes to help. Sara went to shower.

Catherine lay on the bed and tweedled with her phone half wanting to shield herself, from the situation at home, to enjoy tranquillity but half wanting an update. After a quick text to each loved one, she turned off the phone and closed her eyes to enjoy the silence. A silence which ended shortly with Sara's reappearance in a white bath robe and a towel wrapped round her head and claiming regally that, "Tragedy has occurred. I have used shower gel instead of conditioner. What hotel in this day and age has only shower gel and shampoo? Lucky there are no Americans here. They'd sue!"

Catherine scurried through her wash bag and chucked Sara a little container of conditioner labelled 'Cole and Lewis', London, acquired when she and Peter had stayed in Harrogate at the "Cedarwoods" on the way to the Lake District the year they went without the children. Sara thanked her and disappeared back to the shower.

Later, back on the bed, sitting facing Catherine, drying her hair as Catherine remained stretched out on hers, she said, "I do miss my Monsoon shower. It is a bit backward, this hotel. Quaint though, I am really enjoying this trip."

"Lucky you don't have stay in the places that Florence does," said Catherine.

"Yes, and that is something I'd like to talk to you about. Florence told me yesterday that she doesn't use anti-perspirant. Apparently never really has, though did say she has once bought a Mum. I mean what self-respecting young girl would choose that gooey roll-on stuff when they could have chosen, 'Arid Extra Dry'?"

"Oh, I do remember that stuff," said Catherine, "Are we still allowed to use spray cans or are they bad for the planet?"

"Oh, bad for the planet," mimicked Sara crossly. "Everything is bad for the planet these days. Everyone is so censorious. I don't care about this planet. Throw it away and get a new one. They come and go. Four and half billion years is a very respectable innings," Sara insisted.

"Rose said that you have to be careful with sprays and deodorant and stuff not to block up the pores," said Catherine. "She knows all about health and free radicals. I've learnt a great deal over the years on our dog-walks. She says, 'Brazilians' are harmful to sexual health, and the Porn industry, should be more responsible. The hairs, are there for a reason, she says, to collect up the germs. The same principle, as the hairs in the nose, which collect germs to prevent infection."

"Ah," said Sara acerbically. "Remind me not to shave before Nasal sex."

Catherine pulled a face. She actually wanted to enquire about 'anal sex,' as she had a mild curiosity around the subject. Though she had known Sara since she was seven years old and spent many a happy after school swopping plastic ponies there was still taboo subjects and some mystery between them.

"Well, she doesn't smell, does she?"

"Yes, but she goes to all those hot countries and hikes and stuff. How does that even work?"

"Well she showers,"

"But didn't she say that she lived in a twig nest somewhere in Asia for a month?" asked Sara rubbing her hair still.

"I think she was having you on."

"No, it was in Borneo. She just bathed in the river or something or was it the sea, or a pond or something. I mean what about menstruation?"

"Well she's only next door why don't you go and ask her?"

"Don't be silly."

"Anyway, do you still menstruate?"

"No."

"And are you about to live in a hut of twigs in Borneo?" asked Catherine. "So, what does it matter? Anyway," she continued "don't you remember us living on that bus for weeks. No shower and plenty of menstruation, I believe. There were ten of us girls, weren't there? All of whom of childbearing age."

"Gosh, yes we all managed, didn't we? Maybe I have got a little particular, in the last few years. Ten women and ten men, on a bus, for ten weeks," pondered Sara proudly.

"Yes, and I don't think I'll ever forget you swapping a couple of tampons for that item of jewelry, with those women in Nepal."

"Oh lord, I still have that. It's such a pretty trinket. Turned out to be an opium vessel. Don't you remember that guy at customs standing on one leg and sniffing it? That was a Midnight Express moment. I would be lying if I said I hadn't been nervous. I thought at the time, it was because it was a cultural heirloom not to be removed from the country," she smiled "not an Opium pot, ironic isn't it? And then, a few years on, I met Sam."

Catherine looked at her, and then swerved the subject.

"Well lucky they didn't ask for a receipt. What would you have answered? Sorry mate, left it in Boots, Muswell Hill."

"That was a great trip. One day Paris, Munich beer festival the next, then Venice," said Sara.

"And Istanbul with the Blue Mosque and San Sophia and the bazaar. Then all those peculiar sights in Turkey," recollected Catherine.

"Bodrum, was no more than a fishing village. Then there was Damascus, the oldest city in the bible."

"Time ravishes places as well as people, look at Syria," commented Catherine rather morosely.

"That Picasso fellow was good at smoothing things out at borders. Didn't he go mad at Caroline for taking those Israel cassettes into Palestine or was it, Jordan?"

"God yes. I still remember watching that apoplectic guard, jumping up and down on them, thinking someone got out of bed on the wrong side this morning. Picasso was pretty furious, too. I had not a clue of the stress of life, then. Had you?"

"No, I hadn't. I was living in a Rose Garden. We both were."

"Yes, but your Rose Garden was bigger than mine," said Sara. "You were a good sharer. Thanks for letting me win those rosettes on Bandit. I've never forgotten it and never will."

"Yes, that was scary in the Middle East. Really all those guards with rifles. England's so peaceful. We're lucky really. And the Welfare State, at least, Peter and I won't starve. I expect it will be me that has to go to the food bank," Catherine sighed. "I did have this idea that Peter was going to get over this block on long haul flights, and we were going to take off to all the exotic places that have been bandied around all these years. Now that's not going to happen. I'm losing the Rose Garden."

"You've been in one longer than most," suggested Sara. "Change can be hard."

"You've had your knocks, too, known the impact of untimely death."

Sara swallowed and looked away and murmured, "I never did learn to play Song for Guy."

"'Leave a bite in the cherry,' as your grandfather used to say," said Catherine cheerily.

"He was referring to the London Stock Exchange, not learning a requiem."

"I expect he would be very proud of you, making your millions. Not to mention your ability to barter feminine hygiene products on the cutting edge of the Asian Opium trade."

"Yes, I shall tell the 'Great Adventuress Florence' that story tonight, and tell her to put that in her pipe and smoke it."

"Actually, she said she has. She did go through that faze. Claims it was the eighties and everyone was doing it. Chasing the Dragon. I wasn't, were you?"

"Certainly not!"

"And we've been to the Taj Mahal, beautiful wasn't it?" said Catherine triumphantly and then waivered and added thoughtfully "Now that I'm as good as bankrupt, I'll probably never do anything like that again."

Sara wanted to say that she would go anywhere with Catherine, and would certainly be happy to pay, but sensed it was not the time. She would bring it up later and let Catherine choose maybe the Kremlin or Ankor Wat. She was not a one for famous buildings but she did enjoy luxury hotels, service and the mini bar: besides she loved Catherine.

Florence and Rose went straight to their room.

"Sara is bossy!" Florence exclaimed taking off her shoes and stomping round the room in bare feet, "she needs a frigging chill pill."

"Oh, I thought you two were good friends now. London trips and all that."

"Well Caesar liked Brutus. Remember "Et Tu Brutus."

Rose didn't know the play but got the gist and reminded her that Catherine and Sara did go back along way and that she liked the sharpness about Sara. "Well she's got that dry wit, hasn't she?"

"I suppose so if you like that haughty, I'm-so-superior type of wit," said Florence adding that she wasn't too keen in being holed up in the room for three hours until Ms Prim and Mrs Proper got their second wind. "Let's go to that supermarket and buy some nibbles and drinks for this evening. Let's get merry tonight and play the truth game. We'll make sure the spinner lands on Sex."

"What spinner?"

"The one you can whip up. You're a primary school teacher, aren't you?"

"Very well Miss Chief," agreed Rose.

"No, no you can be Miss Chief as you're going to be assistant head!"

"I don't the sound of that one. Can't I be Miss Fortune?"

"No, I bagged Miss Chance and Miss Fortune as my *nom de plume* at thirteen. You can be Miss Shapen," said Florence snorting with laughter, following up with, "I'm only joking. You've got the best figure of all of us. Miss Understood?"

"I'm a teacher Florence! I'll be Miss Steerie."

"Can't see it really," said Florence smiling.

"Miss Right?" suggested Florence.

"Miss Right became Miss Wrong, remember."

"Okay, in the spirit of generosity and our ever-layering friendship I, hereby, christen us, 'Miss Chance' and 'Miss Fortune'. We shall cleave together in times of need. Come on let's go and buy some wine. We can officially toast, our good health and new names, in a lakeside ceremony."

Rose thought they should hurry up and get out of the room as she feared Florence might engage her in a pillow fight or start jumping up and down on the bed. She was reminded of Doug as a puppy tearing round in figures of eight just blown over by the sheer joy of life. Florence put her hand under the back of her T-shirt and fiddled and then whipped off her bra, swung it around in circles and let go, watching it shoot across the room.

"Free, the Florence two!" she called, jumping up and down and collapsed on the bed laughing.

Rose, who was still feeling energetic herself, agreed to go shopping. She wanted a chance to persuade Florence to go on a proper hike the next day and thought she had located the perfect lake to circumnavigate, Lake Tauragnas. It was the deepest lake in Utena county at sixty and a half metres.

On the way to the supermarket, Rose continued to inform Florence of the glacial landscape, that Lake Satai had a shoreline that was the longest in Lithuania and then there was Lake Zuvintas, the shallowest at only three metres deep, but a paradise for birds.

Florence began to wonder if Rose was on the spectrum but enquired about the bird-friendly one and mentioned Catherine loved her birds, too, but Rose said that one was too far away, sadly.

She then mentioned that if they went back to the park that she had since discovered was indeed the oldest established park in modern Lithuania and that from the famous Ladakalnis Hill you could see the six glacial lakes.

Florence, though finding the 'hill' word deeply unattractive, managed to curb herself as she couldn't be annoyed with two of her friends at once and was glad when they got to the shop. It looked exactly the same as it had the day before and had the same woman on the till. Florence loaded up with lager and wine and bags of nibbles and as they walked home Florence chatted about Chadbury. As Rose was reluctant to talk about her work, Florence then discussed the characters in her play, "The Starchers," and that she had had to disguise the old deputy, upright and forthright, as Miss Trout and that she planned for a dark-eyed beauty, with exceptionally fortunate genes, to swish into the village on a metaphorical umbrella and turn it, quite upside down, with her quiet charm and can-do attitude. Rose said though she thought the play "good," wasn't sure about the calling of Miss Fothergill "Trout," even if no malice was intended.

Once back at the hotel, Florence persuaded Rose to sit on the terrace so they could enjoy the lake view as they toasted their new names. She told Rose that she would break her general rule, on this occasion, as wine, especially red wine, was so much classier for their ceremony. Rose was concerned that drinking shop-bought alcohol on the terrace might contravene hotel policy. What policy Florence had said and told her that it was part of the beauty of travelling in a non-English speaking country. There were no rules, or none that you could read anyway.

"Ignorance is bliss, Miss Chance," and poured her a generous glass of wine.

The two of them, pulled their chairs together, and admired the silvery view with a glass in hand. Rose informed Florence that they couldn't circumnavigate Lake Tauragnas, as it was too big, but they could admire the vastness of the lake, from floating footbridges, with lookout points. She said they could go barefoot on the sandy coast.

A blue sky, warm rays of sun, peacefulness of the pine forest nearby and the twinkling lake relaxed Florence and she looked at Rose and thought how lucky she was to meet her. They talked a little about Frankie and Tom, and then of the old days in London, and about the school they'd both briefly worked at, in the East End before Florence had taken off travelling and arrived back pregnant and reticent.

"Shall I call the other two?" suggested Rose. "Didn't we agree to meet up for a boat ride before dinner? I know Sara and Catherine eat late but it's nearly six o'clock. It gets dark around eight."

We are here now. This is the end, my friend.

Chapter 26

On the Lake

"I won't call them, I'm going to knock them up. They should have been down by now, we said five-thirty, didn't we?" said Rose.

"Bring down my jacket when you are up there. Oh, and my phone, too and speaker please," said Florence.

"Florence, we are meant to be going on the lake."

"Yes, I know. I'm looking forward to posing for Lady of the Lake pictures to send Tom. We need music."

"Well I'll be careful. Is it waterproof?"

"I'll put it in a plastic bag inside Frida bag," she said grabbing the string bag as if one of her favourite possesions.

Florence poured herself a small wine and took small sips until the others showed up and Rose passed Florence her phone and speaker and Sara complained, "We've just done an activity this morning, do we have to go rowing? I mean we're meant to be relaxing. That is a far better idea you have. Pour me one."

Florence handed Sara her glass of wine and took out a bottle of beer from their shopping and cracked it open. Catherine sat down, eyeing the wine. You'll have to get a glass from somewhere unless you want one of these. Florence indicated her bottle of beer, taking a cavalier swig. Catherine let Florence open one for her.

Florence tuned into music and connected her little speaker up, assuring them that the girl on reception with the Nordic blue eyes, wouldn't mind as there were no other guests at present, and anyway the thing didn't go up that loud.

Treacherous road

With a desolated view

Distant light

Here they're far and few

"Can you put on something a little more cheerful?" asked Rose.

"How about some romance?" asked Florence and put on Cole Porter.

They sang along with, 'I get a kick out of you.'

Sara poured the wine, out between herself and Rose. Florence, who had swigged her beer fast, rummaged in the shopping bag under the table, for another. She bought one out for Catherine, too. It was decided that they would go after that drink as it getting on for six-thirty, already.

"Well it's not as if we are going to be out for long," said Florence. "I'm joyfully blissful and can't wait to float on a boat. Out on that heavenly lake, a yonder. It will be Rhapsody in Blue."

"Rhapsody in blue jeans. Is everyone going to wear jeans?" asked Rose a little worried that Catherine might spoil her lovely white culottes but anxious there was no time to change.

Sara was still not at all keen. Florence said "Look treats, Sara'" and got out a packet of Tortillas and a big bag of crisps. Only for those that come on the lake. Rose will row you, won't you Rose? She can be your designated driver?" she laughed. "Rose used to row for the village. Bell boating. Well, we three all did. Remember those Christmas outing? I remember it was freezing, one year."

Sara still was not keen, "It looks muddy and the boats don't look that clean. They look all heavy and wooden. Are you sure we can manage them? Look it's gone half past six. Aren't we dining at eight? Can't we go tomorrow?"

"They are little, time and tested rowing boats not the Raft of Medusa," said Florence. "It's a little lake not the high sea. Com'on, Sara, you'll be fine," Florence pleaded.

She put Amy Winehouse on. Sara sat stubbornly, nursing her wine.

"Oh Christ, Sara. Rose is the only child and she occasionally does things she doesn't want to," Florence said.

"I'm not an only child," corrected Rose, "What about Paul!"

"Oh, I don't count him, it's only for the sake of argument," said Florence.

Rose complained and said Paul was a very nice brother, and Florence changed her argument to Sara not having any pets. Sara said that she had had plenty of pets growing up and now didn't on purpose because she chose to be in a position to suit herself and that if she didn't want to go out on a boat she shouldn't be made to feel guilty.

"Oh, come on you two, don't argue," pleaded Catherine.

Florence changed her tactics and broke into another beer, offering Catherine one who took it, even though she hadn't finished her first.

"Rose has been in the rowing club for years. Years of experience. Hey Rose, do you remember our bell-boat got beaten by the WI," Florence burst into laughter.

"Only because we were about the only adults on that boat," Rose defended herself as she was not so keen on losing as Florence.

"Yes, we were beaten by the scouts or it could have been the cubs," said Florence rocking forward in laughter.

"We came last, didn't we Rose,"

Sara smiled and asked Rose if it was true and Rose nodded shamefully. "It was the first time I've ever come last,"

"By contrast I love losing!" Florence claimed, "I find it quite easy especially when playing Pool. I don't think I have the killer instinct,"

"I think I do," said Sara smartly.

"Yes," agreed Florence "With your cold blue eyes and frozen heart I'm guessing you were made in a petri dish. A product of carefully collected warrior genes, by a lab technician, in China."

Sara took a drink, wondering what she was locked into.

'Love is a losing game,' came on and the women stopped, a while, to listen to the song.

"I certainly lost in love," admitted Rose.

They sang along and Catherine said, "Oh I didn't think I liked "Amy" but I certainly do now!"

"Of course, I did have a reputation as a bit of a Mankiller, in my day. Think it was the hair," sighed Florence sweeping back her locks with one of her stylised, flick of the wrist.

"Oh pl-eeese," begged Sara.

"Oh, eat arsenic," joked Florence, waving a middle finger at Sara.

"Don't need to, some of us have a perfect complexion," Sara replied.

"Come on Sara," said Florence "Don't be such a spoilsport. Come on the boat for some, 'Fresh air and fun,'" she pleaded, trying her hand at a Yorkshire accent.

"Show-stopping," said Sara, beginning to get a little angry, and paused before adding, "I told you I didn't come here to do water sport but to relax, to enjoy myself. And to catch up with my dear friends, Catherine and Rose," she added in a lighter tone.

'Valerie,' came on and they joined in:

 "Cause since I've come on home

Well, my body's been a mess

And I've missed your ginger hair

And the way you like to dress."

"Well, sometimes I go out by myself

And I look across the water" Florence sang.

"And I think of all the things, what you've been doing," she continued with Rose. Catherine hummed as she didn't know the words and even Sara joined in.

And I think of all the things, what you've been doing"

"And in my head I paint a picture …..

Rose suggested that they went rowing tomorrow morning instead, all together. Later, she and Florence, would climb the hill and do the big hike and Sara and Catherine could have the whole of the rest day relaxing.

Sara reluctantly agreed.

However, Florence did not.

Amy's voice rang out singing the Rehab song and Florence stood up and half miming with an empty beer bottle and changing the words sang "They tried to make me go on the water and I said No NO NO.

They tried to get me on a boat, on the water

I won't GO GO GO,"

"I'd rather be home with Ant …a,"

She got up waving her bag of goodies, and turned on her heel and started walking off in the direction of the lake, down the path towards the jetty. She turned around and called, "Come on Catherine. Let's do this thing!" and waved the big bag of crisps. Catherine gulped back her beer and followed.

Rose and Sara watched with interest as Catherine caught Florence up and the two of them went on the jetty in search of the right boat. Catherine stating that they all looked the same and asking if they needed permission from the hotel.

Florence handed the shopping bag to her and shook off her bag and fished out her phone and took a photo of Catherine on the dock and then put a song on. "I just love this song."

They waited at the dock for a few minutes and still Sara and Rose didn't come.

"I hope Rose comes without her if she's going to be such a spoil sport," said Florence and told Catherine of their new names. "You're Miss Proper though you're a Mrs really, aren't you," as she unwound the rope and took the shopping bag from Catherine indicating that she should hop on the boat and take a seat which she did and Florence hopped on herself and picked up the oars telling Catherine she would get them out to the middle and then Catherine could have a turn.

"Com'mon you lot," she shrieked back at them. "It's fun!"

They rowed out and the calm water lapped against the sides of the boat. They rowed out a little further. Florence was a little surprized at how much the oars weighed. She couldn't remember the kayak being so cumbersome to manoeuve but thought she would get used to it and was glad there wasn't a wind and there didn't seem a tide. Did lakes even have tides? Catherine was awfully amused by the naming ceremony and wanted to change her name from Mrs Proper to Miss Take or Miss Used and Florence thought it was sweet that she was trying to be a bit more "rock,n,roll."

Florence put the oars down, fumbled in her bag, and took some photos of Catherine and Catherine reciprocated. The lake was stunning with the greenery of the reeds and surrounding pine forest; blue sky and dark mysterious water.

Florence reattached the phone back to the speaker and they played, 'Back to Black' and Catherine said how brilliant this holiday had been and she wished they didn't have to go home.

"About time, too," Florence told Catherine as she noted that Rose was making her way to the jetty with Sara walking behind her, woodenly.

Plucking out the bag of tortillas, Florence stood up and waved them at the women. Then ripped them open and stuffed a couple in her mouth and threw a handful into the air and sat back down and rummaged further into the bag bringing out a beer. "Do you want one?" she asked Catherine, as she slipped the top off one. Catherine did.

The boat rocked gently back and forth, and for a moment the women sat silently listening to their thoughts enjoying their last few minutes of being alone together.

"I hope Sara's brought a jacket," said Catherine. "The temperature seems to have dropped. I'm glad I've got mine."

"It's so lovely out here?" repeated Florence looking up at the sky. "We are in for a glorious sunset." She sat with the oars safe-guarded between her legs and leaned back and stretched her arms in a big circle.

"This is such an adventure for me, Lithuania, a country I'd hardly heard of. New sights, a strange language and time spent with you lot away from the children, away from the dogs."

Florence turned off the music and listened and then quoted Horace Mann, "Lost, yesterday, somewhere between sunrise and sunset, two golden hours, each set with sixty diamond minutes, no reward is offered, for they are gone for ever."

"Ah that's nice. Did you learn it at school?"

"Uni," said Florence.

"It's been such a treat not to look up and see something that needs doing, paintwork, watering, feeding, worming, visiting, cajoling, encouraging, shopping, putting things away and putting more things away. Paying for things and yet more things. Smoothing down feelings. There is always, always something to be done," she said. "It just goes on and on."

She looked at Florence and took a swig. "You just tied things up and travel the world."

"Yes," agreed Florence, wistfully. "I don't think you can have it all, in this life. Aren't we programmed to hunger after things so we won't become bored?"

"I had contented years, when the children were little," continued Catherine. "They were good days although I was always too busy to enjoy them. I do remember wishing for this or that, but I was happy. I could get to like lager. What are they doing hanging about on the bank? Maybe they're not coming in, after all."

The two women were seen, in the distance, in discussion and then Rose seemed to put her arms in the air and turn to unravel the rope.

"No, look, they're launching," said Florence.

"Ah they're both in," said Catherine delightedly. "Shall we row out to meet them?" and started to sing, "Row, row, row the boat," breaking off to say, "I love the word 'merrily' it reminds me of Merrylegs in Black Beauty," and giggled.

Florence was about to regale her with a story about a tribe in Asia, she had once visited, where the whole village used to be very keen on that song, a hand-me-down through the ages from Missionary days, but she decided against it. Instead, she turned her attention back to the other little boat, the boat Rose and Sara had just launched. There it was, brown and chunky, in the distance.

"Look at Sara. Sitting, like an Indian Maharaja," said Florence "A Sultana!" she gaffawed, excitedly. "You can imagine her as a Viceroy, in former days, barking out commands."

"Play 'Valerie' again, Florence," said Catherine.

Florence switched it back on, and they joined in with the words,

"Well, sometimes I go out by myself

And I look out across the water.

And I think of all ……….

Then Florence got up and started rocking gently pretending to be on stage. Catherine looked at her, singing too, and felt euphoria rising in her heart.

Florence navigated herself onto the duck plank and wobbled a little precariously, before sitting back down, with a thump, and rearranging the oars. "We mustn't lose the oars," she grinned at Catherine who had surprised her by getting up on her feet, and standing with increasing confidence. Catherine felt a dizzy light-headedness and was utterly engrossed in the song; the open air; the freedom. Florence was bemused by her friend's enthrallment.

She looked up at Catherine, smiling. There was something vaguely dreamy about the scenario. The sky was turning dusky. The water seemed to have no colour but be a dark and murky, shade of black. It gently lapped around the boards.

"Maybe we should row towards them?" Florence suggested, with a faint feeling of caution. "Would you like a turn?"

"No thanks," said Catherine sitting back down, drinking from the bottle, "but can you turn up the music."

"Sorry, that's as loud as it goes," said Florence, taking the oars, and embarking on steering the boat towards the others.

"Play 'Valerie' again," implored Catherine.

Florence put down the oars and fiddled for the tune. To the sound of the music, once again, Catherine got up on her feet and started swaying, while singing to the words.

"On the water," she rang out. Florence felt a sense of discomfort and the boat rocked a little. She could see the other two in the distance, starting towards them, and felt a sense of relief. She started rowing towards them and found a steady rhythm with the oars. Then Catherine got up on the duck board, and started up again singing into her bottle as if it was a microphone. "The way you used to dress," and just as Florence was going to ask her to sit down she saw Catherine wobble, and then a yelp followed, as her free arm windmilled, and she fell out of the boat sinking into the water, back first. She wasn't to be seen then. Disappeared, underwater.

Florence stared, her mouth open, her eyes straining, her thoughts racing. Dropping the oars, she whipped off her shoes and jacket as she stood up, and then was in.

Sara had seen it happen, too, and Rose caught the transformation of her face and knew something terrible was wrong.

A scream followed. It was Florence who had resurfaced and screamed. She then, drew herself up caught hold of her knees, and dived back under the water. Her eyes wide open, she felt the chill of the water, as she swam down neared the bottom desperately seeking Catherine. Her arms striking forward stretching out for a feel of a body, hoping to grab on to Catherine's flesh, squeeze her arm, pull her up. But Florence couldn't find Catherine. She surfaced for air again and screamed and screamed. Her hair wet and tangled around her with bits of pond weed stuck across her cheek. Please don't take her she thought. Please let her be alright. She screamed again "Catherine. Catherine." And then turning to the others, still in the distance. "Help. Get help." Florence swam around the boat searching in the depth.

The other two were torn as what to do. Rose didn't know whether to row out and help look or to row to shore for help. There was no one about. Sara didn't know who to ring and dialled 999 for England and then googled for help. Rose calculated that if Catherine hadn't surfaced in the next half minute it was all over and they should row in for help. Maybe there was some miracle. She shouted to Florence who was hysterical, still begging them to get help.

Darkness came down on the women on the lake; and Peter was missing Catherine, who was lying on her back, drowned, with both eyes open.

Rose shouted to Florence to put out an oar, cursing herself for not insisting they wore life jackets; let alone took buoys. She looked at her watch and knew minutes had gone by. It only takes a minute to drown she thought. Sixty seconds for an adult. Twenty for a kid and then there was that cold- water shock. She feared the worse and rowed with all her might to the shore. It was over though, she feared. It was over she thought engulfed with a stabbing pain. Early raw grief rupturing through her, as she rowed to shore, with Sara blanched and speechless, clinging on to the bench, where she sat beside herself feeling time slow down, and life turn to surreal, slow motion. She dropped Sara on the shore instructing her to get help and to try Reception first and then anyone in town and then turned the boat round to Florence. Maybe this was damage control now?

Rose was down by the water, among the officials. The receptionist had brought picnic blankets out for them, and stood awkwardly by her two guests as they waited further up the bank.

Rose turned from the men, and started up the slope towards them. Her hand went up to her neck and she started to rub it, looked them in their faces and said, "They've found her." She shook her head. "I'm sorry."

Florence exhaled a guttural, elongated sigh, covered her face with her hands, and turned away.

Sara thought, "With it, or on it?"

Rose thought, "How will they cope?"

Rose said "I'll call Peter," and Sara replied, "I'll call her Mum."

Printed in Poland
by Amazon Fulfillment
Poland Sp. z o.o., Wrocław